Julia Wild was born near Manchester and spent eighteen years working in her local library until the cutbacks came and she took voluntary redundancy so she could do what she loves best – escape into the writing world with a head full of stories and dreams.

She has previously won both the Romantic Novelists' Association's New Writers' Award and the Romantic Novel of the Year Award. *The Secret Notebook* is her first historical fiction novel.

juliawildauthor.co.uk

twitter.com/juliawildauthor
facebook.com/authorjuliawild
bookbub.com/authors/julia-wild

THE SECRET NOTEBOOK

JULIA WILD

One More Chapter
a division of HarperCollins*Publishers* Ltd
1 London Bridge Street
London SE1 9GF
www.harpercollins.co.uk
HarperCollins*Publishers*
1st Floor, Watermarque Building, Ringsend Road
Dublin 4, Ireland

This paperback edition 2021
First published in Great Britain in ebook format
by HarperCollins*Publishers* 2021

A catalogue record of this book is available from the British Library

ISBN: 978-0-00-841858-8

Printed and bound in the UK using 100% Renewable Electricity
by CPI Group (UK) Ltd

Chapter One

Izzie

West Hampstead, Thursday May 25, 2017

Izzie's head sank onto the desk that had once belonged to her late husband, Rufus, as she fought the overwhelming wave of sadness that threatened to engulf her.

'I'm too young for all this…' Twenty-nine was far too young.

She knew it was time she got her act together and found some direction. Grabbing a handful of tissues, she wiped her face and pushed her tumble of copper curls out of the way.

'Get a *grip*,' she whispered hoarsely, but the tears didn't listen.

She felt lost, adrift, throat aching with unshed tears.

Throwing the tissues in the bin, she took a deep breath, pushed herself to her feet and studied the shelf at eye level. She ran her finger along the dark spines of the books written by Rufus, the crime books made famous by TV, the books that made her a wealthy widow.

'When will it stop?' She rubbed her hand against the emptiness in her chest as she was drawn to the wedding photograph perched at the end of the row of books. She touched the picture, her forefinger tracing their outline. They stood close, holding hands, smiling towards the wedding photographer against a background of trees. Rufus, smart in a dark suit and white shirt – his mid-brown hair layered and short – stood several inches taller than her, her dress a cream, knee-length shift; a matching flower held her long curls back on one side.

First there had been the denial, then anger at the unfairness of losing Rufus. She'd made endless bargains with unseen forces to change the outcome, then faced the depression...

And now, finally, the acceptance was growing.

'I know you've gone.'

Despite her tears, she felt lighter inside for the first time in a long time.

The soft beam of early morning sunshine peeping in through the French doors seemed to reflect the nascent sense of hope she felt.

The neighbour's cat, Horace, looked in as if to say a haughty good morning, and then moved on.

The phone burbled, springing her from her indulgent

moment. Clearing her throat and taking a deep breath, she picked up the handset.

'Izzie Dean.'

'It's Justin, Justin Swift. Thank goodness I've got hold of you, Izzie!' His tone was urgent.

'What do you want?' Her words sounded harsh, but it was the shock of hearing from him, his voice tempting her back in time to those first brush of love days.

She fought the seductive pull of memories: a snapshot of hot summer days full of sea and sand and laughter ... of the friendship they had shared for so long before something changed on the day his warm lips closed over hers, making her tremble with heated passion... Just the sound of his husky edged voice tumbled her back in time. It was mere seconds, yet the intense emotions they'd shared swamped her. The way he'd held her so tightly...

'Can you come as soon as possible? Your nan's been taken bad with pneumonia.'

'Nan? No! Oh, no!'

The summer memory medley fell from her mind.

'Nan... God, no.' Not her treasured nan, her favourite person in the world, delicate as a fragile vase, yet so strong of spirit. It was hard to breathe against the sudden panic and sadness swamping her insides.

Justin explained he was visiting his folks, who lived next door to her nan, when he had gone around to see her and found her poorly. He'd called an ambulance and went along with her to the hospital. He gave Izzie details of where to find them when she arrived.

'I'll get the train.' Izzie's words squeezed past the lump

in her throat. 'I was due to come up north tomorrow to visit.' She grimaced, feeling guilty and wishing she was already up in Blackpool. 'Justin, will you ... are you able to stay with Nan? Just till I arrive?'

'Course.'

'I'll be on the next train out of Euston. Thanks, I – I really appreciate ... everything.'

'That's okay.'

She set the phone in its cradle and called for a cab whilst she threw a few things in a rucksack, all the while whispering over and over, 'Please be all right, Nan, please...'

At the same time, she shoved down the gratitude that welled up towards Justin, the warmth his voice triggered inside her giving rise to random visions of them running, laughing, sharing everything and holding one another so tight, believing the closeness they had would last forever.

Promising one another it would last forever.

Those random visions and sensations were immediately followed by the needle-sharp pain of broken promises, the deepest disappointment she had ever known. It was piercing, buried deep inside years ago. It was almost six years since they had planned to meet on her twenty-third birthday. That date was burned into her soul.

Yet, after hearing his voice, it felt like only yesterday.

She didn't want to feel anything like that *ever* again.

He'd let her down.

Until minutes ago, it had all been locked safely away; it was a shock to acknowledge what Justin had tossed aside,

4

and that it still hurt when she let herself glimpse what they'd had.

He would be different now. His successful photography career had seen him travel the world, meet so many different people, dating and photographing many beautiful women, his work appearing in glossy magazines galore.

But as she boarded the train at Euston, the anxiety of reaching her nan, the worry that she might not be okay, took over all of her thoughts. She willed the train faster, faster...

Chapter Two

Izzie

Blackpool, Thursday May 25, 2017

Just a few hours later, Izzie ran into Blackpool Victoria Hospital to be met by Justin.

'Is...?' She could hardly get the words out for a mixture of emotion and the fear of being too late. He held open the ward door and indicated to a single room further down the hallway.

'Molly's hanging on, Izzie.'

Entering the room and easing into the plastic bedside chair, she took the frail, freckled hand in hers.

'Hello, Nan. What have you been getting up to?' She smiled when her nan's eyelids fluttered in response to her words.

'I've come a day early. We can catch up with any plans

you have in mind. I love you.' All the love Izzie felt for this feisty, beautiful woman seemed to lodge in her chest, an overwhelming weight. This strong woman had given Izzie somewhere to run to, a haven to escape to so many times in her young life. Nan was the best; she called Izzie *her little pal*. Loved her unconditionally.

They'd spent hours in the fresh air, either on the beach, paddling, or walking the promenade. 'Do you remember when Grandpop came along with us to the beach, how we always took a bat and ball?' Izzie's memory was jogged by her own mention of her Grandpop. Barely breaking contact for a second, she dug a framed photograph from her rucksack's front pocket and set it on the bedside locker. It was the same one she knew her nan had by her bed at home. Nan and Grandpop in profile, laughing happily together.

'There, Grandpop's with you now, too.'

Izzie ran the back of her forefinger gently down Nan's cheek; the skin was smooth over her cheekbones, lines sinking away.

'Do you remember, when I was seven, I announced to the whole street that you were prettier than the Queen?'

That had been during one of the many school holidays Izzie had spent with her grandparents. Because it had made Nan chuckle with delight, Izzie had made it her mission to repeat it to everyone they met on their walk down to the beach.

A nurse smiled a hello as she entered the room and picked up the photograph Izzie had just set out.

'You're the image of your grandma when she was a

young woman,' she said, looking from the framed snapshot of Molly laughing into Grandpop's face, and then at Izzie. 'You both remind me of Nicole Kidman when she was younger... Beautiful.' She set the photo down again. 'And your grandad was *very* good-looking.'

Izzie made a soft affirmative sound whilst the nurse checked the clear drip bag hanging from a pole next to her grandmother's bed and the nasal canula feeding precious air to her.

All the while, Izzie kept her eyes on her nan's face. Briefly, her eyes opened slightly.

'A ... book.' She gasped, her breathing laboured. The effort it took for her to try and speak was palpable. Realising that she was trying to communicate something important, Izzie leaned closer.

Her words were muffled, almost inaudible. Izzie gently held her nan's fingers and gave them a comforting squeeze. 'Try again, Nan?'

The words Molly spoke were indistinct, but Izzie held them tight, like an audio recording, ready to decipher, replay. She tried again, attempted to be clearer. 'Hid-den. At-attic. Picture. You...?'

'Course. I'll sort it, Nan.' She had no idea what Nan was trying to tell her, but she would work it out. Stroking the sparse but still lively curls from her grandmother's forehead, Izzie felt her heart lurch with love when her nan's pale lips shifted slightly into a ghost of a smile and her pale blue eyes stayed open just a little, just for a moment.

She wanted to beg her grandmother to stay alive – *to not leave her* – and, as if reading Izzie's mind, Nan whispered, 'I-

I'm ready…' Her words again were barely audible, but more easily decipherable now. 'Join your Grandpop…'

Izzie held the cool, bony fingers of her nan's hand and leaned down to press her cheek to the palm. Against the lump in her throat, she whispered, 'Grandpop will be happy to see you again.' Izzie knew it was selfish to wish her to stay. She was ninety-six and clearly ready to leave this world.

Molly's mouth moved in the flicker of a smile, then her laughter lines relaxed, her eyes closed, and a slight puff of air left her mouth.

Grandpop had been gone ten years and her nan had never stopped loving him. *Handsome rascal*, she'd called him many times whilst he'd been alive – and since.

The hand in her own cooled and Izzie felt Justin's palm rest on her shoulder. She had forgotten he was there.

He spoke after a few minutes. 'I swear, she was waiting for you to get here, Izzie.'

The part of her that had visited the past when she'd heard his voice again, that had loved Justin so deeply, wanted to shrug him off, tell him to take a running jump…

But the Izzie of now, stunned by the loss of her most precious relation, shook her head, unable to speak, and laid her free palm over his fingers, grateful for the comfort.

The past didn't matter just then.

The three of them remained unmoving, undisturbed, for a long while.

Chapter Three

Izzie

Blackpool, Thursday June 15, 2017

It was three weeks after Molly Blackshaw had passed. Her funeral had just taken place: a simple service attended by half a dozen neighbours, Izzie and Justin.

The day had been warm and had been both a comfort and a sad affair at once.

Justin stayed for the short service and reception afterwards before leaving for a photo shoot on the Welsh coast.

'I wish I could stick around,' he said as he frowned, 'but this job's been booked for a long time.'

Izzie nodded. 'I'm just glad you came, Justin. Thank you.'

11

He gave a small nod in response, looking as if he didn't know whether to do or say something else.

'Take care, Izzie.' He took hold of her hand and gave it a squeeze. Izzie felt a pang of sadness when he turned to leave, but covered the sensation with a smile as she waved him off from the small local restaurant where she was hosting the reception.

She wanted to ask him when he'd be back, but stopped herself; she didn't want him to know that she might care. She didn't even want to acknowledge to *herself* that she might care, or that she sensed bubbling emotions struggling to break out of the locked box inside, where she'd forced her powerful feelings years ago.

As per Molly's request, her will was read by her solicitor at his offices in Blackpool the following day. The solicitor had arranged for Izzie's mother and stepdad to join them via video call from their home in South Africa.

Nan had left almost everything to Izzie, with the instruction to do with the property as she wished, and to use the money bestowed to enjoy her life. She left a small legacy to daughter-in-law, Valerie, along with a charm bracelet she had once admired. 'I'll send you the bracelet, Mother,' Izzie said, and the solicitor agreed to let Valerie have a bank transfer for the bequest.

'Thanks for organising Molly's send off, Izzie,' Valerie said. 'You know we'd have come if we could, but it's not safe for us to fly these days with David's COPD.'

'I know. Health comes first.' Izzie secretly thought that David's occasional allergies had been upgraded to COPD to create an acceptable excuse for not travelling. The man was as fit as a fiddle and the three of them knew full well that Molly wouldn't have wanted either of them at her funeral service…

After Izzie's father, Tom, had died unexpectedly of a heart attack when she was six, Valerie had hooked up with holidaying South African David just *weeks* later, shocking everyone in their vicinity. Most of all, Molly as Tom's mother.

Molly had called David a money-grabber, and said he needed to pay his own way, not sponge off Tom's life savings. But more than that, she felt very strongly that Valerie should have more respect than to take another man into her house so soon after Tom's death, right under six-year-old Izzie's nose.

She'd felt it was wrong and damaging for Izzie.

Molly's outspoken attitude hadn't won her any affection from her daughter-in-law, and as Izzie had never been close to her mother, the whole thing strengthened her allegiance to the grandparents she already loved to bits.

Strange, Izzie thought, returning from the solicitor's office, but she felt only relief when she waved her mum and stepdad cheerio from the video call screen and returned to her favourite bolt hole.

Maybe it wasn't that strange, really. The peace was liberating, as was the sense of being in her escapist heaven – close to the sea – and the feeling that she was still close to her nan was always present. There was another relief that left her feeling a bit guilty, too. She was relieved to have stepped away from her West Hampstead home. It would help her to put her sorrow at Rufus dying into better perspective. A change of surroundings, albeit for the worst reason possible, offered an unexpected comfort.

She paused at the end of the driveway, letting her gaze travel over the redbrick bungalow: its wide tarmacked drive, side lawn bordered by a mixture of weeds and glorious pads of purple and white aubretia, lavender bushes and heather contained within a low brick front wall.

She made a mental note to do some weeding soon.

The door number was displayed beside the front bay window and picked out in white against a varnished oval of tree trunk. Izzie remembered how Grandpop had carved out the numbers '1' and '2' in the slice of trunk before painting them white.

At around nine years old, she'd sat on a footstool in the back of his garage watching the sweet-smelling wood shavings fall and bounce off the concrete floor; she'd announced confidently to her grandpop that they looked 'like curls'. He'd smiled at her and asked her to bring the dustpan and brush to 'sweep those curls up'.

Relishing the memory, she eased the key from her pocket and moved to the front door, which was actually along the drive on the side of the bungalow and had a tall window off to one side. As she turned the key, the wave of precious, happy memories, the familiar fragrance of muted flowers and the fact that the property was now *hers* struck her in one huge gulping rush.

Eyes streaming, nose running, she thought, *Oh God, I'd*

rather have you both back, but then allowed that thought to alter in her mind to one of, *I'm so grateful you were mine; I'm so happy I was yours.*

Whilst making herself a cup of tea, Izzie phoned her friend and neighbour in West Hampstead to let him know her rough plans. She told him she was considering staying in the bungalow for several months. That thought alone soothed her, as did her neighbour's reaction.

'No problem!' Vinnie said, 'I'll keep an eye on the house here, put the mail out of sight.'

'The key to the letter cage is just on the shelf beside the front door.' Izzie grimaced, 'I meant to remove it, just never got around to it.'

Vinnie laughed, 'It's been there for years, since the eighties when Rufus had a mail chewing pup! I can take a screwdriver round and take it off if you like? It'll only take a few minutes?'

'Oh, that would be great, especially since I may well be here for the rest of the year, Vinnie, there's such a lot to be done.'

Even that news didn't faze her stoic neighbour.

'It's no bother, Izzie. We're both at the end of a phone if there's any concerns – I can easily let you know.'

Before ending the call, they agreed that if Izzie needed to return to West Hampstead for any reason, she could easily jump on a train for a visit.

She phoned Eddie, her boss at DAS – Design, Admin and Secretarial, the agency she had freelanced for, to let him know she was in Blackpool for the foreseeable future.

'Good to hear from you, Izzie!' Eddie added that she

should take as much time as she needed, and when she was ready to take on work again, she could do so remotely if she wished, whilst staying up north.

She also reconnected with her work friends through phone calls. They caught up amidst tears and giggles and promises to keep in touch.

Then Izzie grabbed a little notepad and plonked herself at the kitchen table to make a rough list on how to tackle updating the décor, something she'd regularly thought she would love to do.

Currently, everything clashed colour wise or had a pattern – *just* the way Nan had liked it. Slightly nervous that she would lose the sense of connection with her grandparents if she decorated to her own taste, which was much less, well, *patterned*, Izzie decided she would take photographs first and make a record of the bungalow before she made any alterations. She also decided to use the loft room – which Grandpop had converted many years ago especially for her – as her bedroom and office. That would leave her free to work on clearing the rest of the bungalow and still have somewhere to disappear to without too much dust and chaos; and it would mean she could close the doors on wherever she was working.

The loft had a drop-down ladder that rested in the hallway, and looking at it now, Izzie remembered that when she'd been naughty – which was regularly, according to her mother – Nan and Grandpop would threaten to put her in the loft and take the ladder away.

The thought made her chuckle quietly. The pair of them always had a twinkle in their eyes – especially when they tried to tell her off. She always believed the threat to be her mother's, not her grandparents'.

Izzie photographed all the rooms, pausing to take pictures of all Nan's individual treasures. There was a set of shelves, nestled at the side of the chimney breast, where Nan had always put her favourite bits and bobs. There were photographs of Izzie's dad and herself, Grandpop and Nan, and one of their wedding day – taken when they were laughing and Nan held her daffodils in the air – all in free standing heavy frames. 'I couldn't throw them, Izzie,' she'd told her, 'they were too joyous to go flinging over my shoulder!'

Photographing, hesitating, remembering – it all took Izzie much longer than she'd imagined it would. But then, there was no hurry, she reasoned, and savoured the task. She felt so much love here in the memories.

One of Nan's treasures was a little bowl that Izzie had made from dried penne pasta; it was a rough hexagonal shape, built up on a cardboard base and painted bright blue, a piece of red ribbon threaded through the top layer of pasta and tied in a bow. It had been a rainy day make and holding it, photographing it took Izzie right back to working on it at the kitchen table – kneeling up on the chair, working on a sheet of newspaper, armed with a small pile of pasta and a tube of glue, a tester pot of bright blue paint and a length of red ribbon. 'How about making me something for my special shelf?' Nan had asked, and Izzie remembered how excited she'd been at that prospect.

The dark red rose petals from the garden that Nan had packed into the blue pasta bowl spilt out, spilt their scent... Izzie realised how true it was that smells could evoke the most powerful memories.

The dish looked so simple and yet had taken hours to make. Maybe, she thought, she would put this aside, keep it. It twisted her insides to think of throwing it away, and there was no way that a charity shop would want to take a very dodgy but much-loved pasta bowl... 'Maybe I could use it for paper clips,' she whispered, popping it on top of the cream tiled mantelpiece. How typical of Nan that she would keep a gift so childishly made amongst her other *most special treasures*.

As she worked, Izzie thought she'd get an album especially for the bungalow pictures, and write little notes about some of the photographs so that she could have the best of the memories, without having to physically keep everything. It was hard though – the temptation was to keep so much.

She hadn't thought there would be much to sort out at her nan's bungalow. Every visit for the past few years, her nan had directed Izzie to parcel up this and take that to the local charity shop. Now Izzie understood why.

There wasn't too much but there was a lot more than she'd thought.

She tackled the rooms systematically, ignoring the large kitchen at the back of the bungalow for now and concentrating on clearing the lounge first.

She would keep a recliner chair and the two-seater leather settee and the *'all mod-cons telly,'* as Nan had called it, mainly because it had a remote control. The large upright armchairs and heavy coffee table could go to the local charity shop – they'd know her well pretty soon – and a phone call secured their pickup later in the week.

Deciding to begin by clearing knick-knacks from the fireplace and wrapping them in newspaper, Izzie paused as she held a cast iron, crocodile-shaped nutcracker that was over a foot long. It was in two halves, and the bottom jaw was moved by lifting the tail.

Once, when she was very little, Nan had been looking after not only Izzie, but also a neighbour's child, a boy of about five years old from across the road, whilst his mum went to the dentist. *'Just for an hour,'* she remembered the neighbour saying.

The two of them had played with building blocks on the rug because it was too wet to play in the back yard and Grandpop was having an afternoon nap, feet propped on the step of the tiled fireplace.

Izzie had gone to get them both a biscuit from the kitchen – they'd made some with Nan earlier – and when she came back into the lounge, she found that the little boy, Timothy, had jiggled Grandpop's big toe into the crocodile's jaws, and she saw him leap into the air to jump on the tail. Izzie had squealed as Grandpop's toe was crushed in the jaws.

Her squeal was *nothing* compared to the noise Grandpop had made as he shot upright out of his chair to standing in less than a second. 'Yeoooooow!'

Izzie grimaced at the vivid memory – she'd never heard her Grandpop swear either before or since but on that occasion, she'd heard some new words ... and was told by Nan that she must *never* repeat them. Ever.

Nan had ushered Izzie and Timothy into the kitchen, distracting them with biscuits whilst she got ice on Grandpop's toe, and it wasn't long before Izzie and Timothy had heard laughter from the front room.

Izzie learned some time later that Grandpop's toenail had gone black with bruising, but there wasn't any serious damage.

The crocodile had disappeared onto a high shelf in the hallway cupboard for many years after that, reappearing only when there were no toe-cracking youngsters around anymore.

It wasn't easy, Izzie thought, to get rid of knick-knacks that had such powerful memories attached, but she took a deep breath and wrapped the cast iron crocodile in newspaper, popping it in a bag whilst she reminded herself that *that* was why she'd photographed every single item.

She slid some newspaper-wrapped ornaments into an ancient string shopping bag and laid it in the hallway; she could carry a bag or two up to Cleveleys – the nearest town centre – most days, it'd be a good excuse to get some of that potent sea air.

'*No one's breathed that air before you do,*' Grandpop used to say.

Because her nan had been ninety-six, had outlived Grandpop by ten years and had appeared content to go, the sadness Izzie felt was all for herself and there was a strange ease in that. Nan always said that she'd had a good life despite having lived through the war, life in a boarding house and multiple recessions. And she always spoke with warmth and a twinkle in her eyes when talking about her much-loved husband.

As she continued to dust then wrap ornaments and books before packing them into easy-to-carry bags, Izzie let the memories embrace her whilst she worked, small bursts of quiet laughter escaping her when she thought about things like how she'd believed her granddad when he told her that they had to sweep the dead cowboys out of the back of their TV at the end of the night back when he was younger... She'd been about seven years old and part horrified, part fascinated. But it never occurred to her at the time that the story wasn't true.

The *rat-a-tat-tat* on the door knocker just under a week later made Izzie straighten up from where she was sanding the skirting board.

'Just a minute!' she called out, blowing dust from her face.

She opened the door to find Justin on the step.

'Justin? I – I didn't know you were back.' She mentally shook herself to stop her mind from flying back in time, fighting the urge to leap into his arms so he could swing her around the way he used to when they'd been apart for more than an hour or two.

'Do you want to come in?' Whilst she spoke, a small smile tilted his mouth at one corner.

Izzie froze in place, finding it hard to breathe. Was the fizzing effect he had on her visible?

His dark blond hair had been tousled by the breeze and his clear hazel-green eyes closed a little against the bright afternoon sun. He wore a soft, tan leather jacket, khaki T-shirt and dark jeans. The combination was powerful, *sexy*; she fought that thought.

Unsuccessfully.

'I won't, thanks – I'm on my way out to pick something up for Mum and Dad—' he indicated with his thumb in the direction of next-door '—so thought I'd check in, see if you fancy eating out tonight and taking a bit of a break?'

'Yes.' Why? Why did she say that?

She wanted to recant and say *no*, because, well – was she *forgiving* him by saying yes? Justin was quicker to respond.

'Great! I'll call back in a couple of hours, then. We could walk into Cleveleys?'

'Okay.' Izzie nodded and raised her hand in farewell as he made his way off down the driveway; she watched until he turned the corner of the avenue, out of sight.

As she moved back indoors, she caught sight of her reflection in the full-length hallway mirror and was stunned to stillness. Her cheeks were pink, eyes over bright, and she could feel her pulse pounding a bit too quickly.

She had on a shapeless, blue checked button-up of her nan's, leggings, unwashed hair trapped in a clip, dust smeared on her forehead and shocking pink Marigolds with black fur round the top and a purple plastic bling ring. They were a joke pair she'd bought for Nan once, and she'd happily worn them and then hung them up with a dolly peg each time, *in pride of place*, she'd confided, as they made her feel glamorous.

'Bit grim, Izzie.' She gave a half laugh at her image and it occurred to her then that she hadn't made an effort to look decent for ages; the thought of doing so tonight lifted her spirits. That Justin had just called round seemed a bit surreal. Had she really said *yes* to going out to eat with him?

The flutter in her stomach began again and whilst she cleared up Izzie forced herself to test how she would feel had she said no. She decided she'd made the right choice – or rather, her mouth had. Yet, at the same time, that sense of past hurt began to bubble to the surface, fought with the part of herself that badly wanted to forgive and move on, and told her that forgiving him would be papering over the emotional crevice that would only come back to haunt her. Surely?

After stacking her sanding tools to one side, she took a deep breath, and set the shower to run hot in order to soothe the unrest inside with the promise that Justin wasn't going to hurt her again. Everything was different now. They had both moved on, gone their separate ways to live their own dreams during their time apart.

That might not have happened if Justin *had* turned up that day.

And so, she was going to make an effort to look good for herself this evening, not him.

At least that's what she told herself as she scrunched her unruly curls dry using the fabulous hair dryer she'd bought her nan last Christmas. *'Almost blew my blinkin' curls off,'* Nan had laughed and confided in Izzie that she used it to warm her hands when she didn't want to put the heating on.

After applying a touch of grey eye pencil and a flick of mascara for the first time in months – the sparse make-up that she had stowed away in her rucksack when she'd grabbed it in her haste to leave London – Izzie studied her reflection and thought she looked too pale. She remembered her nan telling her that back as a youngster, if she ran out of rouge, she'd pinched her cheeks to bring colour to them. She tried it and smiled at the mirror when it worked.

'Thanks, Nan.'

By the time she was dressed in a pair of straight legged jeans, sandals and a floaty deep blue top, time had moved quickly on.

Her insides gave a nervous jump at the knock on the door. She finished dabbing on a touch of lip salve in front of the still steamed-up bathroom mirror before hurrying to open the front door.

She was greeted by Justin's familiar wonky smile, the colour in his cheeks raised from the brisk breeze. 'Are you ready to go, Izzie?'

Grabbing her bag from the hat stand, she pulled the front door closed after her. 'Yes, I'm hungry.' She must be – especially if her roiling stomach was anything to go by.

She knew it was more than that though, she was also struggling to push down the anger and upset she'd kept locked inside for so long. Her bubbling emotions asked, *why?* Why had he left her waiting? He hadn't responded to her calls or texts; he'd simply ignored her.

Yet for a reason she didn't understand, she couldn't just ask him why he hadn't turned up that day. And even though so much had changed for them, and they were both very different people now, she still found him as knee-bucklingly good looking as ever. But it wasn't just that, Izzie was sure she still felt that magnetic pull towards Justin, that bond that had once seen their lives so closely entwined. So closely entwined that they had made a pact to meet in August 2011, to travel from wherever they were – certain by that time they'd be ready to settle down.

They walked towards the promenade, a gusting breeze and clamouring gulls negating the need for conversation. When they'd dated, they had never needed to talk all the time either.

For the first time in almost six years, Izzie let herself peep closely at the deeply buried memory of that fateful day…

After waving Nan away on a long weekend break, Izzie had taken her time, revelling in her preparations.

She'd coaxed her hair so it fell in a tumble of curls, carefully applied hardly-there make-up, stepped into a handsewn yellow sundress she had spent all of her spare time making after work especially for the occasion – it had excitement sewn into every stitch. She had also prepared a delicious picnic of their favourite nibbles and packed a bottle of fizz and tumblers.

As she'd left the bungalow, Izzie had known a delicious, building exhilaration, imagined she felt a little like a bride-to-be about to embark on her future with the love of her life…

Justin had to have simply forgotten or been distracted by more important things; there couldn't be any other reason. Distracted by the beautiful models he photographed most likely.

Meeting up with him had been *the* most important thing to Izzie, something etched in stone, the focus of her future; and she would have *walked* from London to Blackpool to keep their pact if she'd had to. It clearly hadn't been as important to him though.

Her gut now seemed to squeeze painfully as they neared the promenade. She forced the emotions back down into Pandora's box, deep inside, tamping the lid down hard. The effort of locking them down again was intense.

The sea breeze blew fresh against her cheeks as they reached the prom, and Izzie raised her face to inhale the sea air, breathing deeply and coming to a halt overlooking the beach, a wide rim of sand darkened by the outgoing tide.

Justin moved beside her and when she heard him take a deep breath too, she almost – almost – leaned against him as she would have in the past. Shaking herself into the present, she wrapped her arms around her middle, and rubbed her upper arms beneath the floaty top to quell the urge to touch him that sprang from nowhere, or, more accurately, sprang from somewhere in the past.

'Are your mum and dad having some work done?' She'd heard some loud banging earlier and had assumed it was workmen his folks had in.

'They wanted the back window out and some French

doors put in to look out on the garden. Mum said you should come over and have a look and a brew with them when you're free.'

'Always such a welcome at your mum's.' Izzie smiled. 'Thanks, tell her I will.'

'How's things going with you, Izzie?'

Bloody marvellous.

Thank God she didn't have a think bubble over her head flagging up how she really felt. By unspoken mutual consent, they began walking slowly again, along the prom.

'It feels easier than it did sorting things out after Rufus died, probably because Nan and I spent some time every visit going through her stuff.'

She touched Nan's rose-gold locket, which hung around her neck. Nan had given it to her on one such visit and Izzie smiled at the memory as they strolled along the prom overlooking the grey, sunlit sea, tips of white that rose then disappeared. They came to a standstill again, the evening breeze salty and warm, the gulls cawing, the tingle in the wind and the whole sea front seeming so familiar to her.

Like home. The perfect place to heal before moving on with her life.

'If you need help moving things, I'm here for a few days before I'm taking off again.'

They both turned to look at one another at the same time.

Izzie's breath caught when Justin's eyes met hers, his pupils dilated and a slight smile twitched at the corner of his mouth; in response, her insides tangibly squeezed. She desperately wanted to keep the lid on her pain. She also desperately wanted to know what he was thinking...

Attraction and heartache twisted together like the strands of a silk rope.

She took a deep breath; it wasn't easy to stay upset when he offered to help.

Was it guilt making him offer these kind gestures?

What was the harm in having him help?

She could use him like he had obviously used her – but somehow that thought didn't ring true...

'Thanks. It'd be a help when it comes to handing stuff down the ladder.'

Gulls cried loudly as they circled overhead, their racket reminding Izzie and Justin they were on their way somewhere...

———

'As much as I love Nan's bungalow, it feels great to escape for a while.' Izzie sipped the red wine, taking a moment to study Justin whilst he concentrated on cutting his steak. Soft music played in the background and the lights were dimmed a little. The restaurant had a cosy, amber glow that glistened in the highlights of his sun-lightened, dark blond hair. He'd always reminded her of a surfer: tanned, mussed hair touched with pale gold highlights, and a constant five-o clock shadow dusting his firm jaw.

'I can imagine.' He looked up, gave a small smile, picked up his own glass and clinked it against Izzie's. 'We always did enjoy escaping.' His smile sank without a trace; pain flashed in his eyes briefly, almost as if he realised that he'd unintentionally brought up their shared past. He looked away from her, then downward, deliberately focusing on his meal instead.

Pain stabbed Izzie unexpectedly at his words, that familiar sense of something lost welling up.

Why did he think it was fine to break her heart and offer no explanation? Never any letters, any word to let her know why he hadn't turned up?

Maybe, she thought, setting down her glass, he had forgotten that part of their past. Maybe it meant nothing to him, especially once his celebrity work began to pour in.

If only it had been that easy for her. Instead, life with Rufus ensured she rarely looked back at her time spent with Justin.

What she hadn't realised when she'd cut off her feelings, was that they hadn't miraculously disappeared as she'd subconsciously assumed, they simply remained to be faced another day.

Unfinished business.

The following day, the hallway at her nan's bungalow – *her* bungalow now, she reminded herself – was stacked with things to go to charity shops, lowered down from where they had been stored in the loft room which was now much clearer. Izzie was closer to having her loft haven sorted, ready to work and sleep in whilst she decorated the rest.

Justin called up to her that he was going to start taking

the stack of boxes and bags out to the car. 'I'll run these boxes to the charity shop, shall I Izzie, before they close? Should get at least half of them moved today.'

He added that he'd ask his folks if they wanted anything whilst he was out and reminded Izzie that his mum had made a casserole they could eat whenever they wanted.

'Shall I pick up the grub when I get back?'

'Sounds good, thanks. Take the key off the side, Justin. And tell your mum she's a star!' She almost added *and so are you*, but stopped herself – she wasn't sure why, and she was equally unsure why she wasn't *liking* herself for holding back her gratitude.

It made her feel petty, ungrateful. Much like she'd been with her mum and stepdad as a teenager. An awkward feeling. Maybe it was time she accepted that she and Justin could be friends – or at least *kind* of friends – despite their past? Could she stop the rushes of emotion? Get them under control enough to be just friends? It certainly didn't seem to be bothering Justin that they'd been lovers – *more* than lovers actually, two youngsters in love so deeply, but *knowing* in their ambitious hearts that they needed to follow their individual dreams before settling down with one another.

Hearing him drive away, she forced herself to put that aside and think about the job in hand.

––––––––––

Every inch of the bungalow held Molly's giant personality in its fabric.

Heavily patterned wallpaper, swirly carpets and a kitchen straight from the 1950s. It had been Molly's idea of perfection.

She'd always batted away Izzie's ideas of bringing the décor up to date, saying that there'd been enough years of plain and drab in wartime. She wanted – and enjoyed – colour and large patterns in her life. *It doesn't matter if they clash*, Nan always said, *colour and patterns make me happy.*

Izzie couldn't – and didn't – argue with Nan's reasoning.

Climbing the ladder to the loft, Izzie wanted to do another check around to see if anything else needed ferrying downstairs.

Smiling and arching backward in a stretch, Izzie looked around the wide-open space of the large loft room.

Her bed, the one that had been hers to use any time she visited and then permanently when she moved in at fifteen, needed to remain for some time yet. A sharp pang took her breath for a moment, as she remembered Justin and herself lying there and kissing...

She had thought she would melt; she'd been seventeen, Justin eighteen, almost nineteen, and they'd nipped up into the loft when they were home alone, Nan and Grandpop having gone to a long birthday lunch with a pal.

That had been right at the beginning of when their friendship became something more. Something far more.

Snapping herself back into work mode to stop any further memories of Justin, she smiled at the sunset seascape painted by her granddad that she had always loved – one she'd hung above the bed beneath the sloped ceiling.

She had sat with him at the back of the bungalow in the sun lounge that ran all across the rear of the bungalow watching, spellbound, whilst he painted.

At the grand age of eleven, she had her own special paper to paint on and attempted to copy how Grandpop painted. He'd showed her how to mix colours, how to put a white froth on the blue sea at the shoreline, but when they were done, she'd announced that Grandpop's painting was better than hers. She'd asked if she could have it for her upstairs bedroom and he'd said only if he could have hers for the kitchen. She'd grinned, well aware she'd got the better deal but wondering if Grandpop realised that.

The painting was going to go in the box of keepsake treasures she absolutely could *not* part with. *Ever.* She reached up to unhook the painting, intending to dust the narrow blackwood frame and put it back in place.

'Oh!' sprang from her as the painting came away from the wall.

Behind the roughly A3 size painting, a rectangle had been cut in the boarding and a small door fashioned and held in place with duct tape.

Curious, Izzie carefully set the painting down beside her bed and eased the door open slowly to reveal a shelf in the eaves resting against the outer brick wall. A package, wrapped in layers of old newspaper and tied around with string, sat on the shelf.

'What's this?' She wriggled the package out of the opening, years of dust rising off it. A shaft of light through the roof window lit the motes as they rose into the air, making her sneeze. Tiny fragments of cement, loosened from the bricks and mortar over the years, scattered from the folds of wrapping, showering her legs and the bed she knelt on.

Moving to sit on the rug on the floor beside the bed, Izzie slowly peeled away the newspaper to reveal a lovely green notebook.

She ran her fingertips slowly over the worn green textured cover, pausing over a small, embossed sprig of yellow flowers decorating the top left-hand side. The book felt as if it held more pages than it was meant to, the reason becoming clear when she opened it up to reveal the stiff inner flap that was covered in an array of what looked like mementos. A border of cream and pink flowered wallpaper formed a strip along the top of the page, a deep, neatly cut border of newspaper reinforced the bottom of the page and bore what looked like ink drawings of dandelions and daisies. Colourful flowers had been cut from magazines and stuck on the newspaper too. A stylised ink sketch of a playing card, the Queen of Hearts, had been drawn on the inside of a cigarette box and stuck on the newspaper border. There was also a piece of card that held a beautifully embroidered flower, what Izzie presumed to be a cinema ticket, and, on a scrap of card that could have come from the inside of a pack of cigarettes, an intricate pencil sketch of a beautiful young woman, curls framing her features, a slight smile playing on her mouth…

'Nan.' She traced the beautiful, delicate sketch. She could hardly bear to drag her eyes away from the drawing.

The sheer care with which it had been crafted was breath-taking. What a gift, to be able to capture the essence of a face in such a simple sketch. Moved to capture the lovely moment herself, Izzie grabbed her phone and immortalised the sketch with her own photograph, before broadening the lens's scope and photographing the entire page. Turning the book over in her fingertips, she touched the edge of the pages, it looked as though extra pages had been trimmed to fit and fixed in place at the back, maybe when more were needed. The pages gaped very slightly because more mementos had been attached to the inside pages. She turned back to the inner front cover once more, fingers gently tracing along the strip of newspaper, an invisible flap lifted unexpectedly.

Questions crowded Izzie's mind. Why was the book hidden away? Was it meant to be found? Why did the discovery make her heart trip faster?

A deep pink rose, cut with tremendous care from a magazine, also decorated the newspaper envelope. There was something inside, she realised. The envelope was very slightly raised, yet she only found the opening by running her finger along the paper. Izzie slid out the contents.

It was a short letter.

A huge spear of nervousness tingled through her with the realisation that it was a letter from Nan. Her handwriting had always been the same; small, neat and loopy, tilted slightly to the right.

It felt like prying where maybe she shouldn't and her fingers trembled slightly, not knowing what it was she had found. Was it private?

Questions crowded her mind, but Izzie couldn't just wrap the notebook up again and pretend she hadn't found it. The lure of Nan's words was greater than her prickling conscience. Yet, the enormity of reading someone else's letter made her breath catch, made her hesitate.

In the end, the enticement of potentially spending more time with her deeply loved Nan won the battle of conscience.

Carefully, she flattened out the thin paper of the letter, eyes growing wide as she read:

1946

I can't tell a living soul what happened. There's only one place I can tell the truth and that's here in this notebook.

This began as a place to record my joy at meeting him, but over time it became somewhere I had to write everything down to help me cope with my life and keep my sanity. No one knows what is written in these pages. I and me, and that's it.

I intend to keep it; it holds precious letters and memories. I intend to keep it for a while and read through it one last time before I burn it. That is my intention, but likely I won't be able to part with it. There's too much here that matters to me. To my beloved husband.

In the meantime, whilst I decide what to do, it's a safe place to keep the secret. M.

'Ah!'

'The book ...' Nan's whispered words when she'd struggled to speak.

'Hidden ... the attic ... the picture.'

Was this it? Izzie closed her eyes as she replayed her nan's struggle to tell her about the book.

Had she said any more? She didn't think so.

Her own response – *'Don't worry, whatever it is, I'll sort it, Nan'* – had drawn a little, unmistakeable smile, a smile that Nan regarded Izzie's hands as safe ones. It reassured her that Nan had wanted her to find this – and nobody else. She hugged the notebook to her chest, silently thanked her nan for trusting her with this – and effectively removing any guilt from her for being inquisitive.

'I'm back, Izzie.' The front door closed and Justin's voice carried up into the loft. 'Got our dinner here.'

'Won't be a minute.'

Shaken back to the present, Izzie carefully slid the notebook into a clean pillowcase and called down to Justin. 'Can I pass you something delicate?'

'Sure. Just let me stick these plates on the table first. Be right back.'

Whilst they ate the casserole, Izzie briefly filled Justin in on what was in the pillowcase.

'It looks like a scrapbook, or diary, or maybe it's a bit of both.' She grimaced. 'Crikey, if my mum had found it, it'd be in the recycling bin by now.' That thought made Izzie gasp, that something so precious to her nan could have been thrown out without a second glance. So precious that it had been hidden away in a specially made hiding place, and had been carefully wrapped in newspaper and string to protect it against damage. It had been hidden in Izzie's room, perhaps on purpose with the thought that Izzie would be the one to find it?

'Nan worked in her stepmother's boarding house in Blackpool during the war. But she was so straightforward and down to earth, I can't imagine her having any deep, dark secrets.'

'It was a different time, Izzie. What folks kept to themselves then likely wouldn't shock anyone now.'

'Do you think?'

'I'd say so.'

They finished eating, and as Justin stood to collect the plates and return them to his folks, he stretched out his back. 'I'll make a move now, Izzie, thanks for dinner. Dad wants me to sort out a dripping tap before I go home.'

She laughed. 'Thank your mum for our dinner, Justin! And thanks for your help today.'

'Anytime.' He gave her a smile that was off the sizzleometer and raked his fingers back through his dishevelled hair. 'I'm working my way through their list of jobs in between my paid jobs. I've some work going on in my house, so it helps that I'm here and I can leave the builder to it during the day. He gives me a call and I pop back if he needs anything.'

'You live nearby then?'

'Just a couple of miles away.' He paused at the front

door, faced Izzie fully and for a moment she thought he was going to lean in and kiss her cheek – she could have sworn he leaned slightly towards her. Her breath caught and something akin to a rush of anticipation followed by disappointment assailed her as he straightened up and away, reaching for the door handle. She caught a fleeting expression in his green eyes – was it hurt? It was too fleeting to identify as pain for sure, but she felt it could be.

'Justin…'

He paused when she said his name.

'Thanks for all your help, I really appreciate it.' She smiled and watched as an answering smile curved his mouth, then wavered. Izzie felt spikes of adrenaline when his eyes met hers and he held her gaze as he spoke.

'You're welcome, Izzie.'

She waved him away, briefly closing her eyes at the effort expended to keep him at arm's length, to resist the lure of that sensual smile that had always had the ability to speed her pulse.

That evidently hadn't changed.

Alone now, Izzie poured a glass of red wine and set it down on a small table beside the large, pink, flowery utility armchair in the back room, beside the French door.

The notebook was a little bigger than A5 size, Izzie thought, the handwriting in dark blue ink and so familiar in style…

Chapter Four

Molly

Blackpool, Saturday November 6, 1943

Dear Diary,
    I should be getting off to sleep, but I'm too excited. I need to write down what happened today, so I never forget.

Dora had just left work and I stood in the doorway of the boarding house to cool off before going back inside to put the cleaning stuff away in the hall cupboard.

Enid shouted from the kitchen that I should answer the front door. I wanted to tell her to do it herself but kept my voice down to a whisper.

I wasn't *that* brave to answer my stepmother back...

I raised my curls away from my hot face and neck; I knew they needed combing. But that didn't matter.

No one ever cared what I looked like – so long as they got fed and a bed.

I whisked open the door to find two tall, dark men, so smart in RAF uniforms and more handsome than *anyone* I had ever seen.

I was transfixed.

'Joe Blackshaw, miss. We're billeted with you. And I'm *very* pleased to meet you.' He held out his hand to shake mine, blue eyes twinkling. He had a smile that took my breath away, and he told me that I wasn't seeing double as he gestured sideways. 'This is my twin brother, Jack.'

Joe Blackshaw's hand was warm and I thought I'd like to hold on to it for longer. His open smile and sparkling blue eyes made my insides flip about like a landed fish. I stood there, smiling like a twerp and then a bit belatedly, I moved my hand to Jack's, and said it was nice to meet him, too.

'How do.' He looked exactly like his brother, his smile a match too, but my stomach didn't lurch about when his hand closed around my fingers. I thought that was strange.

I led them both into the lounge to meet Enid, introducing myself as Molly, stepdaughter of Enid, on the walk along the hallway.

I was kept busy then with a continual stream of billets arriving, right up until mealtime. But I'd a right old struggle to keep my excitement under control at the thought of seeing handsome Joe Blackshaw again, the warmth I'd felt at the touch of his hand…

All the guests settled down for their meal and when it

came to clearing the plates afterwards, Joe brought his pots to the kitchen, followed by several others who did the same.

'Do you go dancing?' he asked without preamble. 'We're off to the Tower Ballroom in a bit. Will we see you there?'

My insides were flip flopping again; I took their plates, aware of Enid standing at the cooker stirring custard.

I whispered that I hoped to go, and prayed that mother wouldn't hear me making plans – she'd a way of ruining them.

'You've a lot of clearing up to do, young lady, before you go off gallivanting!'

She'd heard.

But I could work quick when I'd a mind to.

I was just about to open the back-room door to say goodnight when I heard Enid pipe up that it was time I was married and off her hands. She was talking to a neighbour, Marian Howarth, my friend Dora's mum, who'd come for her regular cup of tea on a Saturday evening. Enid told Marian I'd be left on the shelf at this rate. I was a bit shocked when she added, '*Always out with this one and that, a right flibbertigibbet. I've told her – no funny business with our billets – no good can come of that.*'

That was such an unfair thing to say! I love dancing and the way the band or organ music makes me happy. But *flibbertigibbet*? I enjoy a laugh and a joke, a kiss and a cuddle, but I don't *flibbertigibbet* around!

But there was something I did like about her words – getting wed would mean moving out of Enid's proximity.

Now that idea appealed...

'There's time yet, Enid, the lass is only twenty-one,' Marian responded.

'I don't know, Marian, I think Bill, God rest his soul, let her have all of her own road. She's a bit too keen on enjoying herself, that one.' Enid sighed. 'Most girls her age are settling down.'

Hearing her talking about Dad spurred me into action and I stuck my head round the door to tell them I was off out shortly.

She announced she'd need help traying up the bacon and the like early in the morning.

I don't know why – maybe some latent contrary streak in me – but I shot her a beaming smile and said, 'Six?'

She blinked with surprise, unable to hide her reaction. 'Just before.'

'Right ho.'

I hurried and dressed in the navy tailored dress I planned to wear that evening, quick dab of lippy and a speedy run through with the hairbrush.

The more I thought about it, the more getting married and moving away sounded just the ticket.

I just needed someone to get married to…

Someone I loved – *a lot*.

———————

Dora and I walked arm in arm along the sea front, night bombers flying out across the sea providing a continuous drone.

I told her that I'd looked a right sweaty Betty when I'd

met the Blackshaw brothers and that Joe had asked if I was going dancing and he'd said he and his brother might go too.

I kicked one leg backwards to inspect the eyebrow pencil seam running down the back of my calf, and the light coat of gravy browning used to resemble the colour of stockings. 'Be a shame if the sea mist took it off!'

Laughing, we moved nearer the tram tracks, out of reach of the spray, then crossed the road to go into the Tower – the ballroom our favourite Saturday night destination.

As we shrugged out of our coats, Dora said she was coming around to help out tomorrow teatime to get a proper look at the brothers. I laughed because she always came to help on a Sunday teatime.

Dancing was in full swing when we entered the ballroom. Many of the men were in uniform, some in smart suits, some young women in land army uniform and others in dresses.

Wonderful upbeat organ music filled the room, helping to set aside the press and gloom of the war, the unending melancholy news of injuries, death and destruction, the food shortages, the cold…

Dora went off to dance with an old friend and disappeared into the crowd. I watched as she moved away, and my heartbeat stuttered when my gaze met Joe Blackshaw's; he gave me a nod and my cheeks flamed in response.

'Evenin', Molly.'

None of the RAF trainees billeted with us at the boarding house had *ever* had this effect on me.

In fact, *no one* ever had.

I couldn't understand why he affected me so that I felt short of breath, swept along, *chosen* especially for his attention as though I was special.

'Want to dance?' He smiled his captivating smile, lovely eyes twinkling, and it almost made me forget I needed to actually say '*Yes*'. Then he held out his hand for mine, brow raised in question ... and whisked me onto the dance floor.

He held me and I fancied we floated, waltzing around the heavenly floor. He was so handsome, his easy smile compelling. I could feel the warmth of his palm on my back through my dress, holding me against him – and yet, I wanted more, to be closer still. Whilst we danced, I imagined myself in a beautiful romantic film, one with a happy ending...

My Dear Diary, I felt like the cat that got the cream being whisked around the dance floor, aware that many pairs of female eyes followed Joe, yet he didn't return their gaze.

He kept his eyes on mine and his were filled with warmth.

'You enjoy dancing?' he asked me, and I nodded. He held me a little closer against him.

My sigh of happiness ended abruptly when someone grabbed my arm and jerked me away from Joe.

'What you doing with him?' It was Denis, a past dance partner, a disgruntled expression on his boyish face.

Joe asked, 'Who's this then, Molly?'

'Denis.' He cocked his chin. 'I'm her young man.'

Joe raised his brow. 'Are you?'

'No. We've danced now and again, but he's not my

young man. I would know!' I was cross that Denis had spoilt such a wonderful, dreamy moment.

Taller and stronger-looking, Joe jerked his thumb, indicating that Denis should shift away. 'Find someone else to dance with.'

'Bitch.' Denis spat in my direction, but I didn't care.

I could have burst with happiness; Joe had sent Denis on his way. I felt even more treasured, cared for and protected by this tall, handsome, uniformed man, and the warmth inside me turned molten. I couldn't stop smiling for being so happy.

We danced until it was time for the music to end for the night; for the first time ever at the Tower, I had danced with only *one* partner. Joe Blackshaw. He bought us both drinks, spent all of his time with me... He was so attentive. I felt like a princess; I had never met anyone like him.

Joe held my coat and I slid my arms into the sleeves. 'It's been a grand night, Joe.'

'It has.' He put his arm along my shoulder and smiled in agreement, that wonderful smile again, and I waved to Dora who was also making her way out with Jack and another couple who walked in the same direction home.

It was so dark sometimes and we all bunched together as a rule to be safer.

Joe and I dawdled at the back as we walked along the promenade. I barely felt the bitingly cold November wind tossing the waves and my hair, chilling everything in its path.

Joe chattered non-stop about how he was looking forward to being posted somewhere warm once his training was complete. How he'd intended to become part of the air crew eventually rather than ground support; that's what their extra training was for, he said.

We drew level with one of the shelters and he guided me towards it so we could move inside out of the wind.

He took me in his arms and kissed me then. His mouth and the tip of his nose were cold, yet warmth rushed through me when he held me, his mouth moving expertly over mine. He held me closer and closer.

'You are beautiful,' he whispered, briefly raising his mouth before kissing me again. 'Your hair is lovely.' His fingers tangled with my wild curls and I felt the gentle tug deep inside. 'I felt like one lucky man tonight, Molly, having you all to myself.'

The weak moonlight showed him smiling, 'Every man in the Tower Ballroom envied me. I love that feeling.'

I knew pure bliss in that moment. The waves ebbed and flowed, and the sound of them breaking on the shoreline in the pitch dark below the prom added a magical, romantic soundtrack that filled my heart to bursting.

I tingled from the warmth of his closeness, the embrace of his arms and the loving words I treasured, held close. I felt truly cared about. I'd never had compliments like those before, never been kissed so thoroughly before. I'd never been so happy to be me before. I could feel myself melt against him, but then, just as Joe's palm moved to my hip to gather me closer, Jack called across to us.

'I'm going to see Dora home, Joe, Molly.'

Heartbeat galloping, I pulled away from Joe. The waxing moon cast a brief hazy silver light over the promenade. I waved over in Dora and Jack's direction, called cheerio, breathless because only when I came up for air did I realise that I had been completely carried away, in what felt like a romantic trance – unsure how far I'd have gone if Jack hadn't shouted. I felt like I'd had all my bones removed.

'I need to get home too, time's getting on.' I said those words because I thought I should, but I would rather have returned to the heated kisses.

That engaging smile of his showed in the dim moonlight. He seemed unworried by the interruption and offered his arm for me to link. 'Let's get you home, then, love.'

I wanted to say something, tell him that I did want him to hold me and kiss me, but I was still shocked at my reaction to him, at how easily I'd thrown caution to the wind… I didn't really understand how it seemed so right to be close to him after such a short time of knowing him.

Against the daily tedium of air raid sirens and cold cramped shelters and rationing, Joe was my shaft of happiness, of light, even perhaps escape. His smile, his easy laughter and conversation of home in Manchester, of their postings so far, was a huge contrast to the daily grind, news of deaths, endless rumours of imminent invasion on the coastline, and working with Enid – who, at the best of times, was sullen.

Enid could drain the laughter and fun from me in a heartbeat.

Being with Joe – just walking alongside him – so very handsome in uniform, entertaining and easy to talk to, made my world bearable, beautiful, even.

To be kissed by him and held so tightly, and to feel I was the only one that mattered in his world…

It was shocking how much I wanted him, wanted him even as we turned in off the promenade onto Banks Street and into the boarding house front yard.

Joe squeezed my hand when I said I'd better go in first in case Mother was about and that he should follow shortly along with Jack. He wished me goodnight and I floated into the hallway on a cloud of bliss.

Blackpool, Sunday November 7, 1943

I've been kept busy all day and only just caught a glance of Joe at breakfast, before he and the others went out.

I'd almost finished preparing for Sunday tea, and was wringing out a clean tea towel until it was almost dry to tuck over the tray of butties to keep them fresh, when Dora arrived to help.

I lined up the brown teapots and spooned in tea from the caddy.

Dora shared some sugar around the sugar bowls and asked if there was anything else, she could do to help. 'That's what I'm here for, Molly!'

'Mmm, I'm sure that's *all* you've come for!' We laughed and ferried the plates of sandwiches, homemade scones, butter curls, teapots and paraphernalia through to the dining room, where a mixture of hungry RAF trainees and a couple of civil servants played cards, listened to the radio and wrote letters. They all eagerly awaited Sunday tea.

'I'll take that,' Joe said, taking the loaded sandwich tray from me. 'Jack will bring the teapots.'

I looked over his shoulder to Jack and he raised his thumb and said, 'Will do,' his smile warm and friendly.

'Oh! Thanks.'

'We've been told to help where we can. Is there anything else to bring through?'

'Just cups and the rest of the teapots.'

'We'll sort it.' He smiled, his blue eyes sparkled with warmth and I wished at that moment I'd put some lipstick on, brushed my hair and changed my frock. I smiled back, unable to string a response together because my breath caught at the sight of those blue eyes.

I thanked him again and actually *squeaked* when I spoke to him. I thought I should pinch myself for being so affected.

Luckily, if he noticed, he didn't say anything.

I nipped off into the hallway to sound the gong for mealtime, just in case any guests were still in their rooms, then made my way back through the dining room to check all was well.

'Will you and your friend come for a walk after tea?' Joe piled some sandwiches on his plate. I'd a job not to jump up and down with glee!

I said I'd ask Dora and hurried into the kitchen.

Well, in all honesty, Dear Diary, I ran!

Dora was wiping down the kitchen worktable and said

it'd be okay to go for a walk so long as she wasn't out too late.

Joe, Jack and a couple of the other billeted RAF trainees helped to clear the tables, and wash and dry the pots after tea, whilst Dora and I set the tables for breakfast the following morning. We were finished and ready to go in record time.

Within minutes, the Blackshaw brothers, Dora and I were walking along the promenade, the chill breeze bringing the fresh smell of salt and sea to us straight off the dark sea. We stood and leaned against the huge concrete blocks that protected the Blackpool coastline from enemy invasion and looked out across the sea, the remaining strip of flat sand that the incoming tide hadn't yet covered *just* visible in the dark by the light of the half-moon.

'I never get tired of this view, or the salty smell.'

'Have you always lived here in Blackpool?' Joe asked, a little lop-sided smile accompanying his words. 'I think it's grand.'

'No, I'm not sandgrown. We came here from Royton when I was thirteen – my mum died the year before that, and Dad took the chance of a fresh start. Sadly, he died seventeen months after we moved here.'

'Enid isn't your mum, then?'

'Stepmum. She insists on being called Mother. Dad met her when he came on a work trip with friends sometime after Mum died.'

'It's her boarding house, then?'

'Yes. Dad worked for the railway and he and his pals

stayed at the Bing Lea. He always said Enid was a lost soul too – her first husband died in the Great War. No children.'

Joe put his arm around my shoulder. That new warmth I had never known before filled me from top to toe. It was so overwhelming. I felt complete, as if I truly belonged for the first time.

'Tell me your craziest first memory.' I wanted to know everything about Joe.

'Climbing trees.' He stared out to sea. 'Jack and me swinging on a rope off a branch over the stream.' Then he turned to me and laughed. 'The rope broke and Jack ended up with his arm bandaged up and a good hiding off Ma. She'd told us not to go on it, time and again.'

Jack laughed too where he stood alongside us. 'I was always the one to cop it!'

The slight squeeze Joe gave my shoulder sent tingles everywhere in my body. 'How about you?'

'I was three or four. Playing in a massive cardboard box in the Rope Works Mill with other kids, whilst my mum worked a sort of treadle machine. There was so much noise, machinery – and bits of soft fluff floated in the air, made you cough when you breathed them in.'

'Your mum took you to work, then?'

'At times; not often. I never knew the reason.'

We walked slowly along the promenade; the moon was bright, casting light on the cold, cloudless night, and outgoing night bombers droned and punctuated our continuing exchange of stories. Engaged in listening to Joe – his easy, resonant laughter, his outgoing manner – I almost forgot we had said we wouldn't be out late until Dora called over, 'I need to make tracks, Molly; I've an early start.'

Jack smiled and agreed with her, said we all had an early start.

Reluctantly, we about-turned just past Central Pier to begin the walk home.

'How old are you, Molly?'

'I'm twenty-one. How about you?'

'Twenty-three.'

As we made our way slowly back along the prom, Joe told me both his parents were alive and that he had a sister, Beth, who was turning their Manchester back yard into a vegetable patch.

I told him I thought that was a good idea and that we'd prised up a few flagstones ourselves, in order to plant veg. 'I'm planning on growing some potatoes when I get a minute.'

'You'll probably be another like our Beth. "Green fingers", we call her. She's a proper outdoor lass.'

I curled my fingers into my palms. Constant peeling and washing up had made them split and sore and I wished I could work outside more. I asked Joe where he'd worked before joining the RAF.

'Dad has a small workshop, a fix-it shop, mending anything and everything: radios, furniture, knife sharpening, you name it. I worked for him. Mostly round the local neighbourhood.'

'Does Jack work there, too?'

'No, he worked for a local engineering company – started with Dad first, though. But tell me more about you,

Molly. If there wasn't a war and you could do anything, money no object, what would you do?'

'Oh, what a great thought... I love the coast. I would travel all around the British coast and then choose my favourite place and buy a home of my own.'

Joe laughed. 'Bet you a pound to a penny you'd end up somewhere on the Fylde coast, Molly. It's so lively here and the scenery is grand.'

'You could be right.' I looked at Joe because I felt him looking at me as though *I* was the splendid scenery. Every time he said my name, my stomach trembled. Colour rose up my chest and neck, and heated my cheeks. 'It didn't used to be this lively in winter, but I love it all year round; the sea is different every day. There's somewhere to dance, to sit and relax when the sun's out, the Pleasure Beach is fun, there's loads to do – and miles of coast to walk.'

'I'll tell you what I like about you, Molly, you seem like the kind of girl who's not afraid to try new things. Willing to take a risk. Up for all the fun!'

I smiled at that. I didn't know if I *was* that kind of girl or not, but I did know that because Joe suggested it, I *wanted* to be the bold young woman he saw in me to justify the admiration in his voice.

He reached down, took hold of my hand, then raised it up towards us and squeezed it a little.

'I have another question for you, lovely lady. What would you say if I asked you to be my girl?'

I couldn't breathe in or out. There was *nothing* I would like more. My insides filled with bubbles of joy. 'I'd say yes, but for the sake of my sanity, don't let on to Mother, she wouldn't approve.'

As we made our way along the promenade, nearing home, the sound of outward-bound night bombers negated the need to speak. Too soon, it was time to turn in off the front into Banks Street.

My Dear Diary, I have to admit I thought that I could not get any happier than I was at that moment ... and then as we neared the boarding house, Denis ruined it, striding up to confront me and the others in the street. My heart plummeted.

'What are you doing?'

'Walking home.'

'Where have you been?'

'On the prom. Walking.'

'With him?'

'With Joe and his brother, Jack, and Dora, yes.'

'Walking and what else? Playing fast and loose on the beach?'

'Walking, Denis. And *nothing* else.'

Enid stood out front, arms folded under her breasts, flowery pinafore flapping in the breeze, rollers visible under her headscarf. Her eyes drilled into the moonlit scene that was none of her business. The words *nosey cow* slipped through my thoughts and I wanted to yell at her to go away. Tell her she was getting on my nerves.

'Molly, are you listening?'

'Yes.' I felt the comfort of Joe's palm resting on my back as though in silent support.

'What are you doing going walking with them—' he

pointed at the others '—when I was coming around to say goodbye?'

Whilst everyone watched, I found some long-needed gumption from somewhere inside.

'Why, Denis? I thought we were done with and you did call me a bitch last night. We were only ever dancing partners!' When I said those words, relief washed over me. Surely, he'd get the message now to leave me alone!

It didn't seem right to stand quarrelling in the street, *especially* on a Sunday. I was about to say 'Why don't you leave?' but Enid piped up first.

'You should come in, Denis.' Enid jerked her thumb at the slightly open front door. 'There's a brew on.'

Those were the *last* words I wanted to hear! I swear the woman purposely does things to irritate me.

'I've time. So long as I leave in an hour.'

'I have to go now,' Dora said. She said her goodbyes, gave a sympathetic grimace towards me and turned in the direction of home. Joe and I waited whilst Jack walked Dora to her door but was soon back with us, lighting a cigarette and holding the lit bit inward towards his palm to avoid a telling off from the air raid warden who was doing the rounds.

Denis moseyed into the boarding house as though he owned the place and dropped his kit bag in the hallway. Enid smiled at him and clapped him on the shoulder. She told him to come through to the back and have a cup of tea. 'I've made some scones; a couple will set you right for the journey to barracks,' she said, adding to my dismay.

'Always did like your scones, Mrs Webster.' Denis gave

a smile, shot a look at Jack and Joe as if to stamp his superiority in the household pecking order, like he had some standing.

As Denis was ushered through to the tiny back room, Joe squeezed my shoulder. 'Goodnight then, Molly.'

Jack asked, 'Will you be all right with his nibs, there, Molly?'

'I will, thanks, Jack. And thanks for the walk, both of you, I've really enjoyed blowing the cobwebs off, it was fun.'

'Happen we could do it again?' Joe asked and his sparkling blue eyes crinkled just a little round the edges.

'I'd love to. Especially if you help me clear up first?'

'It's a deal.' His smile made me smile in response, restored my happiness.

As I approached the kitchen and back room, Enid told Denis to go and take the weight off and that I'd bring us a pot of tea through and half a dozen scones.

I put the kettle on to boil and then set down the tray on the table before turning to fetch the teapot and milk.

Denis didn't leave much for anyone else and I found my gaze wandering to Enid's to see if I could gauge what she was thinking, but she just picked up the tea strainer and laid it on top of one of the thick white cups. 'Tuck in, you've a healthy appetite, lad.'

I'd to clamp my lips together to stop the words *'There's healthy appetite and there's bloody greedy,'* from popping out. That was something my mum would have said. She was straight talking, never minced her words.

When Denis had eaten his fill of scones, obviously not a

bit bothered that the jam was meant for three of us, he looked hungrily towards a couple of scones remaining on the serving plate.

I couldn't wait for him to leave.

'You can walk me to the station, Molly. We can say bye proper, then.'

'No. I'll say goodbye now. I told you last night at the Tower, I never was your girl. We only ever danced together.'

I saw him off at the front door, and he muttered his displeasure with me. But I didn't care. I didn't want Denis blundering in and putting Joe off me.

Especially since they'd already had one run-in.

Especially now Joe had asked me to be his girl.

Joe's girl.

It sounded right and more than that, it *felt* right – and Denis wasn't going to wreck it for me.

Chapter Five

Molly

Blackpool, W/C Monday November 8, 1943

M y Dear Diary,
Joe and Jack helped with the teatime clearing up on the Monday evening and we called for Dora on our way over to the promenade to take a walk.

I told Joe I'd made it clear to Denis that I didn't want to see him anymore as we walked.

He smiled at me. 'Ah, I like a young woman who knows what she wants then goes out and gets it. It's grand you know your own mind, Molly, love.'

I knew at that moment what the expression 'jump for joy' meant.

He held my hand in his and we walked towards Gynn Square, a quieter route away from the centre of Blackpool.

The strange thing was that looking forward to spending time with Joe had the effect of seeing Enid's criticisms, grumbles and snide remarks bounce off me. She had a mood dampening diatribe:

'You'll get yourself a reputation, going around with no end of young men; you know folk talk? Watch yourself young lady – Sylvia Bland from down Lytham Road got herself in the family way putting herself about and her mother threw her out. Any shenanigans like that and you'll be out of my door quick as you like…'

Her repetitious nattering didn't bother me. My mood lifted to carefree and stayed there – and I've never felt happier my Dear, Dear Diary. Ever.

There wasn't a dull moment with Joe in the boarding house, he'd sing along with the radio, forever arranging games of cards with his brother and the other billets, having arm wrestles with his companions, and even the house black cat, Minnie, who bore no mind to anyone, could be found winding around his legs.

I told Joe about the sand dunes, riding on the trams, the piers, the Pleasure Beach, the shows kept open for locals, billeted airmen and other servicemen alike in order to raise spirits, the beloved donkeys too – and paddling in the ice-cold sea!

'I don't think my six weeks here will be enough to see everything, Molly.' He squeezed my hand. 'I've a lot of other stuff to do as well.' There was so much I wanted to share, but mostly we walked along the sea front, held hands, cuddled…

'Molly!' It was Dora. 'I was just telling Jack here that we have the best ice cream parlour in Britain – Luigi's!'

'Oh! It's so good, you must both try some whilst you're here. And take us with you!'

Dora, always the opportunist, laughed her agreement.

Jack moved into the nearest shelter to light his cigarette out of the sea breeze. We all stopped for a break and to sit down out of the biting wind. He said that it must be like being on holiday all the year round, living here.

My response to that was, 'Apart from making meals and beds, cleaning, shopping for the food and all those other jobs, it's *just* like being on holiday!' I laughed and snuggled against Joe's side as his arm went along my shoulder. I felt his laugh and looked up into his smile.

'Not quite a holiday, then,' he said.

'How do you and your family fill your days, Dora?' Jack asked her.

'I help Mum; I'll be doing clippie work on the trams soon though, I've been accepted. Dad works at South Shore – foreman at the Vickers Armstrong factory. He was injured in the Great War and was declared not fit for service this time – much to his disgust! Most weekends I also help Molly and Enid in the Bing Lea. I've asked if I can be a member of the Red Cross – you know, drive and roll bandages and things – but I'm not good with the gory stuff.'

'What are *you* training to be, Jack?' I asked.

He went on then to explain that he and Joe would be training together to be Flight Engineers, that they'd already done a lot of training as fitters, but more trainees were needed for the flight crews because so many had been lost.

He explained that up until a few months ago the pair of them had been loading bombs on the planes, seeing to repairs to keep the flyers up there.

I told them quite a few of the billeted lads that've stayed with us have trained for the same as them and Dora said they spent a lot of time marching up and down the prom. She said her dad told her it's called 'square bashing'.

'And here we are being dragged out for a walk on the prom in the evenings too!' Jack said and we all had a bit of a laugh at that.

Joe and I held hands, kissed and held one another tight in the shelter on the promenade.

I knew a pang of sadness when he said he looked forward to finishing his training and seeing active service. I wanted to ask him whether he would be afraid, but it didn't seem right somehow.

So, I didn't.

My Dear Diary, later the same week, Joe and I went out alone. It was a cold, wet night and we went straight to a shelter, the prom quieter than usual.

When he held me, I didn't feel the cold. His hands wandered, his kisses deepened, sending darts of excitement through me.

Aircraft, trams and cars moved in the dark, each unseen in the cloudy night, whilst adding their own background sounds against the suck and crash of the restless winter sea.

'I need you, Molly.' Joe's words were soft, his breath

against my ear making me shiver, heat searing through me. 'Let me…?'

My body yearned for him, I felt hot and could think only of getting closer to him. I pulled him as close as it was possible to be. But at that moment a great clanking noise from a tram nearby made me jump and realise just how close we'd come to making love – right there in the shelter.

My Dear Diary, it made me realise my need for Joe was getting more overwhelming.

'Soon, Joe,' I whispered, pressing my mouth quickly against his before straightening my clothes and standing up to make the move to go home.

He was quiet after that, barely saying a word as we finished walking home. I felt anxious he was annoyed that I'd stopped him going all the way; it had been obvious, Dear Diary, that he wanted to.

Blackpool, Wednesday November 17, 1943

I haven't written for a week. I've been down in the dumps, haven't felt like it. The only time I've seen Joe has been at mealtimes. He said he has to go out in the evenings to do extra studying with some others and the hour he has after eating, he spends with his RAF pals and Jack, playing cards, smoking, having a laugh.

He says that there isn't enough time for us to go out walking before he goes to study, but that it shouldn't be for too much longer, just until he catches up with the work. I'm relieved he wants to see me, once he's caught up. I miss him so much.

I miss feeling like his special girl all the time and the way he makes me feel treasured and loved.

Surely he misses walking out with me, too? I really hope so, but I'm not sure. He still smiles and winks at me when I'm serving up meals, but I can't help feeling a bit uncertain. Much to Enid's delight, I'm keeping busy with work to help take my mind off him – it works for some of the time at least.

Tonight, Joe was out studying and Jack asked if I'd join him and the others for a game of cards.

He and a couple of the lads were sitting around a table and one of the others shuffled the cards. Jack sketched something on a scrap of card whilst the playing cards were dealt to the others, then he shoved the stubby pencil behind his ear and put the small piece of card in his shirt pocket.

All the clearing up was done. The choice was the back room listening to the radio with Enid, going for a walk alone in the howling wind and rain, or an hour or two playing cards.

I said, 'Go on then,' and folded my apron over the back of my chair.

I've noticed that Jack is less gregarious than Joe. There is a kind of patient air about him, in that he didn't mind going over the rules of the card game again and again. I was just about understanding the game of rummy when the other two said they were off to bed, they both had to read through their notes for a test the following day.

I said at least I'll know how to play rummy next time …

with Jack's help. It was probably just the light, but I thought that Jack's cheeks went a bit red. 'You're always welcome to join us, Molly.' He tapped the cards straight on the table and laid them next to their tatty, much used box, then asked if I fancied a game of something else before he turned in.

Jack laughed when I said knew how to play snap. He shuffled the pack, saluting goodnight to the others, then he turned his attention back to me and the cards and suggested, 'Best of three?'

I won two games and remained sitting at the table when Jack stashed the cards in their box and put them on the sideboard along with the draughts board and small chess set.

My Dear Diary, I was surprised that I had enjoyed myself so much whilst playing cards with Jack and the other two billets. I asked Jack almost without thinking whether he'd like a cuppa before bed, then I joined him. He offered me a cigarette and hesitated to light his own until I told him to carry on.

I asked about his sister, Beth, who'd applied to join the Land Army girls.

'Beth, she's a proper outdoors lass.' He smiled, blew out smoke, and told me he and Joe had had a letter from their mum saying Beth was going to work on a farm in Yorkshire and was excited. I imagined that the twins got along with their sister and asked that question. He stubbed out his cigarette in the tin ash tray, blew out a stream of smoke and said they all got along well enough. 'Except,' he confided, 'we don't get on when she's forever trying to pair us off with girls she knows!' He said Beth had a male friend who was in the army and they wrote regularly, as far as he knew, but he thought it was more as pen pals than as a couple.

I finished my tea and set it down, thought about letters and what they would mean to a service man or woman away from home and without thinking, I voiced my thoughts.

'I should think it's a good thing to get letters from your loved ones, for those at home and those away.'

Jack had nodded at those words and asked whether I wrote to any servicemen. I said I didn't at the moment, thinking I would likely be writing to his brother in the future. I glanced at the wooden clock on the mantlepiece.

It was almost ten o'clock. It was my turn to lock the front door tonight; Enid and I took turns during the week, also checking the coals in the grate were out and that everything in the kitchen was turned off for the night.

I told Jack I'd a few jobs to finish off before locking up and I hoped everyone would be in soon.

'It seems a long old day for those who have to study at night, too.' I thought of Joe in particular.

Jack took a breath and responded that my day was as long as theirs. I smiled at that. No one had ever pointed that out to me before.

Then he said, 'If you ever want to go for a walk in the evening and Joe's busy elsewhere, I'm more than happy to keep you company, Molly.' Jack's features broke into a smile when I responded with my thanks. I told him that I'd bear it in mind and that he was kind. 'Tomorrow? If the weather's not too bad? I do love a walk.'

He nodded his agreement, stood and pushed his fingers

back through his dark hair, and a bit of smut from the fire landed on his cheek. 'Bob down a bit,' I told him, 'so I can rub it off with my hanky. Whoops, I'm smearing it and making it worse.' My running commentary made us both laugh before I finally got his cheek clean. 'Good as new,' I announced, shoving my hanky up my sleeve.

I wasn't sure if I imagined it again or if Jack's cheeks really did go a bit red. Probably it was me rubbing at the smut that caused him to colour up. I noticed in that moment that his eyes shone with such gentle warmth that I found myself smiling.

Just smiling.

'Hello, hel-lo!' Joe stopped in the lounge doorway, hands on hips, head tilted on one side. 'Are you after stealing my girl, Jack?'

Jack looked irritated at his brother's words. 'You know me better than that,' he said, then added, 'It's usually the other way round.'

Joe swept into the room, smile and arms wide. 'How's my beautiful girl?' He pulled me close, out of Jack's proximity. Before I'd a chance to answer or explain that I'd just been wiping Jack's cheek, Joe's mouth closed over mine.

My Dear Diary, Joe's kisses were enough to make me forget what I was doing; that melting warmth always took over, making him the most important – the *only* thing that mattered.

He raised his mouth from mine, his eyes half-closed, a small smile tilting his mouth and asked if I would go dancing with him the following Saturday night.

Any insecurities I had entertained disappeared. And I agreed, of course. I was about to ask him how his studying went and if there'd been some female trainees along in his class, though there must have been; he smelled faintly of roses. But then he smiled, my insides heated and he kissed me again before saying he had to get up early and needed a good sleep before the test.

It didn't occur to me until I took our cups into the kitchen, washed them up and checked everything was switched off, that Jack had left the front lounge without a sound. Or maybe he had said goodnight but I hadn't heard him. Joe's kisses affected everything my hearing included.

Blackpool, Thursday November 18, 1943

Thursday evening, Joe brought a stack of dirty plates into the kitchen and winked at me. His broad shoulders fitted his blue uniform shirt, his height and sheer presence seeming to fill the kitchen doorway. The sleeves had been rolled a couple of turns; his tie slightly loosened. I knew for a fact that they all had to look impeccable first thing in the morning when they left for training, and yet, the more casual look suited him enormously – fitted his slightly bad-boy persona. My stomach did a flippity flop.

'So, you meant what you said last night? Will you come dancing on Saturday night? I'd love to take you.'

'I'd love to, Joe – yes!' With him. I loved to dance *with*

him. I could barely wait; just the thought of enjoying an evening with him made me happy.

Once all the clearing up was done, Joe had left to go and do his extra studying, Jack and I hurried over the road to call for Dora, who quickly bundled into her coat and scarf, then the three of us linked arms in the dim light and hurried down onto the promenade to blow off the cobwebs with a brisk walk.

'We should do this every evening,' I turned my face seaward, so the breeze blew the hair from my face, loving the simple pleasure of the salty air, the distant crash of the tide.

Both Dora and Jack laughed, tugged me to keep walking in the cold night air.

Blackpool, Saturday November 20, 1943

Before we went out, Dora and I painted the buttons on our dresses with some red nail polish. It was amazing how it made our outfits look different. And we helped one another to style our hair. It was terribly wet out, so we opted for twist styles, held in place with hundreds of hair pins and grips.

Dora said she's so happy she's walking out with the tall blond American serviceman called Matt. She meets up with him on Saturday nights at the Tower and she finds his accent sexy, she says. I can't always tell what he's saying, but I didn't tell her that!

We got a bit blown about on the way to the Tower, but our headscarves kept most of the damage at bay and everyone had rosy cheeks from the wind.

I noticed for the first time that Jack wasn't short of willing partners, but he rarely stayed with the same one for more than a couple of dances.

'You look beautiful.' Joe pulled me close, leaned down and whispered against my ear, sending shivers through me. When I smiled up at him, he held me tighter still and I knew then what I'd suspected the moment I met him.

I loved Joe.

I could feel my eyes sparkling with the excitement of being whirled around by this dashingly handsome man, being the recipient of his smiles and his whispers making promises against my ear as we danced close.

I experienced sensations I never had before. I'd fallen hard and fast.

At the end of the night we walked with some others going our way so we could make our way back to Banks Street together in the dark, sharing fish and chips out of newspaper whilst walking along the promenade.

'It's like being on holiday,' I said as I stole a fat chip from Jack's serving and he just laughed.

'Do you want to sit down?' Joe asked.

We made for the nearest shelter; the breeze coming in off the sea made our cheeks tingle with cold. The rest of our crowd, four or five of them, called out their goodnights and went off into the dark.

My Dear Diary, Joe and I were alone for what felt like the first time ever. Not literally, because there were lots of folk making their way towards billets and home, but alone in the shelter, just the two of us.

When Joe spoke, his words made my insides swirl with warmth and with love.

'I haven't known you long, Molly, but I feel as if I've known you a long time.'

'That's how I feel.' I turned to face him, his arms went around me, and I moved onto his lap. We shared the longest embrace; the warm firmness of his legs beneath me rose to warm mine, the feel of his torso where we touched felt so powerful.

The words *I love you!* shouted in my mind, but I didn't want to scare him off, so I kept them there. When we broke apart, I traced my finger down his cheek, and was stunned anew by his handsome features, the way his eyes drank in my features, thrilled that he seemed equally besotted with me.

'What are you smiling at, Molly?'

'I'm happy. I'm smiling because I'm happy.'

'Do I make you feel that way?' He looked pleased, expectant, as if there could be no other reason.

I spread my fingers over his chin and raised my lips to his. His chin was cool beneath my fingertips, his breath, his mouth warm. 'You do. I don't know why, you just do.' We kissed again for a long time.

I ached to tell him I loved him; had the feeling I'd like to stay in the shelter on the sea front forever … but then we both became aware of time passing, of it getting late, and I became mindful that we couldn't *actually* stay there forever.

'I think we'd better…'

'Yeah.' He stood and I slid to my feet from his lap, then Joe held out his hand. 'We've about five minutes to get home, love.'

Not so far away in the sky above us, unseen night bombers droned and spluttered as we hurried towards Bank Street and home. We just made it.

It is so strange, my Dear Diary, fewer of Jack and Joe's forty-two days are left, and time is speeding up. It reminds me of the sand in our egg timer, the fine sand falling through the top of the hourglass to the lower one – ever more quickly – as it nears the end.

Blackpool, Wednesday November 24, 1943

A few evenings later, Joe was out. Jack came into the kitchen with a pile of plates, carried them to the sink and began washing up. I dried them whilst we chatted about his family. 'They're keeping all right, by all accounts. Spend a lot of time in and out of their Anderson shelter. Ma's last letter said the sirens are forever wailing. Said she's looking forward to spending a whole night in her own bed!'

'Poor things.' I dried another plate and added it to the stack on the table.

He dropped a stack of washed forks onto the draining

board. 'You should join us in the front room later, we could take another walk first, too if you fancy?'

'Thanks, I might do that if Mother doesn't need me for anything.'

Enid had just finished lining up the teapots on their shelf and shrugged. 'Finish up here, Molly and take care of the locking up – I'll get an early night. Join the billets if you want, but think on there's no funny business.' She wagged her forefinger to emphasise the words I knew were coming, 'I'll not stand for any shenanigans under my roof.' She looked pointedly from me to Jack to be sure her message hit home.

'We just play cards or chat whilst we go for a walk, that's all, Mrs Webster. No funny business.' Jack finished drying the forks and put them away.

Jack and I called across for Dora, but she declined the invite to come for a walk, said 'I'll come along tomorrow, bit busy tonight!'

Then quietly, as we turned to move away, she said, 'Do you two lovebirds good to go out on your own!' And she winked. I rolled my eyes and Jack just laughed and we hurried away – there were very few who could tell the brothers apart – including even Dora sometimes! And neither of them bothered to correct folk most of the time. I linked my arm through his as we listened out for cars and hearing none, darted over the road to the promenade. 'Does it ever cause problems, the two of you being identical?'

'Sometimes, but we've learned to handle it.'

'I'll bet.' We walked quickly because of the cold and

shivering a bit, reached Central Pier and then with just a nod, turned around and made our way back.

After hanging up my coat and running a comb through my hair, I joined the billets in the front room. Jack had a rough square of blank paper and his pencil moved quickly against it as he kept glancing up at Percy, who sat opposite. Curious, I moved to stand behind his chair. Emerging was an incredibly life-like sketch of Percy's face: his dark hair, eyebrows and moustache, the half-closed eyes, slightly wonky nose and thin lips spoke of someone relaxing at the end of a long day. Jack added a touch of shading to the line of his subject's jaw, just a smidge under his cheekbones – and printed the date at the bottom, along with his initials *JB*. 'Here you go, Percy.'

Percy's broad smile spoke volumes, pleased as punch. 'Our Alison will be thrilled with this, Jack, thanks.' He explained to me that his fiancée, Alison, had been bombed out of her house in Stockport, and her photos had all been destroyed.

'It's a great likeness, I'm sure she'll love it.'

I caught Jack's eye, 'That's a real talent you've got there, Jack.'

'I've promised Edgar a sketch, too.' He looked up over his shoulder at me. 'I'd like to draw you, Molly, if you're free?'

I was warmed inside at his suggestion, said yes.

'I'll make us all a brew, then, whilst you draw Edgar, Jack.'

And, Dear Diary, whilst I was at it, I nipped and tidied my hair, pinched my cheeks for colour and made myself look a bit more decent. By the time I joined the chaps in the front room, Edgar was stifling a yawn. 'Think it's the sea air, I sleep like a log here, right from the first night.'

'It does get you like that.' I set down the tray and then moved behind Jack to see how his sketch was coming along. The likeness was nothing short of incredible. Jack had captured perfectly Edgar's pale ginger colouring, very short hair and a neat slightly darker moustache, and the mischievous twinkle in his pale blue eyes.

'Nearly done, Edgar,' Jack said, catching him yawning again. He signed his initials at the bottom of the drawing and handed it to his pal.

'Made me look proper 'andsome!' Edgar nodded, grinned with approval and shifted to an easy chair from the upright dining chair. 'I'll bet Sophie will kiss this every night before bed!'

'More likely she'll cover you up,' Percy said as he handed round the scones. 'Might give her nightmares.'

They all laughed, including Edgar, who broke his scone in half and dipped it in his cup of tea.

'Young mucker needs housetraining.' Percy shook his head and looked exasperated.

'Shame Joe misses this bit of fun, Jack, with having to go out studying,' I said.

Percy and Edgar fell silent, just for a second, and exchanged glances. I caught the look and momentarily wondered what I'd said to warrant the exchange, feeling as though I'd missed something. Then Edgar intercepted the brief thought, held up the other half of his scone, his mouth still full when he said, 'These are good, Molly.'

Percy set out the draughts board on the small dining table in the window between him and Edgar. 'Best of three, Ed? For a couple of smokes?'

Jack indicated I should sit in the dining chair.

'I can't believe how quick the weeks are going,' I said whilst Jack's expression spoke of concentration, his slight smile in place as he made swift yet careful strokes with pencil against paper.

I didn't realise, Dear Diary, until Jack sat up, looked at me, then added some adjustments, that I'd had a similar, slight smile on my expression, too.

It was a little while later when he put his initials at the bottom of the paper along with the date: November 1943. 'About done, I think, Molly?' He held it up at arm's length and the other two looked across from their game.

'Very good,' were Ed's words, and he whistled in appreciation.

Percy nodded in agreement. 'Tis, very.'

Jack handed me the sketch. 'Here you are, Molly.'

I was stunned at how he had portrayed me using just a pencil; although in grey, black and white, my coppery curls looked shiny, my eyes lit with fun and a small smile tilted my mouth. 'You're gifted, Jack.' For some reason a strange lump rose in my throat and my voice came out a bit hoarse. 'No one's ever drawn me before, thank you.' I looked up at him and his eyes smiled in response.

He shrugged, tapped a cigarette out of the packet on the table, caught it in his mouth and lit it. 'I've always drawn, have since before I could write, Ma said.'

'Does your brother draw?' Edgar piped up to which Jack shook his head.

'He thinks it's soft.'

'Well, I think you're a good artist, Jack, and I think you've taken a flattering view of me. Thank you.' The sketch just fit in the large patch pocket on the front of my dress so I slid it in and gave it a protective pat. 'I'll keep it safe. Oh, I'm sure Dora would love a drawing too – she could give it to Matt. Would you mind if I mention it?'

Jack readily agreed, 'Anytime, Molly.'

'I'll get her to come round tomorrow evening then, if that's all right?'

'Fine by me. If it doesn't take too long, maybe the three of us could go for a walk, afterwards? You too, Edgar and Percy?'

'Aye, if I'm not too tired.' Edgar responded. Percy shook his head.

The clock on the chimney breast said it was almost ten. Edgar and Percy chorused their goodnights and went upstairs.

'You should go up, too, Jack. Thanks for your help and for the sketch. It's great.'

'My pleasure.' As we walked down the hallway, the front door opened; it was bang on ten o'clock.

'Hello, hel-lo, are you trying to steal my girl again, Jack?' Joe looked tired out; I thought he must have been working hard.

'Oh, dry up.' Jack looked a bit cheesed off with his brother. 'You shouldn't cut it so fine getting in, Joe.'

I frowned, wondered if I'd imagined a thread of tension

running between the brothers, then the thought evaporated when Joe spoke.

'Yeah, sorry.' He dragged his hand down his face, turned and gave me one of his engaging grins. 'Sorry, Molly, sweetheart, I got talking after – lost track of time.' As he spoke, Jack took hold of his arm and guided him to the stairs.

'Apology accepted.' He did look sorry and I couldn't be cross when he smiled that way. 'I said to the others, Joe, it's a shame you can't join us in the evenings because of your training.'

Joe paused and turned to look at me over his shoulder. 'It is, Molly, a great shame.' His blue eyes shone with sincerity. 'Goodnight, sweetheart.' He gave a slightly wonky salute before moving upward.

'Night, Joe. Night, Jack.'

'Night, Molly.' Their voices drifted down the stairs.

Blackpool, Saturday December 18, 1943

Joe's last Saturday night arrived. He and Jack were due to leave the following day.

Right until it was packing up time, we danced to the music of the big band at the Tower Ballroom – the floor was crowded for both slow and fast dances – and only stopped dancing for a quick drink now and then.

On our way home we stopped off in what we thought of as *our* shelter.

Joe pulled me close against him, so my face was squeezed against his shoulder. The feel and smell of his dark blue uniform, dampened by sea air, was so familiar to me now.

I clamped my lips together; tears stole my voice for a second or two.

'I love you, Joe.' Those words just left me, Dear Diary, they wouldn't stay inside any longer. 'I'll miss you so much.'

I thought I'd never seen anyone look so handsome.

Joe's short fringe fell forwards as the waning moon peeped out from behind a cloud and lit a sparkle in his eyes, just briefly.

'I don't think I've ever been happier or sadder,' I said. The thought of him leaving the following day had seemed ages away for so long.

But it was almost here. I didn't know how to bear it.

'I feel sad, too.'

I nodded, couldn't speak, didn't want him to see the tears rolling down my cheeks.

He put his finger and thumb gently on my chin and raised my face.

Pull yourself together! I tried telling myself, but was reduced to wiping my face with my fingers.

In the privacy of the shelter, no witness but the wind and waves, passion between us was finally ignited by lack of time…

The following day, after lunch, Dora, Mary and I walked with Joe and Jack to the railway station. Some of the others moving on to other training facilities walked ahead too, talking, laughing and shouting.

The Blackshaw brothers leaned out of the train window; they looked absolutely the same, yet Joe's smile was the one to make my insides melt with heat and my heart pound.

'Visit soon!' My voice came out hoarse, Dear Diary, like I'd been shouting too much.

Joe held my hand, kissed my fingers. 'I love you,' I said, and he smiled in response.

And then he was gone and nothing but the sooty smoke lingered in the air.

_____

Blackpool, Friday December 31, 1943

Dear Diary,

Almost two weeks he's been gone and the ache of missing Joe is physical, my stomach churns constantly like a panicky sea, wondering whether he will write. Will he forget me? Did he really feel the same way about me? He *said* he felt sad...

But it niggled that he'd made no promises.

And worse than any of those insecure thoughts, *will he live through the war?*

_____

Blackpool, Saturday January 1, 1944

I felt a big relief when a late Christmas card arrived today from Joe and Jack, signed by them both with a few words saying they hoped I was well, as they were. There was a kiss beneath Joe's name and a note on the back of the card said thank you for the socks I'd knitted and sent them both for Christmas.

I write to him every three or four days, so have neglected you, Dear Diary. I tell Joe all the goings on of my daily life, and I always finish by telling him I love him and that I hope he will write soon.

Blackpool, Monday January 10, 1944

Although it is already January, past twelfth night, I still have the card stood on my bedroom dressing table as my only connection to Joe. Sometimes, I wonder if the happiness I felt was real. Sometimes the time spent with Joe feels more like a wonderful dream.

It's becoming harder to remember every detail; I am grateful that I wrote everything down as it's too easy to forget the small things.

I read this notebook time and again, savouring every word written about the time spent with the man I love, attempting to relive every single moment. The ache of longing for him rarely lets up, the churning in my stomach constant.

Yet, as time moves along, Dear Diary, a question rises up time and again.

How well do I know Joe?

That thought chips at the edges of my thoughts; I flick that stray worry away, feeling that there must be some reason for the lack of letters, a hold-up somewhere. Someone in the queue at the butcher's yesterday said that they'd received a bunch of letters all at once, so I imagine that is what has happened; I am sure I will hear from Joe soon.

I pick up my diary just to write the day to day things, to keep my mind occupied and to give myself something to do whilst I listen to music on the little radio in my room when I want to be alone.

But, my Dear Diary, sometimes I can barely breathe for wanting to see Joe so badly. I close my eyes, wrap my arms around myself and remember how tightly he'd held me; how precious he made me feel. How I felt like the most important young woman in the world to him.

His smile and how handsome he was in his uniform...

Every time a new lot of billets arrives, I wish with all my heart it was Joe's lot arriving – and that they were just beginning their time in Blackpool. Then the dream-perfect love affair could start all over again.

Time, though, gallops on too fast, pays no mind to wishes.

Proof, my Dear Diary, that you have to make hay whilst the sun shines.

Enjoy every moment.

Blackpool, Saturday January 15, 1944

My Dear Diary, I'm writing this as my head swims and I've just stopped feeling as sick as a dog. I managed to get to the bathroom, bilious, desperate to keep the noise down. I splashed my face with cold water, drank some to wash out my mouth after being ill.

I froze at the knock on the door.

It was Enid demanding that I stop being a *'lazy 'apeth'* and get downstairs to do some work.

There's something, something I've suspected for the past few weeks, something I have prayed hard that it isn't true. I have no doubt now. I overheard our neighbour, Phyllis, when she spoke with Enid sometime last year, describing how she had been nauseous in the first month or so when she expected a baby.

I've been feeling that way for several weeks.

I have the growing suspicion that I'm expecting, too.

Chapter Six

Izzie

Blackpool, Sunday June 25, 2017

'Crikey,' Izzie whispered as she rose from the chair and put a bookmark to keep the page. 'That's unexpected.'

At the discovery that her dad, Tom, had been conceived out of wedlock, she tried to imagine how different life must have been back in the 1940s; it must have been immensely difficult, she thought, if Molly could only confide in her notebook. Poor Nan, to keep the knowledge secret – so secret it could only be shared with the written word as the choices for her future seemed so very limited.

Izzie prepared for bed, imagining how it might have been, but the predominant visions from her nan's secret notebook were of her falling in love with a handsome, charismatic man in uniform, making the most of life at a time when no one knew when their number would be up.

She pictured Nan as a young woman, working until she was ready to drop in her stepmother's boarding house, and then laughing, dancing and, like everyone else at that time, taking what she could by way of enjoyment, whilst she could.

As Molly had written: *Make hay whilst the sun shines...*

Whilst she settled down to sleep, Izzie's thoughts focused on Nan's life. Falling pregnant gave Nan what Izzie could see as only one choice – she had to marry the baby's father. Molly had written about how young women were thrown out of their homes because they fell pregnant. It was so sad – and she could only imagine how conflicted Molly must have felt. She was in love with Joe, yet whether she would ever see him again was uncertain. Swamped with the sudden longing to hug her grandmother close, to bury her face in the soft fabric of her blouse, inhale the faint smell of Coty's L'aimant, make her feel better, Izzie whispered, 'I miss you, Nan.'

At that point, Izzie's thoughts drifted to her own marriage.

It had been their choice, hers and Rufus, but the timing had been key to that turn of events.

A pang of something like guilt, or regret, or a cocktail of both, accompanied the acknowledgement that if she and Justin *had* met up, her choice would likely have been different.

She wondered if the emotional pain she had held close on her journey back to London after her fruitless trip north to meet Justin was anything like the insecurity, the undoubted fear and uncertainty for her future that Nan must have felt upon finding herself expecting and alone. Izzie had felt adrift, lost, directionless…

Izzie thought that Nan had had much more to face. She'd likely thought she had a simple choice: marry Joe or be thrown out of her home.

Izzie's choice had been made, perhaps, because it had been a route that opened up and offered a path out of the agonising anguish, a path that allowed her to lock her pain deep inside and take another unexpected direction.

Justin called around the following morning. 'I've come to let you know I've a job in Scotland – Tobermory – for a tourist brochure. I'm travelling up there shortly.'

'How fabulous.' A stab of disappointment interrupted Izzie taking a breath. 'Have you time for a cuppa?'

'Love one.' He followed her into the large kitchen whilst she made them both a cup of coffee and summarised what she'd discovered in the notebook so far.

'I tried to imagine how different life was, Justin, but it's difficult to get my head round. I mean, being pregnant without a husband isn't shocking these days, is it?'

'No, but it would have been shocking back in the Forties. I remember Gran telling me how she refused to stand next to someone at a tram stop who was pregnant and unmarried.'

Grimacing, Izzie said, 'Like they'd catch something? It beggars belief.'

'I know,' he agreed and nodded his thanks for the mug of coffee she set down on the round table. 'It was different then though.'

'Poor Nan. It's as if the life I'm reading about is a different one to the one I knew about her.' She put a plate of biscuits on the table between them and Justin shot her a nod of thanks as he picked one up.

'The job in Scotland, will you be gone long?'

She didn't *want* to care if he *never* came back, but was finding it hard to hold onto the hurt she'd buried inside for years. She wanted to ask him: *Why?*

Izzie still found it hard to believe that Justin had just stopped getting in touch, hadn't responded to her calls and messages...

That day had changed the course of her whole life.

It made no sense – but the question felt too difficult to ask. As though asking would be akin to inviting the intimacy they'd once shared to return and risk ripping the plaster off the agony that lurked inside. It had crippled her emotionally then; it might do the same again if she let it back to the surface.

The reason he never brought it up, Izzie realised, was probably because he never even thought about it; he'd moved on and he must have done way before their arrangement to meet.

He had his photography success, the dream come true that he'd always worked towards. And all the beautiful women in his life...

He really did appear to have it all.

It was so easy to brush over their shared past and blot it out, smother it. They'd always got along – way before they became lovers, they'd been the best of friends. It would be so simple to return to that tried and trusted friendship, leave their painful episode locked away inside...

There was no way though that she could brush aside the enormous help he had been in sorting out Nan's bungalow: helping shift heavy furniture out into the garage, driving her to the local charity shops and recycling centre, mucking in carting stored boxes down the ladder. No matter the hurt caused in the past, Izzie still felt a tangible connection between them.

'I'll be gone until the weekend.' He looked her straight in the eyes then. 'Will you miss me?'

'No.' She raised her cup to give her something to hide behind and something to do rather than gawp at him, then, unable to lie, added, 'Maybe, a bit.'

'Strange thing, Izzie, sometimes I feel like we've never been apart.' He hesitated, then said, 'I have to keep reminding myself that I can't just grab you close and kiss you anymore.' As he spoke, a dimple slashed his cheek and in response, a long-stifled sensation coursed through Izzie.

In that second, she wanted nothing more than to feel his arms around her, pulling her close ... to feel his body firm against hers from chest, hips, legs ... to taste the coffee on his lips...

His words set off a reaction that almost caused her to throw her arms around him, hold him, kiss him. Hearing his words moved her emotionally, handed her a kind of

JULIA WILD

sweet emotional shock. Maybe he did recollect just how close they'd been, how fiercely they'd loved one another.

'I keep reminding myself that we both made our choices.' His words served to bring her back down to earth.

With a bump.

He looked at his watch, finished his drink and stood. 'Better make tracks. If you're about at the weekend, I'll be back working my way down the folks' job list.' He removed his dark framed glasses and rubbed his eyes, then caught her scrutiny of him.

'What?' He gave a slight smile. 'Something wrong?'

'Just thinking.' She probably shouldn't share exactly *what* she was thinking; the vision of him grabbing her close and kissing her made her feel breathless, made her want exactly that.

In spades.

'Then I'm home till just before the New Year, just some relatively local work booked in.'

'Where are you going in the New Year?'

'New Zealand on a wildlife photography assignment for *National Geographic*, one of my life ambitions.'

'I'm in awe. It's great you're doing the work you always wanted to do.'

He smiled at that and Izzie felt a familiar catch inside.

'I've been lucky, that's all.'

'I know *that* saying – the harder you work, the luckier you get!' She walked with him to the front door.

'Bye, then Izzie.'

'Bye Justin, thanks for all your help. Drop by when you're home?'

'I will.' Justin leaned down to drop a kiss on her cheek and his closeness made all the fine hairs on the surface of her skin shimmer. She looked up to see what affect her nearness had on him, but he was already raising one hand in farewell and fishing keys out of his jeans pocket with the other.

———————————

After tidying and boxing up a set of first edition books signed by Rufus for her nan, Izzie set them aside thinking she'd offer them to Justin's parents.

Justin.

She dredged up what he had said that had set her stomach twisting inside: *'I keep reminding myself that we both made our choices.'*

Both?

Sudden anger surged through her, sending prickles to the ends of her arms and legs. They'd *both* made their choices?

Had they, hell!

He'd made his choice by not turning up and she'd been left with the consequences.

Heartbroken.

She'd been as devastated as a jilted bride.

She should have pulled him up on that. But she couldn't have done for fear of letting the pain erupt like red-hot lava; she didn't want him to witness it, didn't want to feel it herself. Once had been enough. It had to stay contained where it couldn't cause damage.

She turned up the radio loud, dancing like a crazy puppet to get her rage out of her system, and then stood puffing, with her hands on her hips, looking around the bungalow to decide on her next job.

Setting herself the task of stripping off the dizzyingly patterned wallpaper from the hallway, Izzie carried on clearing and then cleaning. She planned to call around to visit Justin's parents and take the box of books for them - soon

In the meantime, anything that still needed to go to the local charity shop, she stacked in the wide hallway at the side of the door.

Moving into the back room to pull the curtains against the dusk, Izzie eyed the notebook tucked on the table at the side of the room by the chair and felt irresistibly drawn to read more about her nan's life and how she had dealt with the pregnancy. Izzie felt nervous at what she would find amidst this notebook of secrets entrusted to her. Her poor nan, she had lived for the moment, fallen deeply in love and then fallen pregnant.

She must have worried that Enid would blow her top, throw her out. Izzie wondered if her nan tried to keep her pregnancy a secret and for how long? It must have been nigh on impossible to keep the pregnancy quiet for long whilst living in a house full of other people.

Then she thought how precious a new life would be during the difficult time of war, when the newspapers and radio broadcasts pounded home the loss of life. How uplifting it must have been to have news of a *brand new* life...

It was daunting for Izzie to read about lives already lived – those of her own family. How strange that her grandpop had been a twin and she had never known about it. She wasn't sure if anyone had mentioned it during her young life – would she remember? She couldn't seem to shake anything free in that vein.

And that thought gave rise to the belief that she had always held as a teenager, that she would have children of her own – with Justin.

They'd discussed it casually whilst sitting on the beach one afternoon – as though they could affect the outcome just by agreeing they would have twins.

As if it was that easy!

She groaned at how simple they'd assumed life would be.

Meet up, plan their marriage, twins…

And then the unexpected twist that had altered her life… She had married Rufus – Rufus the celebrity author. Rufus who didn't want any children, but he had only told Izzie that after she'd married him.

She wondered if Justin had any children and wondered why she hadn't asked him. Izzie suspected that if he did have children, then she didn't want to know. Suspected that she may feel nothing but a raw jealousy for his partner. He hadn't mentioned Lorna – the beautiful model he had been reported as dating, and a quick peep at his online profile described him as currently unattached…

If she dug too deep, she suspected she may still yearn for the life she had originally planned with Justin, still longed for a family with him – twins or otherwise.

To hold her and Justin's baby… A misty vision rose for a moment, then disappeared. Sniffing, she took a deep breath against the brief, powerful image, and the lump in her throat that it caused.

Izzie dashed the seductive thoughts from her mind, blew her nose and settled into the chair to read more of Molly's story.

Chapter Seven

Molly

Blackpool, Wednesday January 19, 1944

I still have the growing suspicion that I'm expecting…
All day, whilst I worked, I composed the letter to Joe
in my head. I was certain he loved me, I was sure he would
get leave as soon as he could and marry me before the baby
showed too much. Although I'd spent all day deciding what
I would say in a letter, when it came to the evening, it was
hard to find the right words. In the end, I kept it short,
wrote it first in my notebook and then copied it into a letter:

Dearest Joe,

I hope you're keeping well. I have news that should be certain to
see you write back to me this time! I'm expecting your baby

around September time, so it would be best to be married as soon as you can get some leave. I think about you all the time and even more now I carry your child.

Never doubt that I love you,

Your girl,

Molly.

I couldn't help getting excited at the possibility that Joe would just turn up rather than write – he was always spontaneous and full of fun.

In my mind's eye, he would stride up to the boarding house, handsome as ever in his dark blue uniform, and he'd smile that smile that made me feel I was the luckiest girl in the world.

I'd fly into his outstretched arms and we'd float off into the future in a cloud of happiness with our new baby, to a home of our own.

Those were my daydreams, Dear Diary.

In reality, I felt dreadful – nauseous, tired, worried sick and my appetite shrank whilst my chest appeared to expand. I couldn't tell anyone or let anyone see I wasn't feeling well.

I had to hide everything from Enid for fear of being thrown out before I had a ring on my finger.

Blackpool, Wednesday January 26, 1944

A week crept by and one morning when I hung about in the bay window, I could see the postie getting closer and made an excuse that I needed to pick up some litter blowing about on the front doorstep so I could go out and collect the mail.

Our female postie announced, 'Just two today!' and I looked to the sky to thank the man upstairs that there was a letter for me from Joe. I pushed that one into my pinny pocket to look at in private later on, and took the brown envelope with Enid's name on through to the back room, where she took a break and ate breakfast.

It was such a busy day that the only promise of being alone was at bedtime. I caught up with all my jobs and hurried up to my room earlier than usual, having promised myself total privacy so I could revel in Joe's words undisturbed.

Thankfully, it was Enid's night to lock up and turn everything off.

I pulled the eiderdown around my shoulders and my fingers shook with excitement as I tore the envelope open and eased out the flimsy paper.

I held the folded paper to my pounding chest before finally – *finally* – reading it.

I prayed silently as I held the thin paper tightly, prayed that Joe's written words would be the answer to my prayers, whispered, 'Please...' in the hope that the letter would say all I needed to hear.

My fingers shook as I unfolded the letter. I had no idea

just how my life was about to sink, my Dear Diary, and plunge me into the depths of hopelessness…

Dear Molly,

I'm writing to put the record straight. I'm sorry to hear you got pregnant, but I thought that, like me, you were just after a good time. In any case, I should think there's a good chance that the baby isn't mine because we only got down to business once.

I don't want to settle down yet with anyone. I'm not ready for the responsibility. I was with other girls sometimes when we were in Blackpool, and thought you knew that I wasn't really out studying some evenings.

I did like you a lot, but as I say, I'm not ready to have a family. I didn't make any promises and I thought you'd get the message that I didn't want to go steady when I didn't answer your letters.

I wouldn't have answered this one, but Jack said I owed you the truth.

Regards,

Joe Blackshaw.

The air stuck in my chest; I couldn't breathe.
No! No! It couldn't be right.
Couldn't be right.

I read the letter over and over to make sense of the words that danced before my eyes…

I read it until every word was burned into my mind and clawed at my heart.

But reading the words over didn't alter them. Anger ripped through me in a hot surge; I punched the pillow until it exploded and feathers puffed feebly over the bed. To add to my misery, I was ill in the bucket I'd put in my room.

A sense of denial settled around me. He *couldn't* mean those words. Surely not. He'd been so loving, so attentive, so charming…

Hadn't he said he loved me?

But… *no*…

No, he hadn't.

My Dear Diary, that truth dawned as great gulping sobs rose to the surface. I'd stupidly assumed that he *loved* me because we'd *made love*. I pulled the maligned pillow to my face to stifle the noise of my pain as I wailed out loud … for fear of being overheard.

My dream of a happy future crashed into a nightmare in the time it took to open the letter and read it. I shook with anger, with shock, with misery.

I knew I was in trouble, but at that moment I couldn't think beyond the agony of reading Joe's words, words that held my real-life future. The opposite of what I'd imagined in my own foolish romantic vision of the future.

I felt alone, desperate, could think of no way forward, could think only of my desolation.

My pillow was wet and cold.

Miserable and exhausted and against all the odds, I fell asleep.

Blackpool, Thursday 27 January, 1944

The following morning, my Dear Diary, I felt happy for a split second, then I remembered. Joe's letter... Self-pity overwhelmed me, rendered me barely able to move until Enid knocked on my bedroom door.

'Time you were up. Stop your lollygagging, girl.'

Pride forced me out of bed, shocked at the mess of feathers on the floor and bedcovers. 'I'll be down shortly, Mother.' I was surprised that my voice sounded normal, that apart from swollen eyes and feathers all over the place, there was nothing to betray the cruel news I'd had.

Within minutes, I'd washed and dressed and during that time had given myself a talking to. Enid was not going to know about the misery I felt, I could give no hint of what was happening until I had a plan.

No one, my Dear Diary, except these pages would know.

The trouble was, I had no idea what to do. I didn't know how to carry on. I knew I had to find a way to deal with this, and this was whilst dealing with the waves of misery that I had so stupidly been taken in by Joe's handsome face, his engaging smile, urgent kisses and clever love-making. And then the little details I'd ignored at the time – that slight smell of roses on his uniform, and another niggle I had completely pushed out of my mind:

When I returned from the cloakroom in the Tower one time, I saw Joe leaning casually against a pillar, and a woman who was running her fingers down his chest. He appeared to smile down at her, then glance around. On seeing me, he pointed her in the direction of the opposite side of the room.

On our way out of the Tower, I asked Joe who the woman was and he said it was someone Jack had been seeing and that she had got mixed up between them. Of course, I accepted that explanation and brushed aside the questioning frown Jack shot at Joe, gladly letting myself be distracted as Joe whispered how beautiful I was against my ear.

The worst of it was that Enid and all of her dire warnings about young women playing fast and loose and *'getting caught out'*, now also applied to me. Empty, sick, bereft, I had to think of something.

I still didn't know how I could afford to move out of the boarding house and start my own life away from Enid; she would never put up with the stigma of me expecting, unwed and living in her home.

She has made that blatantly clear.

Dear Diary, one moment I'm weighed down with misery about my future, the next I feel a tickle of excitement, of expectation that a new life has begun.

I dreamt both nights since Joe's letter that Denis proposed and I was trapped into marriage by my expectant state. Imagining marriage to Denis … the sense of dread grew, the thought of Enid, hands on hips, shaking her head, forcing the issue, telling me how lucky I was that such a decent young man offered to marry me, even though I'd behaved like a slut.

In the dream she said, '*I knew something like this would happen... You should have listened to me.*'

Dread increased in the daytime, too. I'd an awful feeling that, any time, Denis would turn up at the door and that, rather than be turned out on the street by Enid, I would be forced to beg Denis to marry me... I could imagine he would be high-handed, so full of himself for taking on a loose woman. That is my worst nightmare.

Dear Diary, there *has* to be an alternative. I *will* find one.

Work is an escape. I am numbed by impotent anger at Joe – but blessedly busy. I had to find work away from here, from Enid ... maybe down at South Shore or further away.

Blackpool, Friday January 28, 1944

This morning, something happened that shone a shaft of hope back into my life.

A letter arrived.

Not from Joe, but from Jack.

My Dear Molly,

I feel badly for the way Joe has treated you and what he has left you to face alone.

I was with him when he wrote to you and I'll admit I made him write because he was going to ignore your letter.

I know what he wrote and I want to tell you now that I won't let any niece or nephew of mine be born in shame. I don't want you to feel alone and I will look after you and the baby as my own. No one need ever know that the baby isn't mine, if you're happy with that.

If you agree to be my wife, I'll secure a pass for us to marry as soon as I can.

I understand if you need time to think about this. I'll write again in a day or two and hope you'll write to me, too. Joe knows that I'm writing and what I'm asking, so don't worry that I'm doing something underhand.

I'm thinking of you and I look forward to hearing from you. I care a great deal about you, Molly, and would be a happy man if you'd do me the honour of marrying me.

Yours hopefully,

Jack Blackshaw.

Dear Diary, tears rolled down my face when I read Jack's words. Quieter than Joe, Jack looked the same but personality wise, could not be more different. I recollected his quiet patience as he taught me how to play rummy, his warm smile. The way he sketched whenever he had a spare minute – people, plants, me... There was a certain sensitivity about him, too, which was missing in Joe.

It took my breath away that Jack was willing to take on the responsibility of the baby and me.

I had loved Joe deeply, but had been wrong about him loving me. His letter though, had left no hope that he would take on his baby. He'd even made certain I knew I hadn't been the only young woman he went around with.

That thought still makes me feel sick to the stomach. As does his assumption that I'd done the deed with some other man – *men*, even.

Jack's letter, when I'd reached rock bottom, was an unexpected offer of salvation. We'd chatted in the evenings, many evenings, played cards, drank tea, talked about his family and shared a joke or two; it struck me that I'd probably spent far more time with Jack than I had with Joe. And I like him a damn sight more than Denis. But marriage?

How strange life is, how one simple letter threatened to destroy me and the future of my unborn child; how another has given me hope. Not only hope, but vigour. I'm afraid to test too hard how I feel about the escape Jack has offered.

In case it wasn't real, in case Jack changed his mind.

Chapter Eight

Izzie

Blackpool, Thursday June 29, 2017

I *felt alone, desperate, could think of no way forward, could think only of my desolation.*

Molly's heartbroken words echoed in Izzie's mind whilst she deposited yet another couple of tied rubbish bags by the hatch for taking down from the attic.

It wasn't just that Nan had been expecting a baby, but that she'd been rejected by Joe in no uncertain terms.

'Oh, Nan.' Izzie held the gold, skin-warmed locket around her neck, teeth biting into her bottom lip as she considered how her beloved Grandpop had offered to step up in his brother's place for the sake of the unborn baby, for the sake of Molly, so she wouldn't be left alone to face an uncertain, unmarried future.

Molly had loved and expected to marry one man, but had she too married another? It had turned out amazingly well though as their love for one another was always, always evident. There was never ever any hint that Grandpop had been anything other than the love of Molly's life.

Izzie wondered because she too had loved and expected to marry one man, but had married another. She empathised completely with Molly's desolation at the time of her rejection.

Desolation. Izzie had felt exactly that when Justin had failed to meet her... Hadn't known how to cope with the misery engulfing her. She'd had no inkling of what she should do next, only that she had to run, get away and return to London where she could hide from reality, bury her pain, lose herself in the routine of work.

And then Rufus had presented her with an unexpected escape route – a route Izzie ran down blindly without hesitation in an attempt to out-run her agony.

Marriage, work, art, admin, caring – all with Rufus as the focus.

She hadn't realised at the time what she was doing; it was only hindsight that allowed her to have a clearer picture of her reaction, to fully recognise that marrying Rufus had been her way of reaching subconsciously for an emotional balm.

Molly's situation, though, pushed Izzie's woes into perspective. 'Just get on with it, Izzie!' she chided herself.

Carrying an old, dismantled bed head towards the loft hatch, she caught sight of the framed photograph she'd set on the desk – the much-loved photo of Nan and Grandpop on their wedding day. She stopped for a second, smiled at the photo and then looked to the ceiling and whispered, 'I swear you are still with me, Nan, thank you.'

Blackpool, Saturday July 1, 2017

A few days later, Izzie handed the dismantled bed in pieces down the ladder to Justin. Luckily, the spare old mattress was thin and spongy, easily bent in half and shoved down through the loft hatch.

'I know a decent decorator if you don't want to do it all yourself?'

'No, I'm going to stay here and do some of the work. It feels good to have a purpose again.'

She watched whilst Justin rolled up the old, disused crumbling foam mattress and tied a length of string around it, then climbed down the ladder.

When he turned back to face her, he had a definite twinkle in his eye. Izzie heard his words in her head before he spoke.

'We had some fun on that.'

Laughing, she felt the heat creeping up her cheeks. 'It was sort of innocent.'

'You think?' There was no mistaking the heat in his eyes when he spoke.

A sharp thrill shot through her at his words, followed by the heated memory...

Laid side by side they'd taken off their T-shirts – *because of the heat*, they'd claimed.

Then Justin had pulled her against his torso and they'd discovered the intense pleasure of skin against skin, his mouth covering hers, his tongue exploring against hers, his palm running up the outside of her ribs; unashamedly, she'd wriggled so he was atop her, her own hands ran over his shoulders, his back ... and their kissing and touching became more urgent, more intimate...

Slowly, she let out her breath. The powerful recollection had taken her right back to that hot summer day.

Their eyes met and Izzie thought Justin's looked dark and sexy, as though he too shared the memory.

'Well, maybe not all that innocent.' She put her hand to her chest in an attempt to cover the flutter inside in case it showed, then wanted to laugh at herself for the daft thought.

His brow twitched just a bit, those eyes of his weighing her up. 'You got that right.' He blew out as though he was as affected as she, before leaning down to pick up the old foam mattress to carry out.

She followed him as they ferried more stacked rubbish to Justin's car boot.

'Fancy a hot date to the dump?'

'Heaven.' Izzie put a hand to her chest in a dramatic gesture. The fluttering inside and deep in her belly still hadn't stopped. 'You do know how to spoil me.'

'I always did.' He gave a short laugh when Izzie threw a work glove at him and then sank into the passenger seat.

Several trips later, the cavernous car boot was empty and they returned to sit in the car to wait for another vehicle to pull away.

'I could leave you the keys for the car in the New Year?' He shrugged one shoulder. 'Might be useful? If you're still about.'

'Wow, that's kind, Justin. I plan to return to West Hampstead early in January, though.'

'Well, in case you're still here? The only downside would be that Mum and Dad might ask for lifts to their appointments. You know, doc's, hairdresser's, that kind of thing?'

'I'd do that with pleasure – I know you always did stuff like that for Nan to save her getting cabs.'

'Molly told you?'

'Yep.'

One side of his mouth lifted in a wry smile. 'Molly always thought that you and I should be together. She liked Rufus, but not as much as she liked me.'

Izzie laughed and glanced at him, feeling instant warmth at the spark of fun in his eyes.

She suspected he was right; Molly had always adored Justin. 'She thought the world of you.' Silently, Izzie thought that she and Justin should have been together, too – but he'd blown that plan out of the water, made his choice. And his choice hadn't been her.

Yet, increasingly, the temptation to throw caution to the

wind and encourage their past closeness beckoned like some sensual, out of reach enticement.

'Do you think she ever guessed what we got up to in the attic when she was out at her lunch clubs?'

He nodded gravely. 'Oh, I think so. All that practice we had paid dividends.' His mouth hitched in a small smile.

Izzie had the feeling he wanted some kind of reaction from her, but just let the memories wash over her briefly. 'We did a lot of that.'

He laughed; the warm sound fizzled around her insides.

'So, you don't get any complaints from Lorna?'

'Lorna? No, no complaints there.'

The car in front pulled away and Izzie glanced down at Justin's hand and forearm as he changed gear to move off. It was a sexy forearm, lightly tanned and dusted with dark blond hair.

'Are you still with her? Lorna?' If he was, Izzie wondered why she hadn't seen her around. The thought of Justin with the gorgeous, leggy, brunette stunner caused an unaccustomed, sickening lurch in Izzie's stomach.

Lorna had been the latest in a long line of glamorous partners; she was in a league of her own when it came to looks with gorgeous, long dark hair, and she photographed like a dream. Their relationship had been featured in a Sunday supplement, Lorna a supermodel on the up and up, a perfect pair to Justin's tall, broad yet rangy frame, his sun-streaked hair as tousled as Lorna's was poster-smooth. Justin had been with some of the most beautiful women and Izzie always assumed that being with such stunning women and having entered a different, glamorous world had taken him out of her orbit and into another realm.

Izzie had peeked at his website from time to time, and his photography was stunning. The early work of fabulous models, both male and female, some celebrity work, giving way more and more to incredible images of scenery in remote locations.

'No, she dumped me when I told her I'd be away again in New Zealand for three months early next year.' He sighed. 'Lorna said I couldn't care about her much if I kept going off for months at a time. She'd had enough. She was looking for something more permanent, she said. I reminded her I'd never promised her permanent.'

'Did it upset you?'

'The first few times she ended it, yes it did. It was a very on-off relationship. But happily, she has another fella now. It's all good.'

He didn't sound troubled at Lorna finding someone new … but then, Justin could be hiding how he felt; she remembered how he could do that, just push aside his feelings so that no one else would guess, yet she'd always thought *she* knew how he really felt. How he'd really felt about her… She stemmed that thought.

Changing the subject, he told her about an upcoming photography commission for a Lake District tourist book. 'It'll be just a few days of a job and I'll travel from here when the forecast is good, stay over if I need to.' Then he asked, 'Will you join me for dinner tonight, Izzie?'

Considering for a moment, she remained silent.

'Or I could bring something round to you and you could catch me up on Molly's notebook?'

'Sounds like a good plan. I'd like that.' A sharp thrill that he sought her company had shot the words right out of her mouth without any hesitation.

Justin seemed able to get a handle on what made her tick as easily as he ever had.

She smiled; spirits buoyed at his easy invitation to share dinner. It almost felt as if they were back at the beginning again – starting with their friendship. And she admitted inwardly that she didn't want to resist the pull of their new relationship, friendship or otherwise. Why shouldn't she just go along with the flow – whether they resurrected their friendship or more, there was no likelihood it would be more than a transient relationship this time. They each had solid plans for their futures, plans that would take them away from one another yet again.

Whilst they ate that evening, they talked about many things. Justin told her he was sorry to hear Rufus had died. 'I was out of the country when it happened; it was Molly who told me when I visited.'

'Tell you the truth, it all passed in a fog. Rufus organised everything how he wanted and I went through it in a daze. The weird thing is, you can know what's going to happen way ahead of time, but it doesn't make it any easier. I kept looking round for him, expecting him to wander into his office at home. Sounds daft.'

'No, it doesn't.' His hand covered hers lightly. 'Are you okay?'

She nodded sadly. 'It was an unusual situation, Justin. Rufus asked me to marry him knowing he only had four or five years to live. He'd an inoperable brain tumour and whilst he was still well enough, he wanted to plan the time he had left, map it out as best he could. Get his ducks in a row, he called it.'

'Did you love him, Izzie?'

She nodded. It had been love.

Justin squeezed her hand and then left it resting on hers as he took a swallow of wine.

She smiled, tested whether she wanted to talk about her marriage and whether it would hurt too much. She hadn't been sure initially, but Izzie found it surprisingly liberating to share...

'It seems ages ago.'

'When did you start working for him?' Justin cradled his wine glass in his palms.

'I worked for DAS, Design Admin and Secretarial Services Agency – as part of a great team for over four and a half years. We'd a lot of musician clients, music venues – exciting stuff – and we worked on some admin for Rufus's books, when his books were optioned for a TV series.'

Justin raised the wine bottle to offer a refill and Izzie nodded her thanks.

'It was after four or so years, around February time, Rufus's assistant moved away. Before that, I'd stood in for her during holidays. He suggested that I work for him, just part-time at first, through DAS as his PA, helping to transcribe and format his bestselling crime thrillers featuring DC Nicolas Riggs, and at the same time taking care of his diary, interviews, contracts and correspondence, sometimes even organising his food deliveries.'

Background music played quietly on the kitchen radio and Izzie imagined Rufus at his desk, back home in West Hampstead, writing by hand in his fast and focused manner. 'Rufus wasn't a fan of mornings, so I worked on other jobs for DAS, then, if I needed to collaborate with him, that'd happen in the afternoons; either from his home office or those at DAS. Come late August it became full-time solely for Rufus when … when I married him.'

She told Justin how Rufus loved the contact of pen with paper; his plan B – when he was tired, or could not write fast enough – was to speak his bestselling scripts into the box of tricks recorder. She closed her eyes. 'During his last year, he would have a large glass of whisky on the edge of his desk, working on his plotlines until he became so drowsy, he could barely speak.' She gave a little laugh, looked sidelong at Justin. 'It used to be my task to unravel and make sense of the written and spoken text, to format it how Rufus wanted it so it was ready to present to the publisher.'

'What a great way to see how well you got along, Izzie. The man was a genius!'

Laughing, Izzie asked, 'What, you mean before he asked me to marry him?'

'Yeah, simple idea and genius.'

Some awfully strange pinging sensations tremored through Izzie, such an ambiguous mixture of sadness, loss and a twist of regret. Whilst she took a breath, she nodded her agreement, pushed down the whirling mixture of emotions.

'It was a good move for both of us. DAS released me to work solely for Rufus, said I could freelance for them anytime.'

After standing and clearing the table, Izzie asked, 'Coffee, tea or more wine, Justin?'

'Tea would be great.'

'I enjoyed going to work – always had – but working with Rufus was beyond my wildest dreams.' She dropped a couple of teabags into her nan's chunky brown teapot, hooked two china mugs off the mug tree and took the carton of milk out of the fridge, whilst Justin leaned against the kitchen doorframe, listening, legs crossed at the ankles.

'He found me funny when I didn't think I was anything more than slightly amusing; he even said I looked pretty when I rolled up for work doing a walk of shame because I hadn't made it home after being out with my friend Ruby or the others – although, admittedly, that was before I became his full time PA. He said I was a good listener, and a genius on the keyboard. But the best thing was we could laugh and talk together and lose all track of time. He never tired of discussing plotlines – airing his ideas and listening when I suggested my own twists.'

'Sounds like a good partnership.'

'It was.' It *had* been a good partnership. She had loved him, he'd been crazy about her, loved her he said, and from a famous, successful writer that was so flattering. Just when she'd badly needed to escape into another world.

But for her, she had realised as she spoke to Justin about Rufus, there had always been something missing in that relationship: a spark of incredible excitement, outright sensuality – something she had only ever known with Justin.

In that exact moment, she also realised that during her time with Rufus, she had tamped down the yearning for more, perhaps subconsciously knowing that giving away her whole heart had emotionally seen her on her knees once before.

Desolate... The word Molly used when she was at her lowest ebb, when she had been pushed aside by Joe. It also described how Izzie had felt when she'd been stood up on her twenty-third, summertime birthday.

She recollected again how she'd felt that nothing would ever be right again.

She looked directly at Justin, pushed on. 'After a spell as his part-time PA, he asked me to marry him. He explained all about his health, how it would degenerate over the following four or five years. What he wanted more than anything was the reassurance that he wouldn't die alone, and to be sure of the dedication I'd give him to work on his books for as long as he was able. After that, I needed to be there just for him.'

Justin's palm rested gently on Izzie's shoulder. 'It must have been beyond painful to lose Rufus; it sounds like you had an amazing relationship. Close to perfect.'

Again, something shifted inside. She touched his fingers where they rested on her shoulder. 'Thanks, Justin.'

The truth was, it *hadn't* been perfect, but she tucked that fact aside for the moment, unwilling to face the unease of that truth just then. There was time for that – when she was alone.

'I got an invite to a pal's wedding,' Justin said, suddenly changing the topic. He hesitated for a moment before continuing. 'Will you be my plus one, Izzie? It's some time off yet, 23rd December, just a few of days before I fly out to New Zealand. I've had a "save the date" card from them and I was just thinking if you wanted to join me, you could put it in your diary.'

The invitation surprised her, and she blurted out unexpectedly, 'I'd love to, thank you.'

She frowned at herself and her big mouth; it continually engaged before her brain did. But the idea of some carefree fun immediately filled her with excitement. The idea of some carefree fun *with Justin* added a whole other shard of anticipation. Sometimes, she thought it was a good thing her mouth made decisions for her!

'Do you remember Mick? We all went down the sand dunes near Squires Gate with him and a crowd of others on high days and holidays? He's marrying Janey.'

'Oh, of course! We had some fun with that crowd.' They'd enjoyed endless summer days together.

A flash of memory surged: bright beach towels, swimming, laughing, their little crew huddled beneath a ground sheet when a deluge of unexpected rain pounded the soft sand. A picnic of squashed sandwiches and crisps, melting chocolate and tins of beer, the smell of suntan lotion. She sat beside Justin; their bodies pressed close together as they held the cover over their heads until the rain passed, their noses touching when they turned to look at one another at the same time ... then the becoming aware of one another and the laughter that followed.

Justin had been eighteen, Izzie seventeen.

'I just had a flashback of us all playing truth or dare.' Just the memory brought heat to her cheeks.

Justin gave a half-smile, a deep dimple showing in one cheek. 'It was fun back then.'

'It was fun – unless the *dares* happened to you!' Izzie laughed; the vivid recollection sent goose bumps over her skin.

'Bet you're remembering the dare when we had to swap tops.' His brow raised and amusement lit his eyes.

'It was all right for you!'

His top had been a big baggy vest and Izzie's a little wrap over blue top. Izzie hesitated. 'I had nothing on underneath it cos I'd hung my bikini top to dry off.'

Justin laughed wholeheartedly. 'You went for it though, Izzie, I thought you'd opt for a truth that time.'

She resisted the urge to fan her face at the memory that rose next.

'A bit later on, I got the dare to kiss the person to my left as though I really meant it.'

'That'd be me you were kissing.' He smiled, a sexy smile that seemed to hit Izzie right in the gut.

'Yeah.'

Izzie lingered in that magical moment for a second or two. Their kiss had sparked something so powerful – a crossroads where they moved between friends and lovers.

The memories flashed through her mind in seconds, but

there were so many – it could have been hours. They dated during her last year at college, when Justin had already finished and worked at his dad's photography business. He'd go to help at special occasions and weddings, carrying equipment, learning the ropes about lighting and all the ins and outs of developing photos, mending expensive equipment instead of replacing it.

Izzie was living with Nan and Grandpop by the time she and Justin were an item, and couldn't bear to be away from him. It was ideal that his folks lived next door.

She and Justin had become lovers around a month or so after that scintillating first kiss; Izzie fell absolutely – incredibly – head over heels in love with Justin. She felt the rush of emotion burst in her chest at the intense memories.

All along, though, they'd both known that Justin had a burning desire to travel anywhere and everywhere, photographing it all. He already wrote articles for local papers and magazines, and did a bit of local celebrity work; he was forever entering photography competitions – and winning more often than not.

They both started applying for jobs, not really thinking much would come of it.

Then something Justin had applied for during their first Christmas as a couple – an internship with *National Geographic* – came up with an offer to begin work in late June.

He was ecstatic, thought all of his Christmases had come at once, and he was paired up with one of their photographers as an assistant.

She recollected Justin punching the air with sheer joy,

unable to believe what was happening. He'd then picked her up and spun her around, they couldn't stop laughing. To say he was happy was an understatement. And his happiness was infectious.

A couple of days before that, he'd spotted the advertisement DAS had put in an online photography and art magazine he read. Izzie would never have seen the advert if not for him and Justin had encouraged her to apply for the junior design admin post; it was in London, just where she'd always wanted to work. It was like someone had sprinkled dream-come-true dust on their lives because against all the odds, Izzie got an interview; they too were happy for her to begin working for them several months hence – in June, once her college course had finished.

Tea brewed, Izzie carried their mugs into the back room. 'Shall we have a read of Molly's notebook now?'

She settled on the wide armchair beside him and wondered why it felt fine to share Molly's past with Justin, then realised that he was the only other person in her life who had truly known Molly. She knew through her nan that Justin called around regularly whenever he visited his own parents next door – and he had certainly been liked by Molly. It occurred to Izzie that any time that she spent at Nan's – even as a *'bit of a wild'* teen, as described by her mother – if she was going out and about with Justin, then her nan and granddad never seemed to worry.

It was only now that Izzie realised how much trust that Nan and Grandpop had had in Justin.

And her.

It occurred to her too that the roles people played in one another's lives changed, and whatever had happened in the past between herself and Justin, he remained a link with Nan and Grandpop. They had been such a huge, happy part of her life.

It was still difficult to accept the fact that Justin had let her down without any attempt at an explanation, and at the same time it was increasingly difficult to deny the attraction that seemed to pull her towards him even now. She didn't know if she could accept that part of her past, look beyond to the friendship they were forging anew now, but she did know that, at the very least, she wanted some time with Justin. That deep inside part of her ached to forgive him, but another part of her didn't know whether he would hurt her all over again if she let down her guard.

She suspected he might still have the power to do so if she let herself be drawn too close to him – the saying 'like a moth to a flame' flittered into her thoughts…

Chapter Nine

Molly

Blackpool, Saturday January 29, 1944

My Dearest Molly,

Here's the letter I promised, written two days after my first. I keep wondering if you've considered whether to marry me, and how you and the baby are. I remember walking close to you and Joe when you suggested visiting the sand dunes, going for rides on the trams, grabbing an ice cream from Luigi's, going to have a look at the donkeys, the Pleasure Beach, paddling in the sea. As far as I know, I don't think the two of you managed many of those things. I would really like to do all of them with you.

I have to go soon so this will make today's post. I will write again very soon in a couple of days and hope that you will write to me and let me know your decision – or if you don't want me, then please, still let me know how you are? Are you still working as hard at the Bing Lea? Is your stepmother still ruling the roost?

With fondest wishes,

Jack Blackshaw

A rough copy of my reply:

Dear Jack,

I am touched by your offer of marriage. It's the kindest thing anyone has ever done. Enid speaks often about local girls who've ended up in the family way outside of marriage. She told me she would throw me out if it happens to me, and she repeats it over and over. This may be why I want to accept. I'm afraid I'll be offering little to you besides affection in return for such a huge commitment from you. I'm concerned that you may regret marrying me. And it doesn't seem fair to you above anything else.

If I'm being completely selfish, then yes, please, I would love to marry you. But if I stop to consider you – then is it fair? I would always take care of you and treasure you as my husband, I can promise you that. Will you think about my concerns before you fully commit, Jack? The last thing I want to do is accept and disappoint you in any way, or make you unhappy.

Whatever you decide, I would love to see you if you can visit? And I'll abide with any decision you make. It is always a treat to hear from you by letter, too, it is like a ray of sunshine warming up a dreary day. And I am keeping well, thanks, I think being busy all the time helps me. I'd like to join the Red Cross along with Dora, even if it is just to roll bandages for now. I will ask if they need help with that.

Dora is still seeing Matt, the American who you met when we all walked along the prom together. He takes her dancing to the Tower or the Winter Gardens on a Saturday night, and sometimes I go along too. He brings chocolate and other gifts, and last week he brought his Box Brownie camera. Matt showed me how to take pictures so that I could photograph him and Dora together. Dora is looking forward to having a photo of him, and he said he would get one for himself too. I hope the photos turn out well. They both love the sketches you did for them, by the way.

Enid is shouting that I need to help her with serving now, so I had better go and bang the gong! I'll write again in a day or so and look forward to hearing from you, Jack. I am very grateful for you writing and feel eager to get another letter from you.

Please keep safe.

Yours affectionately,

Molly Webster.

My Dear Diary, I feel something I didn't think I would ever feel again when I write to Jack. I feel hope – and an inkling of joy. I also feel an amazing sense of gratefulness that Jack should care enough to write, and even more that he should offer to marry me. What is wonderful is that when Jack says he will send a letter, I feel sure he will. He seems to say what he means and mean what he says.

My dad used to be like that, too.

Dear God, keep Jack safe, and his family in Manchester too. And Joe. I wrote his name and it didn't hurt much; the anger I had towards him is less now. I think it was the thought of being thrown out of home or having to settle for marriage to Denis that fed the panic and anger before Jack stepped in.

I make sure, Dear Diary, that I am working in the front room, so I can see out of the dining room window when the postie makes her way up the road.

I don't want Enid to know that I look forward to Jack's letters; I'm afraid if she knew about them, she may hide them, or God forbid, burn them.

My Dearest Molly,

Hopefully, the next time I write I will be able to let you know a date when I'll visit.

Thank you for your answer. I am very happy that you have said yes to marrying me. I did consider your concerns, but I have a strong feeling that everything will work well with us both and the baby. I don't want to frighten you off, but from the moment you shook my hand, I felt something for you. I've a feeling Joe jumped in and charmed you because I let slip that I wanted to pursue you myself. He's always been like that, wanting whatever I want for himself, and he'll do anything he can to get it.

When I read about the photographs of Dora and Matt, I thought how much I wanted a photo of you. I want to carry your photo and show it to my friends so they can see how beautiful you are and how lucky I am, but mostly so I can just look whenever I've a mind to. At the moment I carry a small pencil sketch I did of you on one of the nights you joined me and the others in the front room for a game of cards. It makes me smile, but I would love a photo.

I think about you a lot and hope that we can be together before long, that this war will end soon...

My news here is that we smoke and play cards and football, but most of the time we are kept busy. There're always so many new things to learn and so much equipment to repair.

I have to stop myself from telling you where I am and any more about what I'm doing, the censors cut any of those things out of our letters in case they fall into the wrong hands.

I have a friend in South Shore who said I can bunk at his whenever I visit. He moved there from Manchester with his parents, and says I can sleep in his lounge if he's no beds free;

he's done that for other visitors. He has RAF billeted with him most of the time, like your stepmother. My friend took evacuees back in 1939, from Manchester, mostly, but they went back home later the same year because nothing happened, you know, when everyone called it the phoney war.

That seems like a long time ago. It doesn't feel phoney any longer.

I'll think of you often and hope you will write soon.

With fondest love,

Jack Blackshaw.

My Dearest Molly,

This is just a very quick letter to let you know I can get a pass for the end of February, on the 26th. My pass is only forty-eight hours; I would have to leave on the 28th. I hope that will give us time to be married.

Stan in our squadron managed to marry his sweetheart when he had a weekend pass, so hopefully it can be done.

If this can be, let me know ASAP and I'll contact Ma, who can organise the reading of the Banns in our church at home; that's what Stan did. Could you do the same at yours?

I look forward to hearing from you and seeing you very soon,
Molly.

With fondest love,

Jack.

_____

My Dear Jack,

It makes me so happy that you always keep your word. Your letters lift my spirits.

For years I have had my late mum's wedding dress in an old suitcase under my bed. I will try it on and if needs be, alter it to fit. Dora will help if I struggle with that – and her mum is kind, I'm sure she'll help too.

I've just dashed over to the church and spoken to our vicar, he can perform the ceremony at midday on the 26th, if you can be here by then? Does that suit you? The Banns will be read on the first three Sundays in February. Do you mind if I tell Dora? I will have to tell Enid soon. Do you want me to write to your mother and father and invite them? Let me know?

With love and affection,

Molly.

Blackpool, Thursday February 3, 1944

My Dear Diary, war makes folk realise how precious time is. In the same way, expecting a baby makes me very aware of the passing of the same time that I used to drift through. I have tried the dress and it fits as, fortunately, it is a straight up and down style, ending at the ankles, with capped sleeves and a gauze shawl with a fringe that can be worn over the shoulders, or in a loose knot around the hips. I took Dora into my confidence about the upcoming wedding but didn't mention any reason other than the sad losses we hear about every single day and the need to make the most of time. She thinks the dress is fine as it is, and although she said she was bursting to tell her mum about the wedding, she won't. She promised. Just until I've told Enid though. I will do that soon.

I carried on arranging the things that I could without Jack's final okay, and just hoped it would all come together all right.

Blackpool, Thursday February 10, 1944

Dear Diary, I was relieved to hear from Jack. I know folk talk about post taking a while, but I had begun to feel nervous. The date is only just over two weeks away and there's a lot to do.

My Dear Molly,

I'll be in Blackpool before noon on Saturday the 26th. I'll go straight to the church as I won't have much time before that to do owt else, my train will be due in just before twelve, so hopefully there won't be any hold ups.

Ma arranged to have the Banns read on the same three Sundays (first three in February) as they'll be read at your local church. Sadly, Ma and Pa's house has been badly damaged in an air raid and they've had to decamp to Oldham to live with my aunt. I've written to tell them we'll be wed, but they say that travel is difficult for most. I imagine they would like to come, but'll probably not make it. As time is running out and I need to get this off to post, I will have to let you know any other news from home on the day.

Stay safe and well, Molly, I look forward to seeing you very soon.

With fondest love, your husband to be.

Jack.

Chapter Ten

Izzie

Blackpool, Saturday July 1, 2017

Justin blew out, looked to Izzie and carefully set the precious letter written on thin paper down on top of the open notebook.

'Hey.' He took hold of her hand. 'Are you okay reading this?' His dark green eyes shone with concern and something twisted inside her in response.

'Yes.' Izzie's voice was a bit hoarse with emotion. 'I didn't expect to … you know … feel everything so much. He was so kind, Grandpop.'

It moved her insides further because Justin's hand remained covering hers; a tiny part of her wanted to throw it off, but the compulsion to relish his touch, the warm shocks travelling through her fingers and arm,

133

spreading all through her – that compulsion won. She didn't want to move a muscle in case he removed his hand. At the same time, she wondered if Justin felt anything at all.

At first, she didn't quite have the nerve to look into his eyes again but then she did.

He smiled. 'Okay?'

'Thanks, yes.' Her words were still hoarse and briefly she wondered how Justin knew her so well. Then she acknowledged that he probably knew her better than any other living soul now. 'I'm good.'

Izzie reached out for the letter; she wanted to touch it, marvelling that the neat handwriting had survived intact all these years. Then, she folded it carefully and handed it back to Justin. He slid it back into the small envelope that was stitched in place on the page.

'I wonder where Jack was when he wrote this? Whether he was cold or warm, hungry or full, tired or in danger when he wrote to Molly, I mean Nan.'

'I think it's fine to call your nan *Molly* whilst you read these.'

'Yes, it does seem like two different people, doesn't it? It makes me think, Justin, just how much things have altered. Beautiful, handwritten letters have been replaced by emails and text messages. Things were slower then. How many servicemen and women must have craved letters from home to keep their love alive, to keep their spirits up? It's hard to imagine how much the letters meant to those fighting for their country, and to those at home who kept life ticking over like Nan – Molly. How beautiful that letters from Jack would bring her hope. It's hard to imagine a text message doing that.'

'Yeah,' Justin said, 'and photographs, just a single photograph was carried of loved ones, maybe kissed goodnight or for luck before a mission; these days, hundreds of photos are shared instantly online. Sometimes I delete dozens in a day when I'm on a job.'

'It's so different.' Izzie glanced at Justin, and something in his eyes held her look; she thought there was a trace of sorrow, maybe pain in their depths.

A spear of sadness shot through her; she and Justin had written, phoned to keep in touch, but it had gradually dwindled to nothing. Dwindled in the months leading up to her twenty-third birthday...

How had that happened?

And so soon afterwards she had married Rufus...

Had it been too soon?

'Izzie?' Justin's voice tugged her back to the here and now, where the emotion rose and pushed to the surface. Her throat ached with the effort of keeping down the rise of painful tears for what Justin had let go of so easily. 'You sure you're okay?'

'Yes.' This time, she covered his hand, just briefly, and knew that familiar rush when he turned his fingers to squeeze her own in return. 'Just emotional, you know.'

'Thank goodness things seem to be going all right for them.' Justin stifled a yawn and apologised, and Izzie handed him a postcard to use as a bookmark.

'Shall we call it a night?' Izzie asked. 'I'm getting sleepy too.'

'I've a free afternoon tomorrow. Do you want some more help here? Or would you like to go out – a long walk and dinner or something?

'Yes, to everything.' Izzie was done holding back. Even if she and Justin were only destined to be friends, she wanted to enjoy herself; walking and talking and dinner sounded perfect to her.

He laughed. 'Hard to please, as always.'

They arranged that he'd call around at one, they'd work for an hour, then go out.

———————————

The following morning, Izzie hooked her fingertips around her trusty old rucksack, which she'd found buried deep within one of the eaves cupboards in the loft. She fancied the rucksack still held the scent of the sea and sand.

She'd forgotten that she'd stored an old, filled sketch pad in there; a wealth of her art school sketches. The drawing pad contained several pencil drawings of gnarly trees – one of her favourite subjects back then – and on the pages beneath those were sketches of another of her favourite subjects: Justin.

Her insides lurched at the memory of all the love she'd sketched into his features; it was just his neck and shoulders, but it was the light she'd captured in his eyes that made her breath hitch even now.

His eyes followed her, closed just a little against the hazy sunshine. It was a very sensual look.

A powerful memory of the two of them relaxing beside

the sand dunes close to Starr Gate on a warm summer day hit her. In those days, she took her sketch pad everywhere, stashed along with pencils and a towel in her rucksack. All that mattered then was being outdoors, taking a dip, loving the endless warm days, and Justin. They'd had no cares, no responsibilities, no bills to pay or homes to take care of. They could just ... be.

Taped in the back of her pad was a photograph of Justin that she'd taken around the same time as sketching him, something she habitually did if she wanted to re-do or add to a work in progress.

Setting down the sketch pad, Izzie grabbed her phone to take a picture of the sketch of Justin.

Later, when Justin called around, he ducked in out of the torrential rain. 'Maybe we should put that walk off until later? It's going to clear up.'

'Sure.' Izzie suggested they have a cuppa and a read of Molly's notebook until the weather improved.

'Lead the way,' was Justin's response.

Chapter Eleven

Molly

Blackpool, Friday February 18, 1944

My Dear Jack,

I loved reading your letter and look forward to you coming here on the 26ᵗʰ. I'm going to hear the Banns for the third time this coming Sunday morning.

I will see if I can get a photograph for when you visit and hope that I might be able to get one of you, too.

I will never be able to thank you enough for saving me in this way, at least hopefully now the nightmares I have about having to marry Denis, or someone like him, will stop.

I can't wait to see you. Sorry this is short, but Enid is calling for help. I'll write more soon.

Take care and please stay safe.

With fondest wishes,

Molly.

Dear Diary,
  I told our boarding house guests that Jack and I were getting married on the Saturday and we'd be having a small lunch to celebrate here in the guest house dining room. I asked Enid if we could invite everyone along since they were due to be here anyway. She muttered that it would be more like an ordinary lunchtime, but brightened up a bit when I told her I'd be getting some extra ham from the butcher specially for the wedding.

Matt thinks he will able to get away from Warton, to come and take some photographs. Dora was excited by that prospect, too.

The thought of seeing Jack is like a ball of excitement sitting in my chest just waiting to explode out with a mixture of nervousness and happiness. I feel such gratitude, such warmth towards him and I recollect him drawing his life-like sketches; I love the one he gave me, I should ask him to do one of himself to put here in my notebook, alongside mine.

Chapter Twelve

Molly

Blackpool, Saturday February 26, 1944

Word of our upcoming wedding spread like wildfire around the neighbours.

Everyone I knew seemed to make themselves available to help towards the preparations. It was so uplifting. Lilian, the newly taken on helper at the boarding house, insisted on coming along early in the morning to make extra sandwiches for lunch, a cake from her ferreted away supplies – her *wedding gift to us* she called it – and freshly baked scones.

The grocer found us extra rations, and the butcher handed over a wodge of ham wrapped in greaseproof paper. 'Everybody gets ham for their wedding day, and seeing how you are a special customer, I've put a bit extra in. Only don't tell anyone.' He tapped the side of his nose.

I had expected to have to do everything myself from scratch, but a few local ladies turned up along with Lilian, Dora, Dora's mum and Enid, and none of them arrived empty-handed.

One of the ladies carried a bunch of joyous daffodils, fresh and colourful, picked from her garden, she'd wrapped them in a doily type handhold after surrounding them with some greenery and baby's breath. 'These are for you to carry down the aisle.'

I was thrilled, Dear Diary; yellow flowers are so joyous.

They all mucked in and busied themselves and Enid seemed almost happy for once directing operations.

At that point, as the pushed-together tables heaved with all manner of food, Dora suggested it was time to get ready. We took the flowers and wedding dress and made our way over to her house where I could get ready away from the preparations.

Dora helped to take out the rollers I'd worn overnight, and then teased my hair into a Betty Grable style, curled under in a victory roll. It was lacquered into place so that even a high Blackpool wind wouldn't budge a hair on my head. That was the hope.

There were no visible signs of my pregnancy and it was fortunate, too, that the nausea had stopped for the main part.

Dora helped to put on my lovely mum's dress and the silk fabric of the lining floated downward, soft and warm against my skin. The gauzy overdress had embroidery across the yoke and across the hips, the style reminiscent of a 1920s flapper.

The headdress was a simple band, a silk flower stitched on the top right. A shoulder-length veil flowed backwards from the head band.

The shoes I wore were simple white court shoes, borrowed from Dora. I thought of the something old as being my mum's dress, and the something blue was a little blue prayer book gifted to me by my mum's late brother, Charles, who had also once lived in Royton. That life that could have been a hundred years ago, it seemed so far in the past now, but no less poignant. I closed my eyes and thought of my close family for a moment, all lost now.

As we joined Marian in the kitchen for her seal of approval, she presented me with a bottle of sherry.

'I found it tucked away under the stairs! I'd no idea it was there.' She smiled. 'It'll warm you up on your walk to church, Molly, and settle your nerves.'

Marian poured each of us a small glass. 'I'll bring what's left to the wedding lunch,' she said.

She had also unearthed a dramatic-looking bottle of scent, the stopper like a three-pointed crown, the smell extremely pleasant – she said it was bergamot-scented. I dabbed it on my wrists, behind my ears and behind my knees. I never really knew why this was the place to put scent, but I'd seen my mum doing it years ago and that was good enough reason for me.

There was absolutely no point in having a car, even if we could have got hold of one; fuel was in short supply.

Dora's dad, Bill, had offered to walk me to the church

and down the aisle once we were ready, and I accepted. It seemed fitting since he and my dad had been friends.

The church was only a short walk away and I pulled on my warmest coat, buttoned it up and enjoyed the stroll at Bill's side wearing my mum's wedding dress. My dearest friend, Dora, was with me too, her mum beside us, carrying the flowers. The air smelled so clean and fresh this close to the sea, and that raised my spirits.

As we walked towards the church, neighbours – mostly boarding house landladies – and young children stood out on their doorsteps to watch and wave and shout their good wishes.

I smiled and waved and let myself be carried along on a ridiculous rush of excitement and relief that the baby would have a father. I was still finding it hard to believe, that I was about to be married to someone I hardly knew, and yet, I was so very grateful to Jack whose letters had already begun to melt my heart.

So many emotions crashed around inside me.

I found it difficult to walk because I wanted to run, and at the same time I could hardly put one foot in front of the other because I was so excited, so terribly nervous. This *had* to be the right thing to do, I told the wispy concerns trying to force their way into my thoughts.

I wondered secretly, as I entered the church and removed my coat, if the reverend, like every other mere mortal, enjoyed the opportunity to rejoice and simply be happy during this very dark time for so many.

I was pleasantly surprised to see there were far more folk than I'd expected in the pews, their chatter quieting when the vicar cleared his throat and looked up towards us, giving a slight nod.

The breath caught in my throat when I looked up to the top of the aisle. Jack was there and he wore full RAF uniform, a small smile twitching his mouth. Sideways on, he looked so handsome and again, I had that strange sensation where I wanted to hurry but could only walk very slowly. I felt as though my shoes were weighted, slowing me down.

I had already told the reverend that neither Jack nor I had rings to exchange, we had no money to buy them. He had not been fazed.

I could barely believe my eyes, then, when we reached the part of the service where rings were exchanged, and Bill Howarth passed a small gold band to the vicar. I had to bite the insides of my cheeks to keep tears from spilling down. I did not dare look anywhere but at the ring. Then, unbidden, my eyes flicked to Jack's. He gave a nod and a smile, and I thought if it was possible for a heart to explode with happiness then mine would.

Jack slid the ring onto my finger, accompanied by the words, 'With this ring I thee wed...' How I managed my responses past the walnut-sized lump in my throat I really don't know. But I did, and our responses rang out loud and clear, witnessed by the congregation.

A little later, as we signed the register and the vicar wrote out our marriage certificate, he apologised for the shortness of the ceremony.

'I find that without an organ to accompany the hymns, it is far better to keep the singing to a minimum.'

I don't know why but that made me laugh. 'It was a lovely ceremony, Reverend; it could not have been better. Thank you.' The piano music was fine. It was in desperate need of tuning, but things like that came low on any list of priorities these days.

I had another surprise once we made our way out of the church and into the hazy February sunlight. Matt had hurried out before us and was there with his Box Brownie facing our way. He used an entire film taking pictures of the entire wedding party. First Jack and myself, then Dora and her mum and dad. And even Enid posed for one with us. Then Bill took one with Dora, Matt, myself and Jack.

Matt's handsome face broke into a wonderful sunny smile, and holding the Box Brownie camera against his chest, he dropped a kiss on Dora's cheek. That Dora was thrilled with Matt's presence was clear, in fact they both disappeared around the side of the church for a short while, Dora's cheeks a few shades pinker when she reappeared, straightening her long auburn hair.

After, Matt shook Jack's hand and congratulated us both, and said he would join us all for a bite to eat to celebrate before making his way back to Warton.

'I will get these developed for you both, Mr and Mrs Blackshaw, then you'll have them to add to your collection.'

It didn't seem real.

My name had changed.

My life had changed.

We held hands once Jack had lit his cigarette and took a slow walk back to the Bing Lea for our wedding lunch.

I asked him as we took the last few steps down Banks

Street towards the boarding house, 'Do you have a favourite name? One for a boy, one for a girl?'

'It should be your choice; but I've always liked the name Tom for a boy. If it's a girl...' He looked thoughtful for a moment, and then gave a little grimace. 'Maybe you should choose?'

'I like Tom, too. And, well, maybe you'll be home before the baby comes along. If it is a little girl, we can choose a name together.'

The lunch went well, tea cups were raised to toast Jack and I, and to wish us a long and happy life together. Inside, I prayed silently that Jack would stay safe when so many didn't.

We cut the Victoria sponge cake made by Lilian, and everyone had a bit to finish off. At that point, Jack suggested it was time we went to the Pleasure Beach to begin our honeymoon.

Many of the guests needed to get back to their jobs in any case, having extended their lunch breaks quite a bit already.

Enveloped in the warmth of good wishes, we thanked the guests for coming and I hurried up to my room to change out of my wedding dress and put a few belongings into a weekend bag for the hotel room booked on the prom for Saturday and Sunday night. It was Bill, Marian and family's thoughtful wedding gift to us.

'It's been such a wonderful day, Jack,' I said as I snuggled up beside him on the tram seat on our way to check into the hotel, 'and you – you are a wonderful man for making this happen. I'm so lucky.'

Jack put his arm around my shoulder and pulled me close to his side. 'Hey…' He passed me his handkerchief. 'I'm the lucky one, Molly.' He spoke whilst I mopped at the tears of joy flooding down my cheeks, I swear I could have melted from the warmth of his smile. 'I promise you'll never regret marrying me, I'll always take care of you.'

'And I you, Mr Blackshaw.'

Dear God, I have never been happier.

Dear Diary, life is sweet.

Chapter Thirteen

Izzie

Blackpool, Sunday July 2, 2017

Justin took their cups into the kitchen to make them a coffee.

Izzie looked for a long time at the black and white wedding photograph of Molly and Jack.

Jack looked so handsome, Molly so happy and beautiful. Their faces were close to one another, in profile, as they laughed together. Just looking at the photograph was enough to raise a smile at their obvious joy in being together.

She let her thoughts stay with Molly and Jack. They were so happy, and it reminded her of when she was younger, visiting them when she was little and her nan and granddad were forever laughing and joking.

Grandpop had loved to tease Nan and the memory of her chasing him around the bungalow and waving a slipper around threatening to 'tan his hide' whilst he laughed and then stopped suddenly to face her and said, 'Problem is, Molly, I might enjoy it!' Most days with the two of them were punctuated with laughter – and real happiness.

Looking back and remembering how things were between them, made her want *that* for herself. She wanted that strong powerful love, that crazy laughter, that invisible thread between two souls that never weakened with time. It just grew stronger.

Could she ever have that much fun with a partner? Could she imagine that wonderful laughter ringing around the house, making everyone who heard it smile with pure enjoyment at witnessing such a close bond?

When she closed her eyes and tried to imagine herself in the same scenario with anyone, it was Justin who turned and laughingly tormented her, laughed with her, lit her insides with happiness like she had never known…

She shook her head, took a breath against the worm of guilt because surely, it should have been Rufus she imagined?

Was she in danger of transferring the feelings she'd had for Rufus to Justin? She'd read about that sort of thing happening after losing someone, or breaking up with a long-term partner.

Or … had it been the other way around? Had the feelings she'd originally had for Justin been cut off, then transferred to Rufus but in a different form?

It had all been so unfinished with Justin, the ending messy, one that remained unresolved. Unaired.

With a huge mental effort, she pushed the thoughts aside in order to enjoy the photograph and Molly's words...

Then she snapped out of her trance-like state when Justin joined her again and they continued to read the notebook.

Chapter Fourteen

Molly

Blackpool, Saturday February 26, 1944

My Dear Diary,

Jack and I visited the Pleasure Beach, rode on the scary Grand National roller coaster, a ride on which two carriages chase alongside one another around the wooden track, speeding up and down the hair-raising rises and dips. I screamed all the way around and hung on for dear life, terrified. When it stopped, I turned to Jack, gasping for breath, and asked, 'Can we go around again?'

He laughed heartily at that, called me crazy.

Then we went around again.

We rode on a tram to Squires Gate and then walked amongst the sand dunes, the sound of aircraft louder there than further north. It was warmer amongst the spiky marram grass and we sank down out of the wind against the shelter of the dunes and Jack put his arm around my shoulder. I smiled up at him, noticed for the first time that his eyes were very slightly darker than his brother's, and they sparkled with warmth. I'd to take a deep breath against the rising emotion, the overwhelming gratitude and growing love I felt for him.

My husband.

'I'll make you happy, Jack, I will.' I wanted him to know I didn't ever want him to regret this marriage between us.

He nodded, his eyes never leaving mine. 'You already have, Molly.'

I stretched up so our lips met and we shared our first, real, married kiss. I had the shock of my life.

The sensations travelling through me were all-consuming, heated and tingling crazily all at once.

All my worries about marrying Jack sank without trace. I knew in that moment of clarity that what I'd shared with Joe was flimsy compared to this feeling. It had little foundation, no solid roots. It had been a physical attraction.

What I felt for Jack was deeper, it was the beginnings of real love. He was kind, funny and my hero. Through his letters and the way in which he'd stepped up to take care of me and the coming baby, I had fallen in love with this wonderful man. He had given me a second chance at having the life I wanted, demanding nothing for himself. And he had saved me from the fate of being an outcast. I knew that I could trust him more than I had ever trusted anyone.

Tears rolled down my face, chilled in the cool air. 'I love you, Jack. I really do love you.'

He nodded, his smile making a dimple in his cheek. 'You already know I love you.'

———————————

During that one weekend, Dear Diary, we did so much, squeezing a whole courtship and honeymoon into two days and two nights.

After our visit to the sand dunes, we caught a tram all the way to Central Blackpool and went to the Tower Ballroom for a couple of hours, danced with one another and then picked up fish and chips and ate them out of newspaper on the way back to our honeymoon hotel.

We rarely stopped talking, decided we would like to live in or near Blackpool and that as Jack was due to be going abroad, I would stay and work for Enid.

'The good news is that I've always saved up, Molly, I've enough so we can rent our own place when I'm back home. We can find somewhere together if we need more room when the baby arrives.'

'Dora mentioned they've decorated her sister Katherine's room; she's living in at Blackpool Hospital now whilst she trains as a nurse. It's a lovely big room. We could take that on if you fancied?'

'Good idea. You'd be out from under Enid's roof, but still close to your friends – and work. Probably a good move with our baby on the way.'

'And we could move a bit further north when you come home, just along the coast a bit?'

We both liked that idea.

With our chips eaten and our future mapped out, we walked along the prom but decided we would leave paddling in the sea until the weather warmed up a bit. The wind was bitingly cold, and we huddled together whilst walking back to our hotel for the second night of our honeymoon.

Jack's train was due to leave mid-morning on the Monday. Time sped up again, as it always does, and way too soon we hurried to the station platform.

'I'll write,' I said. I could hear the train approaching as my new husband pulled me tightly against him, the intensity of his farewell kiss conveying love and his sorrow at the short time we'd spent together as man and wife.

Tears ran across our faces, under my nose, leaving a salty trail. Then the shout of '*All aboard!*' made it clear time had run out.

'I love you so much.'

He wiped the tears from my cheeks with his thumbs before climbing onto the train.

Leaning out of the window, he held my hand, his cigarette smoke floating up and across to join the steam building in the air, I thought my heart would break as a loud toot sounded and the train drew away, our fingers slipping apart.

'Come home soon.' I felt the strangest flicker of a movement in my stomach and put my palm there, still waving with my other hand. 'Are you waving to your daddy, too?' I whispered, feeling so sad.

So very sad to see him go.

In my mind I heard Ella Fitzgerald's 'Every Time We Say Goodbye'. The song helped to remind me that it wasn't only me saying goodbye. All along the platform, those left behind faced towards the departing train, until slowly, one by one, each turned away to take a deep breath and get on with their lives.

Chapter Fifteen

Molly

Blackpool, Friday March 17, 1944

My Dear Diary, Dora is going to ask Matt if there is any way he can get hold of blank sheets of paper for me to trim to size and stitch into my notebook because the shortages now even extend to paper and I'm running out of pages. I'm having to write smaller and smaller. I think I would go crazy if I couldn't write out my feelings about how much I love Jack, so I can rough out my letters before I copy them out neat.

It was a relief to move out from under Enid's roof, my Dear Diary. Somehow, going into work and returning to a room at Dora's that I will share with Jack, was much better than being at Enid's constant beck and call by living in at the Bing Lea.

Best of all, it feels like a fresh start, the start of being married and expecting Jack's baby. Dora and her dad helped me to move a nice big double bed they had stored in their loft into what used to be Katherine's room and Dora and I spend many an hour sitting on it, chattering, sharing ideas from magazines about how to make do and mend clothes to give them a new lease of life.

Jack continues to write regularly, mostly short but reassuring letters, all of which I treasure, read and read again, and then stitch in here so they'll be kept safe and I can look at them all whenever I need to.

Blackpool, Tuesday May 9, 1944

My Dear Molly,

I wish I could write and tell you when I can visit, but sadly, I don't know when that will be, but I hope it will be soon, even if it's only for a very brief time. I think about you a lot and hope you're not working too hard and you and our baby are keeping well. I've got to go now, sorry this is so short, I love you and look forward to seeing you and holding you tight again soon.

From your husband,

All my love,

Jack.

I swing between happiness at being married and anxiety about whether Jack will return safely home. Every time an RAF plane flies overhead, I watch and wonder; is Jack flying in that aircraft? Does he know the flight crew? Is he stationed with them?

Always, I send a prayer up to the planes, for Jack, for them all.

How vulnerable they look up there.

I wrote my response out in here first.

I re-live our wedding weekend often, and truly cannot wait until you come here again, and this war is over, and we can be together properly.

I should have the photos from Matt this coming weekend, he says. I'm looking forward to seeing them and looking at them with you when you come home.

I need to go now to get ready to go over to Enid's.

I love you. I will always love you. Please visit soon.

Please take care and keep safe.

Yours always,

Molly.

Blackpool, Friday May 26, 1944

'I still don't see why you don't live here in your old room in the attic.' Enid spoke whilst giving the breakfast plates a vigorous wash. 'I'm having to do a lot more at all hours of the day and night now you're not here.'

What did she expect me to say? She'd hit the nail on the head as to why I'd wanted to move out!

Just doing this and *just doing that* used up hours of precious time – and energy.

I took the soapy plate from her and dried it, and we carried on washing and drying in silence.

'Something you haven't told me?' Enid raised her eyebrows and stared at my stomach.

'Jack and I are expecting.' I felt myself go on the defensive, expecting her to have a go at me.

'Aye? Well, so long as you can keep working for your keep and paying your way for your digs at Marian's.'

I wanted to blurt that Jack was going to take care of all that when I couldn't work anymore because of the baby. But somehow, I didn't want to discuss it, or Jack. 'It'll be fine.' I loaded the last of the dried plates into the cupboard.

'Well, don't hang around gawping, fill the bucket, Molly, and go and give them front windows a shine, they're full of salt.'

It was the last thing I wanted to do; I was feeling tired. But at least I'd be away from Enid. I grabbed the bucket and took myself outside to clean the salt off the front windows.

It was refreshing to be outside after the damp warmth of

the kitchen, the never-ending sound of Enid's voice pecking at my sanity.

Late hazy May sunshine cast a soft pale light across the front yard; I opened up the ladder and started at the top lights of the windows, washing then giving each window in turn a shine with a piece of crumpled newspaper. I'd grown hot, been at it for a while and almost finished when a voice interrupted my drifting thoughts.

'Well, now that's a pretty sight!' Deep infectious laughter rumbled, and I gasped in response, twisted around and clapped my hands, dropping my rag, and wobbling precariously at the top of the step ladder.

'Jack!'

'I've come to rescue you from the workhouse, Mrs Blackshaw.'

'Jack! I can't believe you're here!'

I felt my silly happy grin take shape.

Jack reached up to take the bucket from me and rescued the rag from the ground and set them by the door.

'It's so—'

I never got to say, 'Good to see you,' because right there at the bottom of the ladder in the front yard, Jack's arms closed around me and he lifted me into his arms. His mouth touched mine briefly at first and then he raised his head just a little and looked into my eyes, murmured my name then kissed me more deeply. His cheek was cool against my nose, the heat from his mouth a sensual contrast.

I forgot where I was, that I was wearing a splashed, faded pinny, a headscarf, my oldest scruffiest cardigan, and not a scrap of lipstick.

I could not have been happier.

I thought to object and say we shouldn't be kissing here, but I really didn't care. It had been so long since he had held me and I wrapped my arms more tightly around him to keep him close.

'Jack...' I was hoarse. 'We should go indoors. Come and say hello to Enid. Then I can show you our room at Marian's. I'm due a break.'

His smile at my words was enough to cause a hitch in my chest, and I just wanted to get closer to him and stay there.

'Mrs Webster,' Jack acknowledged Enid, who looked surprised to see him.

'Didn't expect you.'

'It's a quick visit, I've to travel back tomorrow. Any chance you could give Molly time off so we can enjoy a short spell together?'

I wanted to laugh because Enid looked shocked at Jack's direct approach. 'Well, I...'

'I'd really appreciate it, Mrs Webster. We both would.'

'Well...' She looked at a loss for a moment. 'If you nip round to Lilian's digs and ask if she'll work for you—'

'Will do! Thanks, Mother.' I didn't hesitate, just tugged on Jack's hand so we could leave before she changed her mind.

'And to think I always thought you were the quiet one.'

He squeezed my hand and smiled that lovely smile down at me.

'I am. Until I really want something.'

Before going home to Marian and Bill's, we hurried over

to Lilian's on the next road to ask her if she'd fill in until the following evening.

'I'd be glad to, I'm saving up,' she said.

'Great.' Jack pulled a ten bob note from his pocket and shoved it into Lilian's palm. 'That's thanks from me, Lilian, for doing this at such short notice.'

'Crikey, thanks!'

We hurried home then; Jack having surprised me yet again.

On our way through the kitchen, we let Marian know what was going on and she clapped her floury hands together. 'Oh lovely, I'll make this pie a bit bigger, then! Join us for a spot of tea later on to celebrate?'

We said we'd love to and then I showed Jack our room.

'This is big.'

It was. The bay window was huge and let in pale yellow sunlight, and the double bed, wardrobe and dressing table left plenty of room to put a cot when it was needed. There was even a sink in the corner. 'I love living here, it's much more relaxed than living with Enid.'

'They're good folk,' Jack agreed and said, 'I'll nip and settle up with Marian so it's not playing on my mind.'

He was only gone a short time, and when Marian's happy exclamation made it through the open bedroom door, it made me laugh.

'I've some photos of our wedding day you haven't seen.' I couldn't wait to show him.

We lay side by side, propped against the pillows, Jack looking slowly through the small stack of photos. 'This is like the one you posted to me.' We were in profile, laughing into one another's faces.

'Matt got me two copies of it so I could send one to you.'

After he'd looked through them all, he said, 'This is my favourite.' It was the same one I'd posted to him.

'Molly,' he said, his hand resting on my stomach, 'did our baby just move?'

'Did you see?'

'I did. Your frock moved.'

We both laughed.

'Likes to wait until I relax and then starts wriggling about!'

Jack looked suitably impressed. 'Incredible to believe there's a little person in there.'

The whole day, my Dear Diary, felt like a wonderful bonus. We talked and embraced like the new lovers we were and after tea we went for a walk to the Tower, accompanied by Dora and Matt, to have a dance for a while, to enjoy being out and about; and knowing we'd be going home together was the best part of all.

I had the sense that I was still getting to know Jack and that everything new I learned about him built on what I was beginning to find out – that Jack was just as much fun as his brother had been, yet he was different with it. He had a quiet confidence about him that was compelling and when he wanted something, he didn't beat about the bush – he asked for it, or went for it, but quietly. No fanfare.

The Tower band played a fast number and we went to stand at the side of the dance floor and take a break.

I heard a low moan in my own throat as none other

than Denis strolled up. I felt Jack's arm close around my waist; it felt as if he was protecting and supporting me all at once.

'Who's this, then?' Denis raised his chin, nodded towards Jack. 'Your glory boy?'

'Denis, this is Jack Blackshaw. My husband.' Pride welled up in me and I admit to enjoying the jolt of shock on Denis's belligerent features.

He nodded whilst this sank in and inclined his head towards Jack, his eyes glittering with spite. 'Let him get away with all of his philandering then, did you?'

'I saw sense,' Jack interrupted before I could respond. 'And I think that's between me and Molly, pal, nothing to do with you. Right?'

My eyes opened yet again to another facet of Jack. He wasn't afraid of standing his ground, even taking responsibility for what his brother had done in playing around, in order to protect our marriage. And our secret.

'A leopard doesn't change his spots.' Denis shook his head as if he didn't believe Jack.

'It'd be a good time for you to leave, buddy. I'll be tempted to take you outside and knock *your* spots off if you don't.'

'Like to see you try.' Again, Denis cocked his chin at Jack.

Jack laughed. 'It can be arranged, but I think you and I have enough on with fighting the huns.'

Denis stilled; his features morphed to less confrontational. 'Happen you're right. But if I see you being unfaithful again, make no mistake, I *will* tell Molly.'

'Deal.' Jack extended his hand and surprisingly, Denis reluctantly took it.

Denis didn't hang around afterwards.

'How did you do that?' I shook my head. 'You amaze me every time you open your mouth!'

Jack shrugged, unfazed, as if unaware he had done anything much. The music had slowed, and he led me back onto the dance floor.

My Dear Diary, I have to share that I felt as if I was the luckiest woman alive when he held me and we danced…

Chapter Sixteen

Izzie

Blackpool, Thursday August 10, 2017

'I've brought these books round to see if you'd like them?' Izzie asked Justin's mum, Linda.

'Oh lovely, come in, Izzie, have you time for a cuppa?'

'Yes please, I've hit a brick wall scraping off wallpaper in the hallway. It comes off in stamp-size chunks – and not very quickly.'

Linda laughed and gestured for her to step indoors. 'Books, you say?'

The two of them went into the kitchen and Izzie set the books on the edge of the table. 'They were Nan's from Rufus, if you'd like them?' She laid her hand atop the hardback books. 'I've got a set at the house in West Hampstead, so it seems daft not to share them.'

'I'm sure Robert will love them, thanks, chick. You know what a bookworm he is.'

Just then, the new French door on the back of the kitchen flew open and Robert entered, waving a shoe around. 'All fixed, Lindy, and the glue's set now.'

'Ah, my master of all trades.' She reached another cup down from the cupboard, and explained. 'Izzie's struggling with all the layers of wallpaper in Molly's hallway.'

'Hold it right there!' Robert raised the flat of his hand in the air. 'I have just the thing!' Tall and slender, Robert about turned and marched back out of the French door and disappeared to his workshop in the garage.

He returned with something that resembled a small spaceship. 'It's a steamer, gets wallpaper off a treat.' He explained how to use it, and demonstrated using the wide paddle that fixed on the end of a pipe, by holding it flat against the wall whilst the steam piped to beneath the paddle permeated the layers of paper. 'Works best if you scuff the paper up a bit first to give the steam chance to get under the paper.'

'Brilliant! Can't wait to get started!'

Robert reiterated what Justin had told her, that they had the phone number of a good decorator if she wanted help.

'Thanks. I have his number. I wanted to get involved myself, I think mainly because it was Nan's and it feels good to have some direction back in my life.'

'You mean since Rufus died?'

It did seem strange when other folk mentioned him. Sometimes her brain wouldn't supply the details of how anyone knew she'd been his wife. Of who belonged where and in *which version of her life.*

'Yes.' The inner pang of loss was still present, though diminishing.

Linda nodded. 'It sounds like a lot changed for you all around the same time, Izzie.'

'It was a lot.'

She saw understanding in Linda's eyes – dark green, gold-speckled eyes, which were so much like Justin's. 'Didn't your mother offer to fly over and keep you company?'

'They were on a six-month cruise around the world at the time and David's chest wasn't good enough to fly. She's not keen on coming back to this country, prefers South Africa.'

'At the time you needed someone?'

Izzie nodded, but took a deep breath, determined not to wallow.

'I had Nan. I came up to visit her when I needed someone close to connect with. She had great hugs.'

'Molly was an amazing lady. I'm sure you know she and my mother, Dora, were best friends during the war?'

'Yes! And she said that when two properties in this street came up together for sale, your mum and dad, and my nan and Grandpop all sold up and moved here.'

'Is Justin working at his home office today, Linda?' Robert asked, taking off his outdoor shoes and wiggling his feet into navy fur lined moccasin slippers.

'He's got a couple of local weddings in the pipeline and

he's meeting up with the couples this morning. He said something about getting their photo lists.'

'Do you see Justin every day?' Izzie was curious. 'It's fab he lives close by.'

'Usually it's Sunday lunch here – or we eat out. If he's in the country he visits regular. He's been helping Robert with a few jobs lately, whilst he's got more time at home.'

Izzie finished her drink, then stood. 'That was really good, thanks. I could stay and chatter all day, but I also can't wait to try the steamer.'

As Robert promised, the steamer sped up the removal of wallpaper and took the joint jarring out of the job too. Izzie lost all track of time, going great guns at stripping off the paper.

The loud doorbell sounded and she opened the door to find Justin outside.

'Justin, come in!' She held the door wide, took a deep breath of wonderful fresh air – air that wasn't heavy with the aroma of old wallpaper, glue, and steam.

'You're doing well!' He nodded and looked around. 'Good job, Izzie.'

'Well, it's so much easier with this.' She held up the paddle before setting it down, turning it off at the plug. 'I'll clear this lot up then make us a brew.' She was conscious that she likely looked a mess, but it was too late to worry about that.

Justin scooped up a great armful of wallpaper and helped Izzie make short work of clearing up.

Rain began to pound down, bouncing off the flagstones. 'Maybe put off that walk again for an hour or two?' Izzie said as she nodded out of the doorway. 'Fancy a brew? A read?'

'Sure, great idea.'

They sat at the large kitchen table with Molly's notebook opened between them.

Chapter Seventeen

Molly

Blackpool, Sunday May 28, 1944

We sat around the large table bang slap in the middle of the kitchen at Marian and Bill's. We'd enjoyed a hearty breakfast and were all relaxing with our refilled cups of tea.

'It's to be hoped Enid will sort some more help at the Bing Lea, Molly, before you pop.'

I laughed at that expression. It was becoming more difficult to change umpteen beds every Saturday morning, but it wasn't impossible by any means. Not yet. 'I'm a way off yet, Marian.'

'All the same, Molly, she needs to sort some proper help,' Jack said. 'Enid best get someone in place well before the baby arrives.'

'I'll collar her about it today. She's got a widow friend from her ladies' club, Agnes, she helped get the food and flowers ready for our wedding. She's talked about giving her my old room and seeing if she wants to live in and work for the company.'

'When's the baby due?' Marian asked.

'At a guess, I'd say some time in September.' I grimaced at my own words, but Marian's face showed no censure.

She ventured, 'Did Enid make any bother about your dates?'

'I was worried about telling her. She wasn't too bad; she gave me one of her looks and said "Well, at least you're wed. That's a small mercy."'

Marian's brow raised, then lowered. 'Aye, well, as my old mam used to say, Molly, many a slip between cup and lip.'

Marian sipped her tea. 'I've got to admit, Bill, Dora and I could never tell you and your twin brother apart, Jack, I expect it's probably cos I only saw you from a distance.'

'Even our ma can't tell us apart sometimes.' Jack gave a short laugh. 'You're not alone, Marian, many a time we've been taken for one another.'

'All that matters,' I piped up then, 'is I married the right one!' I smiled and at the same time I reached across the table to cover Jack's relaxed hand with my own. My words meant much more than any of the others could know. Things could have been so different for me and not in a good way if it wasn't for this devilishly handsome man.

Immediately as he felt my touch, he looked up and said, 'Do you want to go out for a walk? Maybe a tram ride?'

'Love to. Shall I help you square up quickly first, Marian?'

'Off you pop, chick, this'll take no time with Dora and Bill's help.'

Bill made a grunting kind of sound that was some way between laughter and complaint, and Dora sprang to her feet. 'Matt's coming to collect me at midday today and we're going to go on the beach if it stays nice.'

'Do you know where you're going to be posted next, Jack?' Marian asked, gathering pots whilst she spoke.

He shook his head. 'I don't. We're not allowed to say either.'

'Aye!' Bill rose to his feet. 'It's as all these posters say: *Loose lips lose lives*. You can't safely say anything. Mind you, I think it was a bit crazy taking out the street signs in Blackpool. When you see the Tower, it's obvious that we're in Blackpool.'

We all laughed about that; it did seem a bit ridiculous. Photographs printed in the local paper even had the famous landmark blanked out.

'Will you be having a spot of lunch with us before you get your train?' Marian asked Jack. 'I usually just do a few sandwiches on a Sunday.'

'Yes, please. That'll be grand.'

The tide was out, so a lot of couples had found refuge on the beach, some relaxing, others paddling or walking beneath the piers, others lying down on the sand.

Some locals had begun to complain to the newspapers that the beach was a 'writhing mass of bodies up to no good'.

I might have agreed once, but now, I completely understood. There was an edge to time spent with loved ones.

At the back of my mind there was always the knowledge that saying goodbye was never far off, never knowing when I'd see Jack again ... or worse, *if.* I thought, Dear Diary, that it was the same for so many servicemen and women and their spouses, lovers, husbands or sweethearts. Not knowing gave any time spent together an urgency, a sweet sadness that made every second precious.

I was afraid of losing Jack to a stray bullet, an explosion, a prisoner of war camp, or that he would be shot down in an aircraft; the RAF's losses were large and it seemed to me that their sorties were becoming more and more often.

But when you were with someone you loved, you couldn't voice these fears. Instead, you stayed in the moment and enjoyed and savoured your lover's touch, their kiss, their words.

It seemed to me that I and others in the same boat grabbed what we could of life, be it food, love, money, even fun. There really was only the present.

After our lunch with Marian and Bill, Jack and I walked rather leisurely, as though that would help time to go more slowly, but then we ended up having to run so Jack wouldn't miss his train.

Our goodbye was so brief. Too brief. His mouth covered mine in a fierce fast kiss, and then the train left, Jack leaning out of the window and waving until he was out of sight.

Again, I watched as the train completely disappeared,

leaving behind so many wives and girlfriends on the platform, all bathed in a fog of soot and steam.

It feels like I'm living two lives. One, the humdrum yet perfectly fine daily work life in the boarding house, with a dance some Saturday nights. And the other an exciting love-life enjoyed in snatches of time, controlled by some unseen hand that let Jack have time away from his part in the war. A brief time.

Time with me. His wife.

It always takes a while to get over him leaving, and as soon as he leaves, I begin to look forward to the next visit; I think it's the same for all those left at home whilst loved ones are away doing their bit for King and country. Like me, I think they must surely all yearn for the war to end.

Chapter Eighteen

Molly

Blackpool, Friday July 7, 1944

Dear Diary,
     The baby is kicking and reminding me of his or her presence every day. Some days I can't stop worrying about Jack long enough to enjoy the feeling. Until this morning, I hadn't heard from him since he visited in May. Even Dora's dad, Bill, asked 'When's your young man going to visit again? Is he due any leave?'

I told him that Jack hadn't written for a while and that I was hoping and praying he's all right.

Bill reassured me that there was probably a good reason and that I should keep on writing to Jack to keep his spirits up.

Just hearing him say that helped, but I still spend a lot of time worrying whether Jack had been injured, wondering whether I would even hear if he did.

Coincidentally, it was just after lunch today that a letter arrived from Jack. Dora dashed in with it on her way to work on the trams and apologised that she couldn't stop.

I shoved the letter deep into my apron pocket and then left Lilian in charge of the kitchen and nipped into the little back room, just for a few minutes, to read my letter alone and uninterrupted.

My Dearest Molly,

I, like all the other chaps here, am wondering when we'll get home. There had been talk of leave, of travel warrants, and weekends visiting loved ones, but that seems to have all stopped. No one knows why. It is warm here, at least, and I really look forward to walking on the prom with you in the lovely sea breeze. I promise as soon as I am able, I will visit you, and thank you for all your letters. They usually arrive in a bundle and they keep me going. There has been talk that our letters out do not arrive with any speed, but you must know that I write regularly, and they will arrive sooner or later.

I love you Molly, please always know that, and know that I will come and visit just as soon as I can. Look after yourself and our baby.

All my love always,

Jack.

My insides tugged with emotion and I re-read his letter many times before tucking it in my apron pocket. A little thrill ran through me because I had Jack's letter and could read it as many times as I wanted.

Yet when I took a bite from my lunchtime sandwich, a lump swelled in my throat, making it hard to swallow.

Jack's letter, all the love it held – and knowing that he meant every word he wrote or said – made it hit me that I had no idea when I would see him again and neither did he. I wondered how that made him feel. It certainly made me feel emotional, but he was the one away from home. I sniffed, knew I should be grateful to hear from him, be grateful that he was still alive, but I wanted him home so badly, home safe for when his baby was born. We'd spent precious little time together so far and all I wanted was more, much more. I wanted time to bathe in his generous smile, see his blue eyes crinkle a bit at the corners; time to watch him whilst he carried out mundane chores like clearing the grate, and time to watch him sketch his incredibly life-like sketches.

I heard Enid come in the front door and in order to make a quick exit and avoid any questions, I collected up the ration book for the boarding house as well as my own.

'Going to the butcher's, Mother.' I put my head down in case my eyes were red and gave away my emotional state. Enid responded with, 'Aye, don't dally, time's running on. I'm helping Agnes move into your old room, she'll be an extra pair of helping hands. You'll have to get the meal on.'

I hadn't heard from Jack for a long time until today, but it sounded as though my letters got through to him more easily than those from him. I thought that the next time I wrote I wouldn't mention I hadn't heard from him for so long, in case it worried him too much. He'd enough to think about.

God, keep him safe.

Back from the butcher's and with potatoes prepared and bubbling away on the hob, I cleaned and scraped some beetroots and carrots, popping those too on top of the Aga in a separate pan.

After turning over the chops, I stirred a drop of gravy browning into the dip. Just for a bit of fun, I cut out a chop shape from of a lump of stale bread about to go in a bread and butter pudding, and added it to the tray of chops after briefly toasting it on a long fork in front of the coal fire in the back room. I thought I'd take it over the road and add it to Bill's plate tonight – a little extra covered in gravy, just for a giggle. I desperately needed some light relief.

Thankfully, Bill and Marian were always up for a bit of fun. It struck me then too that they must worry about their son in the Navy; there were very few families who weren't directly affected by the wretched war. I rested my hand on my restless baby bump and prayed that mine and Jack's family would stay intact.

Chapter Nineteen

Izzie

Blackpool, Wednesday September 27, 2017

Izzie and Justin made their way onto the prom and walked to the tram stop. 'You'll have to show me your place sometime, Justin.'

'Absolutely. It's a tip at the moment though, I've had a wall down but it's almost finished.'

'We're both in the same boat then, what with me decorating.'

'Bit more mess at mine, I'll show you when it's less of a building site?'

Within minutes, they'd agreed to jump on a tram and go all the way to Starr Gate, a trip they'd taken countless times as teenagers – both as friends and lovers. It was a trip that seemed like a good idea, an idea Izzie thought belatedly that neither of them thought through at the outset; would it shake precious memories loose?

The tram made steady progress along the sea front, a warm, automated voice announcing the name of each stop. They made their way past North and Central Piers, and the Tower, the illuminations shifting slightly in the breeze from their high trapezes suspended from the tall lampposts. The light shows were a famous draw to visitors from early September to early November.

'I'd love a walk through the lights, Justin, it's a while since I've done that. Does it still get busy?'

'Yeah it does. It's still popular. Give me a shout if you want company?'

'That'd be good.' She smiled, felt warmth rising to her cheeks, 'I remember Nan telling me the 'lights' were turned off during the war so that they didn't map out the Blackpool coastline to enemy bombers...'

She was silent for a while, enjoying the familiar sights of the sea front, 'Looking back, Justin, it always seemed to be sunny.'

'It did. It felt like we spent all our spare time on the sands back then,' Justin agreed.

So many days filled with laughter and fun, sea, sand ... and the friendship between herself and Justin that had unexpectedly ricocheted into something more...

She let her thoughts drift back in time until they snagged on a memory from time in the sand dunes. Their small crowd had set up their daily camp on a flat dip between the humps of marram grass and sand, close to the dunes' edge where the beach flattened out.

'Penny for your thoughts.' Justin's voice broke into her reverie as the tram moved on from another stop and the deep automated voice advised passengers to press the button when they wished to leave the tram. Mingling passenger voices, some high, some deep, some childish and laced with laughter wove a lively background.

'I was daydreaming,' she responded honestly, 'about drinking that strong beer Tony used to bring to the beach in his cool box.'

He turned, his gaze meeting hers directly for a long moment. He seemed about to say something, but then just gave her a brief smile and turned to look out of the window again as the tram slowed to a halt beside South Pier. When the tram continued on its way, there were only half a dozen passengers including Izzie and Justin.

As the tram hummed, Izzie let her mind wander down memory lane again.

Back to their crowd and the times they'd shared…

It'd been a hot day, they'd all swam, played ball in the sea and down on the flat sand, then they'd congregated back close to the dunes to share some beer Mick had carried along in a cooler.

Whilst they drank and ate copious bags of crisps, Izzie sketched each of the friends in turn – three girls, Janey, Wendy and Kay, and four lads, Justin, Mick, Tony and Ian. She passed her sketch pad around the friends to have a look once she was done and they seemed pleasantly surprised at their likenesses.

'These are good, Izzie,' Tony had said, struggling to

manoeuvre his T-shirt over a sea damp torso. 'You should set up a stall doing these for the tourists.'

She had smiled, drank more beer, enjoyed the way it made her feel light-headed. 'Thanks, but I'd rather sketch for fun.'

The conductor called out, 'Any more fares here?' , his friendly voice jolting Izzie from her recollection.

'And I was thinking about when I sketched our pals,' she told Justin.

'Have you still got those drawings?' He looked thoughtful. 'I bet Tony and Janey would love to see them if you have.'

'I have. They're in the sketchbook I used to take everywhere.'

'Do you remember that time when Janey could hardly read out Mick's dare for laughing?' Justin asked, laughing at the memory. Izzie felt her own amusement bubble up.

'I do.' At the time, they'd all erupted into gales of laughter when Mick's dare had been that he should run around on the beach, holding a towel like a sail above his head, singing 'The Hills Are Alive' from *The Sound of Music*.

Most dares were hilarious, especially, Izzie thought, when they happened to someone else.

Justin turned to look out of the window again and Izzie rooted in her rucksack for her water bottle, taking a gulp to cool herself down at the thought of what had followed Mick's dare, when they'd all been spluttering with laughter and aching ribs...

The deep automated voice announced that the next stop was the terminus, Starr Gate.

Her memory trickled back to the dares that had changed Izzie's relationship with Justin.

'Kiss their face off like you really mean it...'

Somehow, Izzie couldn't hold back the memory, her cheeks heating when Justin rose to his feet. 'You good?'

'I am.' She took another swig from her bottle. 'Just warm.'

She wondered in that moment if Justin's half-smile meant he could read her mind, that the unlocked memory wasn't shut away like she hoped, but instead playing like a film in her eyes.

As they left the tram and walked towards the dunes, he held his hand towards her, then retracted it as if he realised just what he was doing.

That hurt Izzie like a spear.

'Don't...' slipped from her. Fighting her pain, she held her hand towards him. 'Don't shut me out, Justin.'

He hesitated, stood still, and she saw something flash in his eyes, something like hurt, and she didn't fully understand it. He took a breath and then he took her hand. 'Sure.' His voice was hoarse and a quick glance towards him revealed tension in his frame.

Confused, Izzie's thoughts ran up against a brick wall. As they reached the end of the dunes, she hooked off her flip flops to let her feet sink into the soft sand, increasingly aware of the palm against her own and the darts of heat zinging up her arm.

Almost like they had stepped back in time, they walked along for a short while and then settled close to the spot where they'd always set up camp; it was a weekday and the beach was relatively empty as school holidays were over. There were only a few walkers along the edge of the far away sea, where the damp sand was firm.

Reaching down to fill her palm with soft sand, Izzie let it run through her fingers and fall back to the beach in small pointed piles until the breeze smoothed them off once again, the tiny grains hypnotising as they found their lowest level.

'I love it here.' She set down her rucksack and used it to lean against.

Justin leaned back on his elbows, staring across the flat sands to the glistening sea beyond.

'Izzie...'

'Justin...'

They both spoke at once and then Justin gestured for Izzie to carry on. But she felt suddenly shy. She'd been about to say something about their relationship, but even as she'd begun to speak, she wasn't sure what it was she wanted to say. She wanted it to be easy between them, like it always used to be. She searched for a way to tell him that; picked up another handful of sand and let it slip through her fingers again.

'I – I'm still attracted to you, but I don't want it to be awkward with us.'

What? Why had she spoken the unvarnished truth? Was she mad?

'If it helps, I'm still attracted to you, too, Izzie. But I've got long-term work plans that involve a heap of travel. I'm not looking for anything more serious than friendship, maybe a fling – maybe a mix of both. But definitely nothing more. I learned, to my cost, years ago that long-term involvements don't go well with my job.'

Turning to lie on her side so she could see his expression, Izzie said, 'I think at this point in time, that's enough for me, too. No rules, no ties. Nothing serious.'

Unbeknown to Justin, his words were just what she needed to hear. After her increasingly isolating marriage to Rufus, she wanted to do whatever, go wherever and see whoever she pleased – whenever she pleased – definitely with no one to answer to.

A no-rules fling sounded near perfect to her. Why shouldn't she grab what she wanted out of life? Especially if they both wanted the same thing at the moment?

Justin turned his attention from looking out to sea to face her. His darkened hazel eyes were lit with a kaleidoscope of greens, browns and yellows in the hazy sunlight.

'Does that take care of the awkward?' He smiled and that smile – the one that could light up the darkest corner – reached right inside Izzie. That smile that made her smile back turned to laughter when she responded, 'I'll tell you in a minute.'

He raised one brow; amused questions danced in his eyes.

Feeling bold, wanting what she wanted, Izzie closed the gap between their lips and kissed him gently, her eyes closing when his soft yet firm lips kissed her in return. Then his fingers moved to lightly caress her jaw and neck as the kiss deepened and Izzie's own palms reached around his neck to bring him closer, fingers threading into his hair as she wriggled to align herself to him where they lay on the soft sand. Hot pinging sensations rushed around her, and heat flared in her lower belly.

It had been such a long time since she'd been held. Such a long time since she'd been kissed for pure pleasure and not as a pre-cursor to sex. A soft moan left her when Justin pulled her closer.

Since their very first kiss, they had always enjoyed the closeness, the titillation and the promise of what may come next. Part of the thrill was not knowing if they would take it any further – or not.

The embrace went on for a long time, until a seagull overhead made a loud caw sound and both of them opened their eyes at the same time.

There was a warmth in Justin's eyes, and a smile. Izzie knew – for certain – that a fling with this man was just what she needed. It could last only until Christmas at the latest ... then Justin would be flying off to New Zealand, and come the New Year she would be going back to London, back to her job at DAS, and her home in West Hampstead.

'Do you remember how we became an item – that game?' A smile hitched one side of his mouth and that delicious dimple dented his cheek.

'You mean whilst I was wearing your giant T-shirt and you had my little wrap top over your shoulders?'

They lay facing one another, both propped up on an elbow. Izzie fancied she could feel a magnetic field crackling between them.

'Janey read out the dare and cracked up, it said, *kiss their face off like you really mean it.* I didn't realise for a minute I'd be the object…'

Justin had been reclining, his back propped against a dune, beer bottle in one hand, sunglasses reflecting the sand and sky, and it took a moment for the penny to drop that he'd be the object of Izzie's dare.

Izzie had been emboldened by too much beer on an empty stomach and crawled closer to Justin. She straddled his hips, leaned forward and dropped a soft little kiss on his mouth, before going in again and flattening herself against him, shivering with bliss at the feel of his warm body against hers. She was shocked by how good his mouth felt beneath her lips, how welcoming the heat of his tongue as it moved against hers. His eyes opened behind his glasses and he reached up and shoved them on top of his head, then let his fingers trail down to her cheek, spreading there to hold her face gently, their kiss growing hungrier.

Justin's other hand moved to her side and touched bare skin through the large arm hole of the giant T-shirt, causing a soft moan to escape Izzie. Tingles ran through her, shot outwards from his fingertips, her eyes opened with surprise – to be met by his gaze.

A low whistle rose from the group behind them and someone clapped.

'Wow…' broke from Justin as Izzie shifted to sit back from the embrace. 'That was … wow.'

She stayed where she was, perched on Justin's thighs for minutes or seconds, she couldn't tell, his forest-green eyes held the same happy shock that Izzie felt deep inside. A small smile curved his lips, and he looked as if he wanted to say something…

It was the first time that Izzie had revisited that particular memory with her feelings fully engaged.

It had been raw, passionate and there had been no reason to hold back. It struck her that their kiss just moments ago had roused those same sensations within her, and there was something inherently sensual about revisiting the episode along with Justin.

Suddenly clouds rolled in and the gathering wind began to blow the surface of the soft sand hither and thither. Justin rose agilely to his feet and held both his hands down to Izzie. 'Think there's rain coming. Shall we make tracks?'

'Yup.' It felt so good to have someone else make suggestions, make decisions, knowing that if she wanted to do something different, she only had to say so and it would be fine.

It was liberating, like finding a sense of freedom that she hadn't known for a long time, a sense of freedom she hadn't known had been missing. But even feeling it, she didn't fully understand why, didn't want to start exploring it. She just wanted to enjoy the freedom of being herself and living her life for herself.

For the moment.

The heavens opened as they laughed, stumbling, along the sand, and soaked the pair of them from head to toe.

On their tram ride back towards home, Justin suggested they each go home and shower, dry off, then he'd drive over to Seniors chippy, pick their dinner up and bring it round to hers. Izzie said she'd open a bottle of wine and have Molly's notebook handy for when they'd eaten.

After showering, Izzie found herself dressing with care. Picking out a turquoise sundress, she twisted her loose waves into a scruffy bun and rooted out her hoop earrings. That delicious sense of freedom, a growing feeling of new happiness, saw her smile broadly in front of the hallway mirror. And because they had set the boundaries of their relationship, Izzie allowed herself to look forward to Justin arriving.

Rain pounded down and when his car pulled onto her drive, Izzie opened the front door, ready with the table set and a bottle of wine open.

'Hi!' Her broad smile answered Justin's as she noticed that he too had made an effort. She stood aside so he could hurry indoors with their food, took in his white pilot shirt and black trousers. The word *hot* flashed up in her mind. Some men, she thought, just wore their clothes so well…

'Go straight through, Justin, everything's ready.'

'Got a towel, Izzie, love?' He turned to face her in the hallway and she swapped a hand towel for the bag of fish and chips.

Drops ran down his face, spiked his lashes, did nothing to diminish the light of laughter shining in his eyes.

Just minutes later, dried off, Izzie and Justin enjoyed their feast, music played quietly in the background, little need to fill any silences.

'We should take another trip to the beach on the next dry day that you're not working, before it turns too cold,' Izzie suggested once they'd finished eating.

'I'll drink to that. Cheers,' Justin said. They clinked glasses and Izzie felt the tight spring of emotion within relax another notch whilst they chattered, shared some memories. 'You'll probably laugh, but I remember being insanely jealous,' Justin admitted, 'when we played spin the bottle with our crowd and you kissed Daniel Topping.'

'You were jealous?' She shook her head, grimaced. 'You had no need. I only fancied you. Do you still see Daniel? Any of the old crowd?'

'Sure. Not Daniel – he lives in Australia now – but I see the others now and then.' He brought her up to date on what their friends were up to these days.

'I've really enjoyed today, Izzie,' he said when they were done eating, then stood and took both their plates to the sink, to plunge them into the soapy water there. He looked at her over his shoulder when she moved behind him and wrapped her arms around his waist, pressed her cheek into his toned back.

'Me too.'

He turned around in the circle of her arms, his mouth finding and closing over hers in a long, delicious kiss, one of his soapy hands holding her cheek, his other pulling her close into him. A familiar sensation spread through her. It was as though every single nerve ending in her body remembered him.

Justin raised his mouth from hers when the doorbell

rang, rested his forehead against hers and gave a slight grimace. 'Bet that's my mother.'

Rising up on her tiptoes, Izzie kissed his lips briefly and went to see.

It was a delivery company wanting to leave a parcel for the neighbour on the other side to Justin's parents.

'Ah…' Izzie shrugged as she set the parcel down in the hallway. 'What do you think? Shall we have a read of Molly's notebook?'

Laughing, Justin ran his fingers back through his hair. 'That might be a safer bet than where we were headed.'

Chapter Twenty

Molly

Blackpool, Saturday September 9, 1944

Dear Diary,
  I think that one good thing about working in a boarding house is that I'm kept busy and there is no time to dwell on things. Something worrying though, word is that the Jerries are now sending over buzz bombs – there's no pilot even though the bombs look like small planes. They just arrive, buzzing, then go silent and drop, destroying everything around them. What a terrifying weapon.

Some of our billets bring stories of these awful weapons; apparently, they have so far reached as far as Oldham. That brings to mind Jack's parents, and his aunt who lives there. I can only pray his family stays safe.

As I grow bigger, Enid now has Agnes to share the

work, which is a blessing. My bump is too big to even tie up my pinny; I've had to extend the ties with string! It seems to suit Enid having Agnes around, the two of them chat and sometimes even laugh. It makes the whole experience of coming to work at the Bing Lea more pleasant.

Agnes is a good sort, too – she noticed my ankles getting swollen earlier today and said I should go and put my feet up for a bit till they go down. She also said that in her opinion it was time I stopped work now and take it easier.

So, after talking it over with Enid, we decided that tomorrow will be my last day and I'll just help with breakfast and finish at lunchtime. I only have a week or two to go before the baby is due so it's a relief.

Enid seems easier to get along with now and I'm sure it's having Agnes around that helps.

I haven't heard from Jack for almost two months; I pray he's safe. It's like living with a stomach full of nerves against the wash of hope that everything is fine with him, but as the saying goes, no news is good news. I have to hang onto that.

I write here because it's been so long and sometimes, I think I will sink into the dark misery that lurks like a swamp waiting to swallow me up. I just want Jack to write, to say he'll come home soon ... but there has been nothing.

I write to him at least once a week, tell him every kind of news, small things that happen in the Bing Lea. How Dora's doing with her job on the trams and anything that might interest him.

I feel as if I go through the motions of this life, but then – I imagine everyone else does too. A lot of folk have lost people; I think of every reported death and how many other lives in turn that must ripple out to, devastating loved ones.

Dora is in love with Matt, the US serviceman, and he is lucky to have escaped a tragedy that hit Freckleton last month – so many died when a US bomber crashed there.

It was doubly tragic because there were evacuees from London attending school there – killed when they had gone there as a designated 'safe area'.

Dora told me that Matt and many of his fellow servicemen helped with the clear up and they were all deeply saddened and distressed.

Dora and I walk most days, usually late on, once she's finished on the trams. It helps to keep us both sane, I think!

She tells me tales of the workers cramming onto the trams.

'They grumble like mad about folk who're travelling for pleasure taking space up, because they're workers, they should have first pop at the seats!' Laughing, she added, 'Someone said – loudly – that those who weren't travelling to do a job should get off and walk!' Dora shook her head then. 'No bugger took any notice, they just carried on chattering – and smoking if they were upstairs.'

Me and Dora talk about everything, Dear Diary.

Except *the secret of who is the baby's father.*

That stays in these pages. I don't talk about that with anyone.

Blackpool, Saturday September 23, 1944

My Dear Diary, I am happier and more exhausted than I have been for a long time.

Today, after a long labour in my room at Marian's, I gave birth.

Tom Blackshaw was born just after eight in the evening. He weighed in at seven and a half pounds.

Enid was a great support. It was a joy to see a different side to her. I never knew she could be so, well, in charge – and kind with it.

She left Agnes and Lilian to deal with the evening meal for the billets and guests, and joined Marian to help and keep me company. The two of them were marvellous. I wanted to write everything down so I can remember it to tell Jack, copy it out into a letter to him.

I was surprised to learn that Enid trained as a midwife a long time ago, before going into the boarding house life with her first husband, but as she rightly said – childbirth is something that doesn't really change.

Once I had the warm bundle that was Tom in my arms, his wispy brown hair, unfocused eyes searching, lips rooting and perfectly formed fingers closing around the tip of one of mine, I thought nothing could match the emotion expanding inside me. I felt such an overwhelming rush of love.

I told baby Tom that his dad would be so happy he'd arrived.

'Would you like to hold him, Mother?' When I offered

Tom to Enid, the gentleness in her features brought tears to my eyes. It really was a different side to her.

'Hello Tom.' She smiled down into his face, her forefinger tracing his sturdy little chin.

'I'll go and get you a brew and a spot of something to eat.' Marian excused herself. 'Back in a few.'

There was only one more thing I wanted in my life – *Jack*.

Always, the thought of him gave rise to a sharp pull of emotion. Tom gave a little squeak then, distracting me from those thoughts and rather than dwell I let myself be swept into the magical moment.

'He's a lovely little soul,' Enid said, surprising me yet again and handing him back as he rooted and fussed, saying she'd better get back to the Bing Lea.

'I'm so grateful for your help, Enid, you've been wonderful. Thank you.'

She smiled, a rare sight, but a welcome one. I hope we may be turning a corner, becoming friendlier.

No sooner had Enid gone than there was a knock on the door.

'Come in!'

Dora and her sister, Katherine, came into the room quietly sporting a duo of smiles.

'Mum sent this.' Dora popped down a small tray that bore a large mug of tea, a plate of corned beef hash and carrots, and a great chunk of Victoria sponge. 'She said you're probably ready for something to eat, coz you were busy with Tom over mealtime!'

'Oh, it's lovely to see you, I'm excited to show Tom off.'

Marian followed the others in. 'He's very handsome, like his dad, Molly.'

It's strange, but I have to remind myself regularly that no one else in the world – except Jack and Joe – knows *the secret*.

'Jack will be thrilled.' Dora settled on the side of the bed to take the offered baby. 'I'll send him a telegram from you, shall I? Just put Tom's weight and "Mum and baby doing well"?'

'That's kind, Dora, thanks.'

'Do you mind if I tell Matt? It might help to cheer him up. They've had a rotten time lately.'

'I imagine he's still upset about the Freckleton disaster?'

'Well—' Dora stroked Tom's soft cheek '—he is, they all are there, but there's been another accident, at Warton this time. One of his close friends was killed.'

I had never even considered losing a close friend like Dora, it was something I didn't want to contemplate, but I imagined that the pain for Matt must have been immense, especially as he and his fellow airmen were so far away from home in the States. Friends could be more like family, bonds formed quickly. I'd seen it happen amongst the billets, they laughed, fought, talked and fooled around once they got to know one another – much like family.

'Poor Matt. Yes, of course, tell him and bring him to visit so Tom can meet his Uncle Matt.'

Dora rocked Tom; I couldn't take my eyes off him whilst I savoured the corned beef hash, cake and the tea. I was ridiculously hungry; it was the first meal since going into labour and I was more than ready for it.

Blackpool, Saturday October 7, 1944

Dear Diary, Tom is two weeks old and I've started to get out of bed and potter about after my lying in. I've decided also to keep a note of what happens here so I can remember to tell any news to Jack.

Tom feeds well and takes so much of my attention that I don't think about Jack *all* the time.

Just a lot of the time.

I wrote to Jack yesterday and Dora posted it on her way to work. I told him how Tom's nails look almost translucent, like the inside of those pretty seashells – pink and delicate and perfect in miniature; how his skin is softer than a cloud and his eyes are blue. I wrote, too, that Enid told me an interesting thing – sometimes the colour of a baby's eyes changes as they grow. Another interesting thing she said was that their eye colour always changes from light to darker if it does alter, but she'd never seen it go the other way around – from dark to light. As always, in my letters all my news to Jack is light and I told him the truth: that I couldn't wait for him to meet our baby son.

I told him, too, that I couldn't wait to have him hold me tight again like he did on our honeymoon and on his visit since. I told him that I thought about him endlessly and the photograph of us laughing into one another's faces takes me back to that exact moment on our wedding day every time I look at it and I feel such love and warmth and complete happiness held in that moment. I wrote that I thought I might be getting to grips with being a mum and that it was a lot different to how I'd imagined. It was nothing like playing with a doll as I'd done when I was much younger!

I realised it was high time that I wrote to Jack's parents and let them know about Tom, too.

My Dear Mr and Mrs Blackshaw,

I write in case word hasn't got through to you to let you know you are grandparents. I had a son, Tom, seven and a half pounds, on 23rd September.

He is a contented soul and his smile reminds me so much of Jack. My friend Dora says it is wind making him smile, but I'd rather think that he's already a happy soul.

As I wrote those words, the longing to see Jack was so intense, I gasped, and then gulped down the rising emotion. When I managed to pull myself together again, I blew my nose, tucked my hanky up my sleeve and carried on.

I hope this finds you well and settled in at your new address in Shaw. Mum, Dad and I used to live close by there, too, on Highbarn Road in Royton.

I was very sorry to hear your home in Manchester was bombed, that must have been awful.

I hope that I will be able to introduce you to your grandson before too much longer. Hopefully, it will become easier to travel soon.

I'll close now, but if I can, I'll see if my friend can take a picture of Tom, and I'll send it to you, just in case you can't travel for a while yet.

Do take care and very best wishes to you both, and of course your family.

With love from your daughter-in-law, Molly Blackshaw, and your grandson, Tom.

After Dora took the letters off to post, I thought that one thing I'd learned about being a mum was that there was nothing – *nothing* at all – to compare to what I felt for the warm bundle when I rocked him in my arms, sang – not well, but he didn't mind – and held him close, the clean baby smell of him bringing home love so consuming it was beyond words.

Blackpool, Sunday October 8, 1944

On my way to the kitchen today there was a loud knock. I moved silently along the dark hallway and opened the door. Black dread squeezed me tightly as I was handed a telegram addressed to Mrs Blackshaw, though it took a moment to realise that was me as I was still getting used to my new name. The type was squarish, unfamiliar and official looking, and the word 'priority' struck a chill into my insides. I felt sick with fear, my breath shooting from my lungs, leaving me dizzy; I felt like a vice had squeezed out all the air, black spots dancing on the edge of my vision.

Struggling back to my room, I opened it, checked Tom was sleeping, a good thing he was because I came over all faint and sank to the edge of the bed, I didn't trust my arms not to shake if Tom needed holding.

It read:

Deeply regret to inform you that your husband, Flight Engineer Sergeant Jack Blackshaw, has been reported missing. Letter following.

My Dear Diary, I swear my body turned to water. My arms turned shaky, I sweated profusely despite the chill in the air, my breath felt to be stuck in my chest and would not come in or go out, funny noises left me like gasps. I put my hand to my head to try and stay sitting upright.

I became distantly aware of a tap at the door; it was Marian, she asked whether I'd like a cuppa, but I couldn't answer. I couldn't get my breath to respond.

Slowly the door creaked open and I must've looked pale or something or just strange because Marian came in, her eyes going wide as she took in the open telegram as it fluttered to the floor.

'Molly, what's happened?'

My shaking hand pointed to the telegram. 'Missing...' I

said, 'Jack is missing.' The voice speaking didn't sound like mine. More like the timid squeak of a young child.

Marian picked up the sparsely worded communication and asked if she could read it. I nodded and she scanned it quickly.

'I'm sure he's either laying low, or he's been taken prisoner. He'll still be alive, Molly.'

'Yes.' At last I took a deep breath and got some control of my shaking limbs. 'Yes, of course he is all right.'

As though agreeing, Tom made a little squeaking sound, his small fists pummelling the air. 'Your daddy wouldn't leave us, would he, Tom?'

'I'll fetch us both a pot of tea.' Marian's hands took one of mine between them and she added gently, 'Everything will be all right Molly. Just believe that until you hear any different.'

I smiled a watery smile at her and nodded my thanks. She was back in no time with a cuppa for us both. I asked Marian whether she thought that Jack's mother would have been told that he was missing, or whether it was just the next of kin. 'I think it's just the next of kin.' Marian set down our cups on the dressing table.

I was the next of kin.

Something shifted inside me when I realised that I was now considered a more fitting contact than even Jack's parents. I wondered silently, too, whether Joe had gone missing at the same time, or whether he was in a different squadron. There was no way to know, unless I contacted Mrs Blackshaw by letter and asked her if she'd heard anything about Jack or Joe.

Again, my Dear Diary, it felt wrong to give her more worry that she must already have. It was a concern I could not imagine – having two of your offspring away from home fighting for King and country.

How Mrs Blackshaw, like me, must dread the telegram stamped 'priority' arriving, bearing the terrifying news of loss or lost.

I asked Marian if she knew what happened now and she said she had a couple of friends whose husbands had also been reported as missing in action. She said that quite quickly after the initial telegram a more detailed letter came with the results of their investigations. The news had been good for one friend – her husband was a POW – and not so good for another friend.

She added then that it was very important not to lose hope and not to let nervous worries make my milk dry up, for Tom's sake.

My two overwhelming thoughts, my Dear Diary, were *Please, God, let Jack be alive* and *Thank God for Tom*.

Blackpool, Tuesday October 17, 1944

I couldn't function properly for days, couldn't stop the pain of not knowing from swamping about inside me, like thick black treacle that I couldn't be free of, or the tears that welled up time after time until my eyes were permanently swollen. I didn't write any words until I made the decision to write to Jack. I know he would not receive a letter so I've decided I will write any and all news – little but important things about Tom – here in my notebook. That way I can copy out the news and send it to him when I hear he is alive and well. It gives me something to look forward to – a positive thing.

As the telegram had said a letter turned up just now. Like the telegram, it knocked me for six but somehow the added details did offer some hope. I've stuck it in here:

From Wing Commander G D Garner

Royal Air Force Station

Dear Mrs. Blackshaw,

May I be permitted to express my own and the squadrons' sincere sympathy with you in the sad news concerning your husband, Sergeant Jack Blackshaw.

The aircraft of which he was the Flight Engineer took off to attack a strategic target in France on 28th September 1944, and nothing further has been heard.

You may be aware that in quite a large percentage of cases aircrew reported missing are eventually reported prisoner of war, and I hope that this may give you some comfort. This is not to say that any further information about him is available but is a precaution adopted in the case of all personnel reported missing. Rest assured that you will be notified immediately by Air Ministry when any information is received.

Your husband's effects have been collected and will be forwarded to you in due course through Air Ministry channels. Your husband was a most proficient Flight Engineer and his loss is deeply regretted by us all.

Once again, please accept the deep sympathy of us all and let us hope that we may soon have some good news of the safety of your husband.

Yours very sincerely.

Blackpool, Friday October 20, 1944

It was later the same week, Dear Diary, Enid came across to visit. She rolled a big pram into mine and Jack's room, a warm smile on her face. She said it was ours to use for as long as we needed it as Agnes's daughter had stored it in her garden shed and no longer had any use for it. She added hurriedly that it had been given a good clean up, and I found for the first time I was moved by something other than misery to step over to where Enid stood by the window and hug her close whilst whispering my thanks.

I told her it was a wonderful gift to bring me because it meant now that I could take Tom out for a nice long walk on the promenade and blow the cobwebs of weeks of confinement away. And I felt the sudden need to feel the sun on my face. Even cold sunshine – or even fresh air and no sunshine would do.

I was surprised anew at Enid's kindness, this different side to her.

'I wonder if you and Marian would like to come for a walk on the prom with me and Tom?' Normally, I would happily walk alone, but I felt strangely vulnerable.

'I would, actually. Agnes is taking good care of our billets just now and it's quite warm outside.'

Marian declined to come with us; she said she was halfway through making the evening meal but she would love to come along another time.

Whilst we walked to the end of Bank Street and then across the road onto the prom, I found myself speaking without thinking.

'I like us getting along this way, Mother, I feel like I'm only just getting to know you properly.'

'Aye, well, I used to love working with babies. When I married my first husband, he was already up to his elbows in the boarding house so I didn't really have a choice but to leave my chosen work to support him.'

As we continued to talk and walk, Enid shared that she had been a very young bride the first time and her older first husband, Walter, a dour chap expected her to slave away whilst he drank the profit and did the bare minimum of work. She'd realised over the years that he only married her to be a skivvy, and he'd had no intention of having a family of their own. 'I was heartbroken that having sacrificed my work as a midwife, learned all I could from my own mother, he'd denied me what I wanted the most. A child. A family.'

She said she had no freedom of choice to start a family,

and no time to do the job she loved and had spent a long time learning. 'He would not even let me come and go as I pleased, allowed me no opportunity to go out and dance or have fun because he ranted that my place was in the home, doing for him.'

She added, 'I'll admit I felt envious of the freedom you had in your life to just come and go with no ties. You had so much independence; you walked, you danced, you went out and had a good time with Dora, friends, and you didn't seem to answer to anyone. Even your dad never thought to clip your wings or lay down the law.'

She said when she'd confided in my dad about her first marriage, he was always offering to take her dancing, to the pier to shows, or just for walks. 'But it was strange. Too many years being married to a slave driver made me find it hard to just let go and live a little.' She smiled then. 'Although Bert and I did have some happy times. Your dad was a good man.'

She seemed to find it easier to confide in me now that I was married, now that I had a baby. I was surprised when she told me that she would like to get shot of the boarding house once the war was over, because whilst she was very happy to serve her country that way, it wasn't what made her personally happy as a job. She said that life with my dad had been much better than with her first husband, because at least my dad laughed and talked, and mucked in readily with anything that needed doing.

'My one regret is that by the time I married your father,' she said, 'it was too late to have children. I would have liked Bert's babies. Your dad was a good man.'

I nodded, said I thought so too and that I still missed him.

Our chat, Dear Diary, helped me to better understand Enid and clear the decks between us. In exchange, I confided in her about the telegram and how upset I was, and about the letter that had arrived today. She reiterated what Marian had said, that I must not lose hope, and that no news would be good news. She also said she knew someone who had had a telegram like that – and that had turned out well.

I'm writing this just before I get into bed. Tom is settled and asleep so I got on my hands and knees and prayed, *hard*, for Jack to be safe and that I'd have good news before too long.

I promised Him I would go to church every week and never miss, made any and every kind of bargain I could bring to mind.

If He would just protect Jack.

Just let him be alive.

Chapter Twenty-One

Izzie

Blackpool, Wednesday September 27, 2017

'Takes your breath away, doesn't it? What they went through. Not knowing.' Justin glanced at his watch. 'Bugger, I'd best make tracks, Izzie. I've to leave home at five in the morning, I'm hopeful to catch a break weather-wise up in Ambleside.'

Izzie put the postcard bookmark into the notebook and lingered over the inner front page of keepsakes, her palm running lightly over the different textures out of habit. As she did so, Justin's eyes stilled on the sketch of Molly. 'Your granddad drew Molly? That's good. Reminds me of your style, Izzie.'

'I used to spend hours watching him draw and paint, trying to copy what he did. That is, when I wasn't making biscuits and buns and then eating them all in the kitchen with Nan.'

They both laughed and Izzie closed the outer cover and set the notebook safely to the back of the kitchen table as she stood to walk Justin out. 'I've really enjoyed today,' she said when he turned to face her at the door. She suddenly felt emotional and, as was her habit, her mouth engaged without her brain taking part. 'I'm glad we're friends again ... you know, friends having a flirt but no ties,' she added quickly at Justin's light frown.

She thought she saw a flicker of intense pain in Justin's eyes, but then it had gone and she thought she must have imagined it.

'Yeah.' She sensed him come back into himself. 'It's been good.' Tentatively, he leaned towards her and landed a kiss on her lips, then, when Izzie returned the embrace, palms resting on his shoulders, the kiss deepened.

'I – I'm not sure when I'm back, should be late tomorrow, it all depends on the weather.' He gave a wonky smile. 'You know what it's like in the Lakes, one minute there's glorious sunshine, the next there's a monsoon!'

'Difficult when you're trying for a certain type of photograph, I should think,' Izzie said. 'Well, ping me a message or call round when you have some free time – I'd be glad of some help decorating if you want to be a real hero.'

He laughed at that. 'A hero, aye?' His wonderful face-lighting laughter that made Izzie's insides hitch in response and made her smile broadly.

'Or we can just hang out.'

He moved along the driveway and raised his hand in farewell before getting into his car.

As she closed the front door, Izzie leaned back against it and enjoyed the sensation of a real glow of happiness inside, a feeling doubly appreciated because for so long she'd hovered in the darker worlds of disappointment and sadness.

She was determined to enjoy the brief part that Justin played in her life for the short term.

Again, she knew a delicious rush of freedom.

Tomorrow, she thought, whilst she got ready for bed, she would take a long early morning walk on the promenade and then see if she could crack on with some more wallpaper removal. And if she didn't manage it, what did it matter? She'd given herself until the New Year to finish. She was also getting an itch to contact her old boss, Eddie, at DAS, to see if there were any jobs she could do remotely and ask if he could set her up with work when she eventually returned to London. She planned to fire off a bunch of emails to her workmates, too, to reconnect properly. Just a little reach out to her other world.

Blackpool, Thursday September 28, 2017

'Oh, that's great, Eddie, thank you!' Her boss was sending her some work outlines that could be dealt with remotely – their client wanted a set of watercolours of specific trees that were being featured in a short book about native species.

'Great timing, you ringing! I thought of you when the job came good, Izzie, as I know you love that medium and you didn't get to do much artwork when you worked for Rufus. And the upside is – there's no rush. Early next year is pencilled in for delivery of the originals, with photo updates online of your progress.' Eddie sounded buoyant and the general open office hubbub played out in the background. She'd missed that friendly work atmosphere so much more than she'd let herself admit. Until now.

'Course, if you come south for a visit, come and see us.'

Izzie assured Eddie that she would and felt better for touching base and knowing work was still available for her.

After working all day stripping off wallpaper, Izzie, exhausted, had a hot bath and an early night. The gentle buzz of her phone on the bedside table roused her just long enough to read the message with one eye open...

Just to say goodnight and let you know I'm staying over in the Lakes; weather didn't work out today, fingers crossed it'll be okay tomorrow. J

Izzie pressed 'x' on her phone in reply and dropped straight back to sleep.

Whilst she took a break the following afternoon, Izzie again read through the most recent pages of Molly's notebook that she'd read with Justin. She replaced the postcard bookmark after reliving Molly's shock at receiving the Missing in Action telegram and subsequent letter and she thought again about how she had never known anything about this part of her nan and granddad's lives. She racked her brains to try and remember whether there had ever been an Uncle Joe in her very young life.

Had he ever been mentioned or had his existence been swept under the carpet? Had he died in the war? Had he married?

Izzie wondered how the heck Nan had carried on whilst not knowing whether Grandpop was alive, had been captured, injured or killed.

At least, she thought, they *had* been reunited. But that was knowledge that Izzie had. Poor Molly had had no idea where her beloved husband was.

The train of thought stayed with Izzie whilst she returned to the endless task of steaming off the wallpaper.

She thought how strange life was sometimes. Her dad Tom's birth had clearly revealed a gentler side of Enid. She had had a gruelling life during her first marriage and the legacy gave rise to her resentment of Molly, who Enid saw as a footloose and fancy-free young woman without a care in the world, doing just what she wanted.

She thought how different the way folk saw one another was to the reality of how someone *actually* felt – sometimes the inner truth was a long way from the face shown to the world.

That thought triggered memories of life with Rufus. There had been good times, certainly, but as time had moved on through their four years and four months of marriage, the face Izzie showed to her husband and the world were completely different to how she felt inside. As Rufus became a snowballing part of her daily life she'd had to squash down her own personality, become more isolated, take up less room in her own life, to make room for all of Rufus's needs, his moods, his fits... It had happened so gradually at first that she hadn't fully identified the progression; she had only known how it made her feel. But she'd had to hide her emotions.

Somehow, in the safe space of the bungalow, Izzie dared to look honestly at her time as Izzie Dean whilst she systematically worked on removing wallpaper.

She opened the front room windows and the fading scent of lavender wafted in by the warm afternoon breeze brought back a powerful memory of something she'd been ashamed of feeling when it happened back in West Hampstead...

It was in 2014, three years and a couple of months into their marriage and work arrangement when Izzie had asked Rufus if he minded her going out for a meal with her ex-work pals.

Ruby and the crew had invited her to join them for a meal and she wanted to go because she had missed them all so much since she'd started working solely for Rufus.

Since she married him, she'd transcribed three books for his crime series from his scribbled notes and recordings, she'd handled all the professional and household admin, and in order to meet the deadlines, they'd had very little social life outside a few walks together, and a few days off to wander around Regent's Park or Kew Gardens. There was less and less time for Izzie to meet, visit or chat with her friends – just a few hurried phone calls to touch base.

Izzie admitted to herself, as the scent of lavender drifted indoors that she hadn't fully understood when she'd said yes to marrying Rufus and becoming his full-time companion, was that he'd really meant *full-time*. And during the last couple of years of their relationship, it turned out to be to the exclusion of anyone and everything else.

His degenerating illness meant even the very quick phone calls to her work pals dropped away during that time; only her set-in-stone phone calls to her nan on a Sunday night endured of her own routine.

At first, he'd reminded her of a Cockney pub landlord type, one that was full of life, chat and charm – so sociable. He had joined Izzie and her friends for barbeques, held them in their back garden, joined in her life-affirming fun and friendships. In the early days, it didn't seem possible that he would ever change as much as he'd warned he may.

Rufus's health was beginning to decline, and the effect was that when the seizures began, she couldn't leave him to fend for himself anymore. It also meant that after three years of working and socialising normally, things began to change quite rapidly.

So, when her friends invited her out for a meal at a local restaurant, said she should bring Rufus if she didn't feel comfortable leaving him alone, she'd had to turn them down.

'I don't feel well enough, Izzie, to be home on my own,

and I really don't want to have a seizure away from home.' He'd looked tired when he'd said that and his eyes had held sadness.

'Okay, no worries.' She smiled and dropped a kiss on his cheek, not wanting to make him feel guilty. 'It's not a problem.'

But she had felt the sharp stab of disappointment and had stepped into the garden to take a deep breath and fight off the sense that she was living in a shrinking world.

She missed her pals.

Back then, as she had brushed against a lavender bush, the joyous hum of happy bees failed for once to raise her spirits; instead, there in their West Hampstead garden, the fragrance accompanied the sense of isolation she'd felt.

Brought back to the present by the scent carried through the bungalow's open window on a light sea breeze, Izzie took a deep breath to better enjoy the perfume, to remember the lazy Summer buzz of the bees that loved the copious buds.

When Rufus asked her to become Mrs Dean and all that it would entail, she hadn't fully understood what it meant.

The timing had been everything – the absolute clincher.

Attractive Jack the Lad, Rufus Dean, crime writer and all-around good time chap, handed her an escape route from pain, a clawing pain that continually felt like the expression: the first cut is the deepest.

Rufus offered her a home, something she had always wanted, an income and security for the rest of her life, for doing a job she enjoyed.

She said yes – it was a no brainer.

And she had rarely had regrets over saying yes. There was little time or emotional breadth for introspection whilst he was alive.

It was just that one day that she'd felt it most powerfully – the day she'd had to turn down her old work friends' invitation for the first time, when she walked out into the garden and inhaled that beautiful scent that she began to fully comprehend the scope of what she had taken on and once she had taken some deep breaths, raised her face to the sky and told herself to *get on with it*…

After that she did her best to push aside any caged feelings she had. It was her side of the bargain to simply be there for Rufus and care for him and love him.

Be there for him in every aspect of his life.

Turning off the steamer, Izzie tackled bagging up the lengths of sticky wallpaper, then she photographed her progress, which amounted to bare walls, and pinged the photo to Justin along with the message:

Just so you can see how I'm doing! Izzie x

Whilst she ran a bath and made a cuppa to take along, a breath-takingly beautiful photograph came through on her messages from Justin.

Finally managed it. Sunset over Ravenglass. J

'Wow.' He'd caught a stunning moment in the photograph. A mountain with a dip in its dark profile appeared to hold the white-yellow setting sun, which was throwing off an intense pale-yellow light from behind purple clouds. The sky was a pure orange reflected in the water surrounding the finger of land running out from the mountain into the lake. In the foreground, deep blue water was touched with a blaze of orange. After staring at the photo for ages, Izzie sent a message back:

Truly awesomely stunning. Izzie x

Thanks. I've some good shots, will show you. Driving home soon – just got a hike to the car park! Will message when I'm back, see if you're up for a visit. No worries if not. J

Smiling, Izzie sent an emoji of a thumbs-up and turned off the bath taps as bubbles arched up above the top of the deep bath.

A delicious hot soak and a bit of curl taming later, Izzie flicked on a touch of mascara and pulled on jeans and a bright blue and black checked shirt, grabbed her notebook and settled at the kitchen table. She wrote down all the memories of Rufus she'd visited whilst working earlier, added a few more that needed to be aired.

She cast her mind back to the course of events that had seen her marry Rufus. Theirs had been a different kind of relationship, and that suited her – Izzie had been determined not to love anyone as intensely as she'd loved Justin.

The day after Justin's no show, Izzie returned to London in excruciating emotional agony from Justin's rejection. She remembered she could barely breathe for the anguish. She could only ever recollect snatches of the train journey back down south; it was lost in a sea of torment, questions, disbelief, misery, and self-pity. Every attempt to contact him failed…

She thought it must be serendipity when Rufus popped the question within a week of her return to London.

As she wrote down her memories, Izzie wondered if Rufus had sensed her heartache and sought to help – or if his timing had been pure fate.

'You don't need to marry me; I'll stay here and look after you as long as you need me to. I promise I won't leave you to be alone.' Surprise had shot the response from her.

He'd said, 'Izzie, I've had the best time these last six months you've been working part-time for me. We both know I've not got long left and the only way I can protect your future, make sure you never want for money or for a roof over your head is to marry you. You don't have to let me know straight away, and I don't know whether you want a big wedding. I certainly don't; I'd be happy to have one of those standing on a beach on a tropical island with just two witnesses that neither of us know.' He laughed then, because Izzie clapped her hands together and said that would be her choice too.

Her battered self-esteem, the clawing agony she still fought to squash down inside after a week of pure grief…

Like a thirsty plant in need of water, she grasped the opportunity as a means of escaping the pain, flattered that Rufus Dean, famous crime writer, had offered her a different version of the life she'd dreamed of. It never even occurred to her that it was a rebound. She only knew that she would make it work.

'I don't need to think about it. And I don't care what kind of ceremony we have. I'll still be your personal assistant, won't I?'

'Yes, that's a huge part of the deal.'

She hugged him then and their wedding took place a couple of weeks later on the 31st August, by special licence at the local registry office.

Becoming Mrs Dean had provided Izzie with the ability to completely shut off the agony of having gone up north to meet with Justin ... and Justin not showing up.

Somehow, it had been a natural progression to shift the focus of her emotions to concentrate on Rufus and cut all the love she'd had for Justin off.

Literally.

In the kitchen of her nan's bungalow she wrote down the tumbling thoughts, hoping that writing it all down would help to make sense of things, help her to come to terms with her losses and the choices she'd made.

Her phone buzzed to herald a message.

You up for a visitor? I'm home.

Izzie responded with 'yes.'

'I love this photograph.' Izzie marvelled at the way a soft white mist hovered over the water of Lake Windermere, the evenly coloured pale blue sky holding a narrow wash of pink close to the horizon. It was perfectly reflected in the water below. The mist softened the shape of the land around the edge of the lake, the effect incredible.

'It looks so tranquil, Justin.'

'It was just before the sun came up.'

They sat side by side at the kitchen table, glasses of wine in front of them as Justin shared some more views that he'd captured: some of the black-headed sheep that roamed freely in the Lake District, many capturing the terrifyingly steep roads of Hardknott Pass and the beautiful, scenic hills. Justin had caught it all with stunning clarity and showed the effect clouds had on the side of the steep hills as the greenery began to turn autumnal and golden.

'You've always been good, but these are beyond that, Justin, they're breath-taking.'

'Thanks, Izzie.'

The next photo was one of a similar aspect, but the sun was setting behind the surrounding hills. A dark jetty drew the eye into the water, which reflected the pink and yellow blush from the sky. Above the vivid colours, the sky darkened into a delicious mixture of blue tinged with purple.

'I've a meeting with the chap who wants these photos tomorrow, but I should be done around midday again if you want some company or help?'

'Oh fab. Yes please.'

'Show me how far you got, Izzie?'

After looking around and seeing that she had finished stripping the lounge, front bedroom and hallway, Justin asked, 'Do you want a lift into town, get what you need to do the job?' For a moment, whilst he looked around, Izzie studied his features. *Kind eyes*, she thought as his gaze returned to her own face and he smiled. 'Well done.'

'Sounds like a good plan. We could grab some lunch here after?' she suggested.

Rolling her stiff shoulders, she gave a little grimace.

'Found some muscles you didn't know you had?'

'Yup, I had a hot bath, but the effect has worn off now.'

'I do a mean shoulder massage.' He lifted a brow, eyes filled with fun.

'I'm sorely tempted,' she said. He'd given her shoulders some fabulous attention in the past, when she'd spent way too long drawing or painting, sat in the same position without moving.

He gestured she should sit in the dining chair. 'Tell you what, why don't you read Molly's notebook out loud to me and I'll work on your aches.'

Izzie could swear that only Justin could suggest that and send her insides into a whirl.

She picked up their glasses and when he took one, Izzie clinked hers against his.

'Deal.'

Chapter Twenty-Two

Molly

Blackpool, Thursday November 16, 1944

It is now November, my Dear Diary, and I still have heard nothing from the RAF about where Jack might be.

I wrote to them last week and asked if they had uncovered any more news of him, or if they hadn't written specifically because they had no news.

I told Marian and Enid what I was doing and they both said they were sure I would have heard if they had any news, and Enid reiterated it's likely that *no news was good news*.

It's certainly better than bad news, but *not knowing* feels a bit like carrying around something that won't stop eating away in my chest.

I think I have to be grateful that no matter how worried I am it does not seem to affect me feeding Tom.

On the advice of Dora, Marian and even Enid, for Tom's sake I make sure to go for a long walk in the fresh air every day. Tom is now seven weeks old and bonny as all get up.

Today I flipped back through these pages and read every single word since Jack and I began to write to one another.

I read his letters, which bring a tear to my eye and budding happiness within, and I read everything, every emotion I recorded here in my precious notebook. Never have I been more grateful that I noted everything. Just the thought that I may not have the ability to recollect those magical moments clearly were it not for the fact I had written everything down is terrifying because I've already forgotten so many little details.

I am going to join Enid tomorrow for some tea and scones; she and Agnes are going to set it up in the little back room at the Bing Lea. They're having an hour off and I feel quite touched that they've asked me to join them. I will of course be taking Tom, who is like a good fortune coupon to get me welcomed into any gathering.

I still write letters to Jack in here, or rather, I keep notes of everything that happens so that I can copy it into letters and not forget anything.

I especially do not want to forget anything that Tom does. Like how he makes me laugh when he puts his little perfect toes in his mouth and bites down and then looks surprised, his perfectly round eyes opening wide; like saucers, Marian says.

Matt has enjoyed cuddles with Tom and the last time he

came to Blackpool he brought his camera again. He said something that gave me so much comfort: 'I'll take some photographs of Tom, ready for when Jack comes home so that he won't feel like he's missed too much, I'll write the date they were taken on the backs of them.' He agreed, too, to pick out the best ones and make extra copies to be sent to Jack's parents.

His kindness stole my breath. Indeed, I find any time that folk are particularly kind to me these days, my emotions lurch way too close to the surface, like a high tide splashing up onto the promenade, and tears threaten to roll and splash down my cheeks.

I feel certain that Jack is alive, and if wishing made dreams come true, he would already be home, and the war would be over.

Every time I settle Tom down for the night, I pray that tomorrow Jack will come home.

I imagine that happening every way possible.

I imagine myself standing in the front yard at the Bing Lea, rocking the pram to and fro whilst taking deep breaths of beautiful salty sea air. In my mind, Jack's dark-haired, so handsome figure turns into the street, catching my eye, the choked whisper of his name leaving me as he comes closer. His smile is unmistakable, and that he is pleased to see me is in absolutely no doubt.

I imagine his walk becomes a run and when he reaches me, he picks me up and spins me round holding me so tight, my own arms clutching around his neck as his face buries in my neck, tears of joy pouring down my face.

Sometimes I awake in the night and my mind plays

tricks. I think he sleeps beside me, but as I reach for him, he disappears.

Those are my dreams, my wishes, Dear Diary.

Blackpool, Sunday November 19, 1944

I was clearing up in the kitchen alongside Marian when there was an insistent knocking on the front door, earlier today, after tea.

Marian was up to her elbows in washing-up water. She glanced at the clock on the kitchen wall and said she wondered who it was at that time. I said I'd go, thinking it would be a neighbour.

I'd the shock of my life.

I gasped, hand on chest, at the tall figure in blue uniform lit by a slither of moonlight.

I thought it was Jack.

My whole body felt to be in the grip of an electric shock. 'J-Jack?' But even as the word left me, the man shook his head, blew out a stream of smoke.

Cold air wafted in as he asked, 'Can I come in?'

'Have you heard anything? About Jack?' The words were out before Joe made it over the threshold.

He shook his head. 'That's why I'm here. It looks as though he's gone, Molly. We've been stationed at different bases for a while now – I managed to blag a twenty-four-hour pass so I could visit you.'

No, no. I started to shake, feeling faint, not enough air in my lungs, much like I had when the telegram came.

'It's a quick visit, that's all.'

Behind me I heard the kitchen door open; it was Marian, drying her hands on her pinny and asking who had been knocking at the door.

'Is that you, Jack?' Her hopeful words filled the hall, the frozen silence.

'Joe.' He raised his hand in greeting.

Marian said I should bring Joe through to the back for a brew to warm up.

I felt puzzled though.

Why would Joe bother to come here? I asked him as such once we were alone.

His words turned me cold. 'I want to meet my son. And I wanted to see you.'

I didn't want any kind of discussion along those lines where it could be heard by *anyone*. I reached up to the coat hook and pulled down my warmest coat. Checking my key was in the pocket, I stuck my head into the kitchen and told Marian we were going for a short walk, and asked could she listen out for Tom.

Anything I had to say wasn't going to take long at all.

I rounded on him as soon as we reached the pavement. 'How *dare* you come here and start spouting that you want to meet *your* son? You gave up that right when you left me in the lurch.'

I was *so* angry on my own and on Jack's behalf.

That Joe should so easily disregard his own brother's

feelings, the fact that his own brother was *my husband* and that Jack *was* officially Tom's dad.

We had made it down to the sea front by this point. Joe shook his head. 'I honestly don't see what the problem is. Whether I'm Tom's father or his uncle, I'm visiting as part of the family.'

'Is that all, Joe?' I asked him. Something that Jack had once said nudged at the edge of my mind, but I couldn't quite bring it into focus.

It was something uncomfortable.

'Well, the thing is, Molly, I've been thinking I was a bit hasty turning you away. I mean, what's the harm in the two of us getting together. You don't want the baby to be without a dad, do you?'

It came back to me in that moment what Jack had written of Joe.

It was that if Jack had something, Joe wanted it... The written words flashed up in my mind:

He's always been like that, wanting whatever I want for himself, and he'll do anything he can to get it.

I put my hands on my hips and turned to face Joe straight on. 'I doubt very much whether you would even be here if I wasn't already married to Jack. I think the only reason you *are* here is because *I am* married to Jack and as far as I'm concerned, unless I hear differently, he is still alive. He is *missing*, that is the only news I have had of him.' I raised my chin. 'I am Jack's wife and am going to stay that way.'

He looked surprised for a moment, astonished, I guess.

I sensed he expected me to fly thankfully into his arms

and repeat those words of love I had once spoken to him at a time when I fully believed them.

'And yes, you are family Joe, and you are more than welcome to come indoors at Marian's and visit your nephew as his Uncle Joe. But you are *not* welcome to call yourself his father. His father is Jack. Jack's name is on Tom's birth certificate, along with mine as his mother.'

My Dear Diary, cold wind blew in off the sea, tossing my hair across my cheeks; it was chilled enough to make your head ache, and I pulled my coat tightly around myself.

'The thing is, Molly, if Jack has been killed, you might need me to step into his shoes without anyone knowing. You would still be married and we could be together like we were once before. I know you love me because you told me, many times.'

I shook my head, hardly able to believe Joe's words. Anger bubbled inside me that he should presume I still loved him.

'I *thought* I loved you. I *know* I truly love Jack.'

He didn't seem to hear what I was saying.

He shoved up his overcoat sleeve to look at his watch. 'I'll come back to say hello to Marian and Bill, meet Tom, but I won't stop long. I have to be on the next train back to barracks.'

In the cold whipping wind, we made our way back to Marian's, and once there Joe popped into the kitchen just to say hello and goodbye and that he would see them again soon, and he then followed me into the bedroom.

I put my finger to my lips so that he wouldn't make too much noise as he peeked at the baby – at mine and Jack's baby. I whispered to a sleeping Tom that this was his Uncle Joe, just to be sure Joe understood his place.

Joe looked quite shaken, I have to say. In my mind he was weighing up all that he had thrown away and handed to his brother. I must admit to a tug of emotion watching Joe as he stroked his forefinger down his nephew's cheek. 'Hello, Tom.' He gave a wistful smile. 'I think I made a big mistake, little fella,' he whispered to a still sleeping, unconcerned Tom. 'I should've...' He took a deep breath, stood straight and nodded, as though he was finished. His expression was serious, tormented. I showed him out into the hallway and wished him a safe journey.

He paused for a moment.

'Just know you don't need to be alone Molly. If Jack doesn't come back, you don't need to be alone. I would step up to the mark this time. I would make sure I was a good father.' He leaned in and kissed my cheek and for a moment, I warmed again towards Joe, even felt sympathy for him. Our eyes met and held briefly.

There was so much I wanted to say, my Dear Diary. Like, *You should have realised that before Tom was born. You should have realised that whilst you were out with other women whilst you let me think I was the only one for you. And you should have realised that when I wrote to tell you I was pregnant, and you dashed my heart and my dreams against the rocks with a single letter.* But I said none of these things. He seemed to have realised all that for himself.

He was family, after all, and he seemed to mean well now. I raised my hand to wave at his salute as he turned away, only then letting out the breath I held.

I had witnessed Joe's regret for turning me away when I expected baby Tom.

He was the one who had lost so much. It was hard to witness Joe, identical to Jack yet different in nature, hurting, showing real emotion for once; not the flippant, flirty side of his character, but the side that acknowledged he *had* made a mistake.

It was clear to me in hindsight that I *had* loved him, I had lusted after him and been enchanted by his inherent charm, yet I had not been *in love* with him, as I'd thought.

He had been exciting, he had been gregarious, fun, attractive, always the centre of attention, and that had attracted me far more than it should have done. He still had the power to make me angry though. To think that he thought he could just swagger back into my life and push Jack out of it...

I knew as sure as eggs were eggs that were I to attempt to have any sort of life with Joe, he would at some point in the future stray. His sociable nature would attract any number of affairs, and any wife he chose in the future would be certain to feel the pain of betrayal once the novelty wore off.

How do you trust someone with your emotions when they have already broken that trust?

I have been the lucky one in the long run, the winner.

I married Jack.

I am so lucky to love him without any reserve.

I checked that Tom was still asleep and then went to join Marian and Dora in the kitchen.

'By heck, lass, I thought it was Jack home when I peeped

in the hall. How on earth do you tell them apart?' Marian said.

'Just for a moment I thought it was Jack, too, Marian.' I told her that my heart felt as though it had stopped beating when I saw him. 'I didn't used to be able to tell them apart easily, but it's just the little things.'

'Did Joe have any news of Jack?'

'No, nothing new, he just wanted to call in and pay his respects, meet his nephew.' It was easier all around to simply bend the truth.

There was nothing to be gained by sharing secrets.

'It's bonkers really, Molly, I used to get so mixed up with those lads, I always thought that you were seeing Joe not Jack! I could never tell them apart!' Dora tucked into the plate of food Marian had covered and set aside for her on top of a pan full of boiling water, 'Mind you, come to think of it, you spent a lot more time with Jack than Joe over at Enid's in the evenings, didn't you?'

I nodded my agreement, added, 'Oh, I think they tricked me once or twice in the early days when they were staying at the Bing Lea, but you know how it is, the right one always comes to the fore.' Those words were spoken from my heart, my truth-bending setting off a twinge of guilt which I dismissed quickly.

'You're right,' Dora said. 'The cream always rises to the top of the milk.'

'Enid said you spent many an evening in the front room playing cards and chattering with one of them, but she could never tell which one!' Marian yawned, excused herself then – it was getting late, she said – and I could hear

Tom getting restless in my room, so I went and got him and then brought him back to the kitchen so Dora and I could admire him together and spend some time catching up.

Dora said that Matt was bringing some more photographs on his next visit and there should be some of Tom.

'That'll be lovely!' I said, grasping a reason to smile.

I realised whilst talking to Dora that I needed to keep as cheerful as I could for Tom's sake; being a miserable mother was no way to be when I was so blessed.

I'm determined to believe that Jack is alive, repeating that mantra that *no news is good news* in my head. It doesn't stop the nervous rush swirling around inside me every time I think about Jack though.

I have hope.

I *have* to have hope…

Chapter Twenty-Three

Izzie

Blackpool, Saturday September 30, 2017

Izzie touched the written words and felt closer to her nan than ever, felt such admiration for her. She was so glad that Justin was with her so they could read the entries together.

There was a yawning emotional gap between how Molly felt about Jack – she had complete and total trust in him, complete and total love for him – and for Joe – she had a soft spot for him because she had loved him, but he had destroyed the naive trust she'd had in him. Izzie wondered, as she put the bookmark in place and used both hands to close the notebook, whether she would ever trust Justin again – trust him not to hurt her again.

But then reality dawned: she didn't need to trust him in

that way. What they had now was casual, it was a transient relationship to suit them both. It suited Izzie whilst she got to grips with the emotional turmoil within in the safe haven of the bungalow; and it suited Justin whilst he did local work and oversaw the alterations on his house before he took off on his latest photography assignment just before New Year.

Justin's clever fingers had worked out most of the knots in Izzie's shoulders. There was something so sensual about the way he relaxed her muscles. 'Did that help?'

'Yeah, I'm practically drooling!' She laughed. 'Thanks.'

Before he left, Izzie told Justin she'd been in touch with her boss, Eddie, and lined up some work she could do whilst she was in the north. 'I kind of missed that outlet, you know?'

'I understand that. If I wasn't lucky enough to do what I do, I'd probably take photos just to keep sane.'

'I'll check I've got some watercolours here before we go shopping tomorrow.'

'I'll pick you up tomorrow, then, unless I hear differently from you? Just let me know if there's a change of plan.'

She walked him to the front door. 'Thanks for sorting my shoulders.'

In contrast to the previous evening, he said, 'You're welcome, Izzie,' and stepped into the night.

As she closed the front door, it struck Izzie that they seemed to move between friends and something a little more so easily. There was no pressure. She also admitted to a touch of disappointment, because she would have liked him to kiss her again.

Blackpool, Sunday October 1, 2017

First thing the following day, as she'd been doing every week or so since being in Blackpool, Izzie contacted her neighbour in London to check that everything was okay in West Hampstead. Vinnie assured her all was fine and that he'd been in and picked up the post and free papers from behind her front door and tucked them out of sight on her hallway table.

Working on her laptop on the desk upstairs in the loft, she opened the email from Eddie with full details of the illustrations required by their client and a reiteration that if she journeyed south, she should call in and see them all. Besides that, there were a couple of documents he'd sent on for her to check, print, sign and post back to DAS. There was also a new contract in her emails from the TV production company who had optioned the rights on Rufus's other books; they were interested in the TV rights to his last three books.

It felt good to step back into the design world, even taking the small step of taking on this one job from Eddie gave her the sense that she was picking up the reins of her life, that she was rediscovering herself, the person she had been before her emotional roller coaster ride of the past years.

After checking the contracts and documents and ascertaining that they were standard, just like the ones that had been signed by Rufus in the past, she printed them out and signed them so they were ready to post back. It took her breath away to see her name at the end of the contract in place of Rufus's. But the sadness drifted away again before too long.

The growing feeling was a fizz of excitement at the thought of being productive again, the thought of adding more variety and forward movement to her days.

As she finished up and turned off her laptop, Izzie reached into a desk drawer to unearth the sketch pad that had been in the rucksack in the loft cupboard, making a mental note to show it to Justin when he came around.

'I've got to show you what I found when I was tidying up, Izzie.' Justin said later as she opened the door to him. He handed her an envelope.

'Oh! Photos?'

'Yeah.'

Deciding on a brew whilst they looked at the stack of photos, she sat at the kitchen table.

'Oh, I remember this day,' Izzie studied the photo of her; the bright, jazzy towel she used for the beach a lovely contrast to her lemon cotton sundress, her copper tousled curls glistened in the early evening golden sunlight, her skin very lightly tanned. 'You told me to put my sunglasses on top of my head, so you could see my eyes.' The way the light fell on her made her look amazing. 'Crikey,' Izzie said when he sat beside her to look at the pictures with her. 'You made me look … I don't know…'

'Sexy?'

'Well, kind of, but with all my clothes on!' She felt the heat rise up her neck to her face and a twang in her chest. Silently, she cursed that her mouth came out with that stuff without warning. 'I remember you saying the hour before sunset is the golden hour for the light.'

'It really is. And that's still a good photo.'

'Oh!' The next photo was one that Justin had let her use his camera to take – of him.

Izzie had caught a lovely moment. Justin's eyes were half-closed against the brightness, yet the light shone from within him; his tousled dark blond hair shifted in the breeze, and his slow smile oozed sensuality.

'My God, wait there! You won't believe what I unearthed from upstairs to show you.' She nipped up to the loft and fetched the sketch pad to show him the sketch of the exact same photograph.

He smiled one of his half-smiles and gave a nod when he saw her sketch. 'I remember this.' He studied it for a while. 'You definitely inherited Jack's talent.'

'Thanks.' She took the pad from him and set it aside in order to turn their attention back to Justin's photos.

There were some that he'd taken as possible entries to the local photography competition. One was the weather competition. There were stunning sunsets, rainbows over the sea, and one that had won him third place in the over-eighteens section: white lightning against the dark backdrop of the promenade, Blackpool Tower and the sea. He'd been so pleased – there had been thousands of entries. 'This is so good.'

'Do you remember this one?' He handed her a series of photographs of her at the water's edge. Shots of Izzie paddling, then kicking a foot in the air. She'd called to him, 'Come on in, Justin, it's fabulous and warm!'

The sun had caught the myriad of droplets with a prism of light, turning the drops into miniature rainbows. Izzie was laughing, her head thrown back, arms wide, copper curls tossed in the breeze, most of her bikini top and shorts clad figure obscured by the dewdrop splash and jewel like drops of water that spangled the foreground.

'Oh, Justin, that's – well – that's a beautiful shot.' She said that without any vanity, all of her admiration for the rainbow prisms of light. 'I don't think I realised just how beautiful it was at the time. I mean – I knew it was lovely, but...'

A fast flash of the powerful memory, the deserted beach, Justin setting down his camera way back on the flat, dry sand, on top of Izzie's sundress, sunglasses and rucksack, and folding her colourful towel over the top of the pile before dashing into the water to join her.

Following the initial chill, the seawater had felt warm – the sun was relentless and after swimming for a little while, Izzie had stopped and stood, looking around for Justin. Unable to see him, she'd rubbed the salty water from her eyes.

Suddenly, he'd broken from the water behind her and she'd spun about. She had been struck again with just how good-looking he was: water droplets ran down his face, his neck, his chest and he smiled down at her, hands resting either side of her waist. Then he'd leaned down and kissed her, pulled her scantily clad form against his firm body, their arms wrapping around one another.

'You feel so good...' His whisper had sent sensual shockwaves through her, then they'd kissed for what felt like a long time...

Eventually, Izzie had shivered and Justin responded by giving her a squeeze. 'Let's get out and get warmed up.'

After only a few minutes, they had been warm again, Izzie wrapped in her towel whilst she slipped off her wet things then pulled on her sundress. She'd unearthed her sun lotion from her rucksack and reapplied it to her fair skin.

She returned from the powerful memory to take a longer look at the photo where she kicked up the wave.

'That's a truly fabulous photograph, Justin.'

'Sometimes the magic happens when you least expect it.' He shrugged, gave a wry smile, and added, 'And sometimes it takes hours of watching and waiting for the right moment, and sometimes it still never happens.'

'It was such a good day.'

At that moment, her phone buzzed, her mother's name flashing up on the screen. Izzie grimaced. 'S'cuse me?'

'Sure.' He reached into his pocket and palmed his phone. 'I've a call to make, too. I'll make it in the front room?'

She held up her thumb and greeted her mother, then proceeded to drink her tea whilst she listened to her mother's monthly monologue of holidays, cruises, safaris, how good life was and how Izzie should have moved out there, but it was her loss. She made a hmmm sound every now and again, nothing more was expected of her – or wanted.

Valerie went on to say that David was much better now than he had been, and that his breathing seemed to be back to normal. Before she signed off, she did ask Izzie if she was well and whether Rufus's estate was worth much. That question annoyed her so she said she didn't know yet. If she'd been brave enough, she'd have told her mother it was none of her business. Then, shortly afterwards, Val said, 'Right, got to go. I'll be away next week, so I'll phone when we're back.'

The call finished, Izzie searched out Justin and found him looking out of the window, his call obviously done with too.

'Hi.' She stood beside him in the front bay window. 'Mum phones once a month to let me know what a fabulous life they have, and where they've been on holiday lately.'

'Some things don't change, then.' He gave a wry smile. 'Shall we shoot to town?'

Izzie nodded, realising that Justin was one of the only people who knew that she had opted to stay in the UK and live with her grandparents rather than move to South Africa with her mother and stepfather, David.

From the moment he'd married her mother, David had attempted to discipline Izzie, his favourite mantra being that 'children should be seen and not heard'. The resentment Izzie felt towards him for stepping way too quickly into her beloved dad's shoes had never ebbed.

But it wasn't just that – as soon as David entered their lives, her mother had less and less time for Izzie.

In response, she rebelled at every opportunity; she understood now, with hindsight, that as a child she had likely been influenced by her nan's dislike of him. The man had, after all, taken the place of Tom, Molly's son, in the lives of Izzie and Val within a very short space of time. Izzie remembered the words *'indecent'* and *'immoral'* escaping from her nan's lips; she hadn't known what the words meant, but it was easy to gather from the tone of voice that neither of the words were compliments.

'I gather you don't miss your mum and David, then?' Justin asked whilst driving towards the shops in Blackpool, and she thought how she certainly never regretted moving in with her grandparents. The bungalow always felt more like home after David moved into the family home – and she certainly felt more welcome at Nan's.

'It sounds awful, but I don't. They only bother about one another so there wasn't room for an interloper in their lives.' She blew out and shuddered. 'I can't stand David. I always had the feeling he was hovering, ready to step into Dad's shoes, like they'd already been having an affair or something. It was just weeks after Dad died that David McMoneyGrabber moved into *our* house.' She sighed. 'I know I was young, but even at six, it just felt so wrong. I know Nan was shocked too. I think I picked up on that.' She glanced at him as he drove, 'Tell you the truth, I was happy when Mum and David went off on their travels and then settled in South Africa.'

At fifteen she'd already spent as much time as she could at her grandparents' home, and as much time as she could with Justin and his pals.

'I think all my rebelling arose from David laying down the law constantly.'

She had been a wild teenager and during those years she had struggled emotionally. In the cold face of her mother's slavish agreement with David's attempts at discipline, turning to her nan had felt like her only option. Nan allowed her the freedom to make her own mistakes... Her friendship with Justin added stability to the mix and the change had ultimately brought balance back to her life.

It was freeing, Izzie realised, to know for certain that she had done the right thing by always making for Nan and Grandpop's when she needed somewhere to escape to.

And then she realised that she was beginning to feel more energised and attributed writing down her thoughts to helping her journey back into mental shape.

How strange, she thought, that beginning to keep a notebook, as her nan had, should give her the sense that she was beginning to get herself back on track. She realised too that the optimism she felt bubbling anew may be because she had only herself to please – there was no longer the daily need to make sure that Rufus was happy. She could admit now, too, that what had begun as a pleasure during her marriage had sadly become a burden by the final months and the guilt that truth gave rise to was helped by recognising it; she made a mental note to write that down, too.

They returned to the bungalow sometime later, Justin helping Izzie in with her bags of decorating supplies and tins of paint.

'My folks have a pasting table, if you want, I could bring it and come help tomorrow? I've a day off. Or we could make a start now, if you've no other plans?'

'Great!' Izzie agreed on the condition that she made dinner for them both nights and that they read some more of Molly's notebook when they knocked off.

Chapter Twenty-Four

Molly

Blackpool, Monday November 27, 1944

My Dear Diary, one thing I have discovered about being a new mum is that there isn't much room for self-indulgence anymore. I can't remember what I did with my time before Tom but I love being a mum.

I popped over to see Enid and Agnes earlier and they seem to be managing the work between them just fine with Lillian's help. Agnes says she likes living in the guest house as she likes the company. We shared a pot of tea and then Tom was getting grisly so we said our goodbyes and nipped back home.

There was a letter behind the door addressed to Mrs Molly Blackshaw and I was relieved that this time it was a hand-addressed envelope, not an official one.

Whilst I fed Tom, I read the letter, which turned out to be from Jack's mother.

Dear Molly,

What good news to hear that baby Tom has joined the family. Thank you for letting us know. I will have strong words with our Jack for not telling us straight away. That's men for you, although I'm allowing that perhaps he is unable to write.

We've settled in Shaw, and it'll do us here. At least we're close enough to friends to get together now and again. As any parent, all we hope is that the twins and Beth return home safe. We've had word that Joe was injured recently and that he will be sent to convalesce, his arm was badly broken during a mission and he is unable to function normally just now. We are so proud of all three of them for doing their bit. Beth is still working on the farm in Yorkshire and adores it. She tells us she has fallen in love with the farmer's son! So, if Beth gets her way, we will have another marriage in the family, and no doubt more babies to follow Tom.

I will sign off now and just before I go, I must say that we would love to receive a photo of Tom if at all possible, and once travel becomes easier, Frank and I would like to visit our new grandson. Thank you again for writing and hopefully like you say, we will meet soon.

Best wishes,

Mrs Elizabeth Blackshaw.

Jack's mum sounded friendly in her letter. I pushed it into the pocket of my pinny whilst I pondered her words.

Her letter left me with a bit of a dilemma. It was obvious she didn't know Jack was missing in action. Should I write and tell her? Or should I leave her with the bliss of ignorance? It seemed to me that Joe hadn't told his parents about Jack being missing – and I already knew from experience that Joe wasn't the best at keeping in touch by letter.

I thought I would ask Dora what she thinks, but I do know that at the end of the day it will be up to me.

I tried to think what Jack would like me to do but that didn't really help either. I thought I would wait another week to see if I had news that he was a prisoner of war. If I didn't hear, I thought it was only fair then to write to Jack's parents and let them know. I thought it was probably better to do that than to leave Joe to tell them.

Because it was on my mind, I wrote the letter and I'll tuck it here, inside my notebook.

My Dear Mr and Mrs Blackshaw,

I recently had word that Jack was missing in action after flying in a raid over France. He and his crew were not heard from after this. I apologise for not telling you straight away, but I desperately wanted to have some hopeful news and thought that by leaving it a little while, I might hear from the authorities that he had surfaced as a POW. I am still very hopeful that this is what has happened, and I will of course write immediately if I get some news.

I am sure that Jack is still alive.

As promised, I will send a photograph of Tom as soon as I have one.

With love and best wishes, your daughter-in-law,

Molly Blackshaw.

When Dora came back from work, I showed her letter, and I said I thought I ought to send it now rather than wait. She agreed and I decided I'd post it the next morning.

'When you get some good news, you can get in touch with them by letter, or send a telegram,' she said.

Blackpool, Tuesday November 28, 1944

I posted it the following morning. I wrapped Tom up warm, put my winter coat on and then pushed the pram onto the promenade. The tide was on the way in; it was mesmerising and somehow watching the waves as they ebbed and flowed eased my constant anxiety over Jack.

I thought how on our very short honeymoon we had visited Starr Gate, seen the sand dunes, been on the Pleasure Beach, taken a long tram ride and walked along the promenade for miles.

They were wonderful memories, but I wanted more, more of Jack.

I closed my eyes and just listened to the waves, and then when Tom started to grizzle, made by way back home.

For a moment I let myself imagine what life would be like if this was it.

If I, like so many other new wives and mothers, would be left alone to raise Tom. I had no doubt that I would manage one way or another just like all the others – I would have no choice. Joe's visit pushed into my mind, I had no doubt that he would step up to the mark as he said and be a good father. But I knew, I knew – for sure – that I will never love Joe the way I had grown to love Jack.

No, if the fates were cruel, and if Jack does not return, I will bring up Tom alone.

Blackpool, Monday December 4, 1944

My Dear Diary, within days of sending the letter to Jack's parents, I received one back.

Dear Molly,

What terribly upsetting news. I cannot tell you how it grieves me. I have no doubt that you will let me know as soon as you can when you hear anything further about Jack. We've had word that Joe has had surgery on his arm, but no other news as yet.

I look forward to receiving a photograph of Tom, and hearing from you anytime you'd like to write.

I will pray for Jack's safe return, and like you say, I am sure he is still alive.

With love and very best wishes,

Elizabeth and Frank Blackshaw.

I don't write every day, my Dear Diary; only when things happen that I think Jack would like to know.

It is sometimes difficult to keep believing he is alive. I had another very brief letter from the RAF in which they stated that they had had no further news of Jack and they were sorry but they had nothing more to tell me at this time. They did say if their investigations turned up any more information, they would let me know.

I passed this news on to Jack's parents, and they wrote a brief letter back thanking me for the news and for the photographs I had sent of Tom.

Blackpool, Wednesday December 27, 1944

I had a wonderful surprise two days ago at Christmas when Elizabeth and Frank turned up to meet their grandson, who to their delight was smiling and laughing. Elizabeth had knitted several pairs of blue bootees for Tom and bought him a small teddy bear with arms and legs that moved. We put the bootees on Tom but that didn't stop him putting his toes in his mouth!

We all settled around Marian's large kitchen table along with Dora and Bill, and I nipped over to the Bing Lea to fetch Enid and Agnes.

Elizabeth confided that Joe wasn't well enough yet to return to service, but he had at last been put in a convalescent home not too far from them. She said that Beth and her boyfriend, the farmer's son, were spending the day with Joe and that they were going to visit him the following day.

Jack's parents were lovely people, Dear Diary, down-to-earth and despite all of their trials, they had a good sense of humour. I thought how Jack would enjoy this get-together. It turned into a lively party despite the lack of turkey, few gifts and a very limited menu and just a drop of gin. The company was splendid and there was much chatting and laughter.

I imagined that Jack would look like his father when he was older; Frank was still a very handsome, slender man, his hair greying slightly at the temples but still dark for the most part. He had the same twinkly dark blue eyes as Jack and it was obvious that he and Elizabeth still thought the world of one another even after what must have been many years together. I could imagine Jack and me being a lot like that, too.

It was late in the evening when they left, and there was much noise and waving out in the street before they drove away in their borrowed vehicle.

Chapter Twenty-Five

Izzie

Blackpool, Monday October 2, 2017

'Looking great, Izzie.' Justin scanned around the front lounge. 'It looks lovely and light.'

They'd spent the entire day papering the room and they'd had plenty of laughs – and some minor disasters. Izzie realised she had far more fun working alongside Justin than she did working alone. The radio had provided background music and both of them had sung along when they knew the words – and Izzie had made them up when she didn't.

Justin laughed as she sang now. 'You do know those are not the words?' He caught the damp cloth she threw him to clean off the pasting table.

'Honey?'

'It's "horny",' he said, laughing whilst he cleaned then closed up the folding table, 'not honey.'

Izzie felt her face heat up. She'd been thinking how hot Justin looked when he laughed.

'Oops.' She caught the rag he threw back towards her. 'I fancy a walk, do you?'

'Sure. Do you want to take a walk to my place? The work's finished now so it's finally ready to show you.'

'Love to.'

———

His house was just a couple of miles walk away along the front.

'It's gorgeous, Justin!' The house was a sturdy redbrick semi with cream-coloured corner stones. The front door opened into a wide hallway and Justin gestured for Izzie to go inside.

'I've more or less got it how I want it now.' He gave her the tour: the kitchen was large, a table at one end, and white cupboards lining the walls at the other. The backsplash was made up of subway tiles and the worktop was dark with little sparkly bits in.

'That's ... so similar to the one I've decided on for the kitchen at Nan's. I love it.'

Izzie wasn't sure if Justin flinched, so quickly asked, 'Did you do any of the work yourself?'

'Some, between jobs, but it works out easier to get my pal in to do most of the work whilst I'm away.'

The lounge was huge and ran the full length of the

house, the doors at the back of the room opening straight onto the luxuriant green garden.

The rooms were plain, the focus on the stunning, enlarged photographs spaced artfully around the walls. There were sunsets, sunrises, beaches, lakes, hills and snow-topped mountains, steaming hot jungles and palm trees on tropical white sand.

'Did – did you take all these?'

'Yeah, they're some of my favourites.' He let her take a good look at the pictures and when she looked towards him gestured towards the stairway.

Justin's bedroom was at the front of the house and overlooked the sea. Noticing the view before anything else, she went to stand in the bay window. 'Oh, Justin, what a view.' The sea was slate-grey with a rim of white frothy peaks in the October twilight, the waxing moon laying a glistening path over the surface of the sea.

The room was painted a cloud soft blue-grey and the bed faced the deep bay window. 'How brilliant. You can sit up in bed and watch the sea.' Izzie took a deep breath of the sea air drifting in through the open window. 'It's perfect.'

He stood beside her and eventually said, 'The view sold the house.'

'It would've for me too.' She glimpsed his slight frown before his expression cleared. She asked, 'Show me the rest?'

Next was Justin's office, which carried through with the plain theme; a desk sporting an angle poise lamp, a thick diary and chair to one side, the walls the palest yellow, giving the impression of the room being bathed in hazy sunlight. A laptop and a couple of screens sat on the desk and three beautiful photographs adorned the wall opposite.

Her heartbeat skipped as she recognised a photograph of herself – the one from that day at the beach. 'Is that...?'

He gave a slight nod. 'Still one of my favourites – one of those happy accident photos. I had it enlarged recently when I unearthed that pack of photos.' He glanced at her. 'I change the pictures around now and again, depending on what I'm working on – I've some of those Lake District photos being transferred to canvas just now, too.'

Despite the fact that Izzie was scarcely visible in the picture, its presence in his office caused a strange pang inside that she couldn't christen.

Another dramatic enlargement was of lightning on the sea front at Blackpool, icy jagged light reflected in the wet pavements along the promenade.

'Pure drama,' she said as she studied the sharp lines, the incredible moment he'd captured.

There were shelves above his desk with labelled CDs and many photo albums. Over to one side was a beautiful wooden filing cabinet. 'Looks like a great work space, Justin.'

After peeking into the bathroom, which was mainly white with a row of bright blue tiles running through the centre of the white ones, Izzie followed him back down to the kitchen.

There was something so solid about his home; Izzie thought all of his colour and décor choices were similar to those she had picked out for the bungalow. She wondered if he'd noticed their ridiculously similar taste.

'I love what you've done, Justin.'

'Thanks.'

'How long have you lived here?'

'A few years.' He opened the back door to show her the garden, which was mostly lawn with shrubs around the edges. 'There was a lot of work to do on it, so when I was home at first, I stayed at my folks' house and worked here till I'd got the bedroom fit to live in.' Justin slid his phone from his jeans pocket and checked the screen. Izzie had the feeling he'd just remembered something.

'Are you okay?'

'Yeah, Mick's having a barbeque tomorrow evening. He sent a reminder. Would you like to come?'

'Will he mind?'

'Course not. He said to invite you.'

'I'd love to then, thanks. Do you want to share that casserole I put on to slow cook first thing this morning? I'm hungry.'

'Sounds great.' He smiled, grabbed a bottle of wine from the kitchen and they made their way from his house back to hers.

They ate, drank and again admired the work they'd completed. Then, at Izzie's suggestion, they settled in to read some more of Molly's notebook.

Chapter Twenty-Six

Molly

Blackpool, Tuesday May 8, 1945

Dear Diary, Tom is now just over seven months old and he is a constant source of delight. He is also undoubtedly the apple of Enid's eye.

And today ... Tom's excited shrieks and laughter reflected the mood in Blackpool, in the whole country.

The news is that the war in Europe is over. It was the welcome trigger for so much celebration.

Winston Churchill spoke on the radio and the allied world listened. He said, *'We may allow ourselves a brief period of rejoicing, but let us not forget for a moment the toils and efforts that lie ahead.'*

'It'll be a better world for the likes of Tom, God willing,'

Bill said. 'All we need now is his daddy to make it home safe. That'll just be the icing on the cake, Molly.'

'It would.' I was almost overcome with emotion, but concentrated on Tom, lifting him from the small tub of water and wrapping him in the soft, warm towel.

To the world I present a face of hope, of love for Jack, the fitter armourer – then lately Flight Engineer who risked his life by joining his flight crew.

But inside, all the months of silence lay heavy. It doesn't bode well.

Dora, her parents, Agnes, Enid, myself and Tom had gathered in the back room of the Bing Lea Boarding House and we all raised a glass of Bill's rum – it made my eyes water – and toasted the end of the war.

Baby Tom, pink and gurgling from his bath, was rolling about and kicking his feet in the middle of us on the rug. The radio played lively band music and we had a warm and wonderful night of chatter and celebration.

Outside, more ebullient celebrations could be heard. The streets were full and when Dora and Katherine went to investigate, they returned to say that all the neighbours were out in the street, dancing and singing and drinking.

We went to join them for an hour, and when Tom became restless, I said my goodnights and slipped away indoors to put him to bed in the cot in our room at Marian's.

The noise outside was endless, but it made me smile, Dear Diary. After so much whining from air raid sirens, the sounds of damaged aircraft struggling back to base at Squires Gate, the endless streams of trainees marching on the promenade...

Happy celebration sounds were so wonderful.

I watched Tom sleep, spellbound. I noticed, too, that as his baby fine hair grew, thickened and darkened slightly, he began to resemble Jack more and more. It was a comfort and a painful observation.

A comfort because I love him so much, and a pain because I love his father so very much too and badly wanted to get to know him better than I have done. I feel as though we've had so little time together.

I'm happy, ecstatic that the war is over, but I am so, so sad for myself, and for all those who have lost a loved one, for the gaping holes left in their lives. It's a happy time, but still I cried myself to sleep.

Chapter Twenty-Seven

Izzie

Blackpool, Monday October 2, 2017

Closing the notebook, Izzie stared with wonder at the inner cover, the pages that peeped out of the edges very slightly when it was closed, the mementoes fastened securely within the pages. She thought she would treasure forever her nan's diary and the treasure trove of photographs, emotions and memories inside.

'You really never know what folk have gone through, do you?' Izzie asked, refilling their glasses with the Malbec Justin had brought along.

'You're so right. It's crazy. All that past and no one knows about it.'

'Except us.' She sipped her drink and then clinked her glass to Justin's.

'I'm glad you've shared it with me, Izzie.' His eyes shone with sincerity. 'It's a pretty amazing journal of tough times.' He took a deep breath. 'And having known Jack and Molly, that makes reading the book all the more meaningful.'

'You're the only one...' She hesitated before continuing. 'The only one I'd feel comfortable sharing it all with.'

He raised a brow. 'Because I knew them?'

Suddenly, for a reason she couldn't pinpoint, Izzie felt a lump form in her throat. 'You were part of their lives, Justin, and a huge part of mine.'

There was a definite flicker of pain in his eyes that time. She imagined it was for the obvious reason that Molly and Jack were gone now. She felt something similar within herself, a sense of loss, of yearning.

A yearning for a past that should have been – but one that wouldn't happen now, she thought. Again, those words, *we made our choices*. Those words that had rankled her before echoed in her mind again now – made her want to yowl with the unfairness of what he'd said.

He'd made the choice. She'd had to face it. In a strange way she was grateful for the reminder that she shouldn't allow her feelings to soften towards him too much further.

This was casual – *casual*, she reminded herself – and she could cope with that.

Whatever happened here would stay here. They could revisit their past together, work together, have some fun together and then they would both move back to their real lives.

'Do you remember the time Nan and Grandpop went off to Morecombe Bay on a coach trip?'

'Remind me?' He gave her a wonky smile and took a long swallow of his wine; Izzie had the feeling Justin knew full well it'd been the first time they'd made love. 'Wasn't that the day you finished that sketch of me?'

'Yes.' Izzie nodded. 'Nan told me that she and Grandpop were going on a coach trip and they'd not be back till late on.'

Izzie remembered her nan putting her glasses case into her handbag and snapping it closed. 'There's a meat and tatter pie in the fridge that you and Justin can have later.'

'Aw my favourite. Thanks, Nan.' Izzie had hugged her nan. At eighty-six, she'd still looked so spritely in her flowery bright green tunic blouse with pink roses, bright pink trousers and brand new, *'very comfy'* trainers. 'You look joyous.'

'You know I love my colours.' She'd chuckled and taken hold of Izzie's forearm. 'Izzie, I've seen the way you and Justin look at one another – and I'm happy for you both – but do get yourself on the pill, sweetheart; there's no point in taking risks. I'm sure you want a family one day – but it's best when you plan it.'

Izzie had been speechless, then thankful. 'Thank God it's you saying that and not my mother.'

'Ah!' Nan had flapped her free hand. 'She'd love it if you slipped up. She could play the martyr card because her daughter is … well, human! She'd paint Justin as the devil.' At that, she'd chuckled and so had Izzie.

'Thanks, Nan. I'll sort it.' She already had – just in case –

but somehow it hadn't felt right to say anything when there was no need.

'I like Justin, always have.'

Whilst they'd waited for Grandpop to finish getting ready, Izzie had told her nan about Justin's plans to travel. 'Oh, good on him, he should grasp all the opportunities life offers.'

'That's what I think, too.'

'And what are your plans, Izzie? Will you travel with him?'

'No, my plans are the opposite, if anything. I want to live and work in London – something arty – and make gorgeous clothes in my spare time for special orders, or just for myself.'

'Well, I'm sure you'll do it all.'

'But will you mind? Will you mind me moving out?'

In a typical Nan gesture, she'd batted Izzie's hand. 'The way I look at it, I've had – in fact, I've still got – the best of everything. I've got Jack and I've had you for the best part of your life. It all went a long way to making up for your dad going too young. I don't know many at eighty-six who spend so much time with their granddaughter.' She'd laughed. 'No, Izzie, when you go, you go with my blessing. You'll know when the time is right, and I'll always be here.'

Izzie remembered nodding, swamped with gratitude towards her nan. Always, the freedom to come and go was given; both on a daily basis, and for the future in a wider sense.

'Right ho!' Grandpop had emerged from the bedroom then looking as smart as a tack. His hair was pure white and his dark blue eyes sparkled with fun. He had still been incredibly handsome, even in his late eighties. 'Are you ready to rumble, our Molly?' He'd looked at his watch. 'We've half an hour to get to the coach stop.'

Laughing, Nan had dropped a quick kiss on Izzie's cheek and linked Grandpop's ready arm.

'By George, Jack, you're a handsome devil.' She'd squeezed his arm tightly. 'Let's go and paint the town red!'

Izzie had seen them to the door. She had always loved the banter between the two of them and how they revelled in one another's company, even after all the years they'd been together.

'Don't do anything I wouldn't do!' she'd called after the two of them.

'Making no promises!' Molly had called over her shoulder. 'And neither is this fellah!' Their laughter rang out in the quiet neighbourhood avenue.

Izzie had watched them down the road, full of admiration for the two of them. They really were her favourite people in the whole world. Besides Justin. *The three* of them were her favourite people in the whole world, she amended mentally…

Izzie came back to the present. 'Yes, I was so proud of that drawing, I'd sprayed it with fixative to keep it from smudging.' She'd then propped it on the back windowsill in the sun lounge, thrilled at the end result and heeded Grandpop's 'Let a good thing be' advice when painting or drawing.

'We'd been dating about four weeks,' she said, slipping easily back into the memory, along with Justin this time…

'Come and take a look?' She took Justin's hand as soon as he arrived and led him to the back of the house. 'What do you think? I've just finished it.'

He didn't respond immediately and Izzie heard him take a deep breath.

'I think...' He hesitated. 'I think it's fabulous. And ... I think you love me.'

Izzie laughed, turning to face him. 'You can't tell that from a sketch!' But she suspected he was right.

'I can tell a lot from a picture.' His mouth covered hers softly, then with pure passion, his arms closing around her back, holding her tight.

The kiss sent ripples through Izzie. She reached up and rested her palms on his shoulders, then ran her fingers around his neck, increasing the pressure of his mouth on hers, whilst his palms moulded her against him.

'Justin...' She gasped. 'Let's go up in the loft?'

'Seriously? Are you sure?' he whispered against her mouth.

She gave a nervous laugh. 'I'm sure I want to... I'm just not sure my legs will get me up the ladder!'

'I don't have any.' Justin grimaced, patting his pocket. 'You don't need anything.'

His green eyes opened wider with surprise, darkened with need. 'You...'

'I'm on the pill.'

He raised his mouth from hers, palms shifting to hold her face gently in his fingers. 'I'll take care of you, Izzie,' he whispered, then pulled her close in a fierce hug. 'But I don't think I can carry you up the ladder...'

They both laughed and Izzie said, 'Follow me, then?'

He looked, she thought, as though he couldn't believe it was happening – dazed – as if it was happening to someone else. Justin gave a nod and gestured that she go first into the hall and up the ladder before him.

Izzie stood beside the loft opening once she was at the top and held her arms wide when he joined her.

'Izzie, are you sure about this?' He set his hands on her waist. 'Really sure?'

'Are you?' she countered. 'Because I really am sure.'

'Yes,' he whispered, his mouth covering hers, and laughing along with her when he scooped her off her feet, pretending to stagger as he moved them towards the bed. 'God, you're a weight!'

She loved that he made her laugh at what should be the most romantic time of her life, that he was still Justin, her friend ... about to become lover...

———————

Izzie brought herself out of the memory that seemed so long ago and moved towards the mug tree. 'Fancy a brew?'

Justin's pupils had dilated at the shared memory, eyes darkening.

'Right now, I fancy you.' He smiled that slow, face lighting smile and Izzie thought he looked mildly surprised at the words leaving him.

She turned to face him. They'd kissed – properly kissed

– just a couple of times, but why not repeat the embrace, she thought. Moving closer almost without realising, Izzie let the magnetic pull in the small space between them close the gap. She raised her mouth and he lowered his for a brief, gentle kiss. Then Izzie threaded her hands around his neck and his eyes searched hers for a moment as she flattened herself to him, gasping when his arms pulled her hard against him and the kiss deepened. It felt so good to be held in his arms, to be kissed.

Izzie silenced the little voice in her head that asked, *What are you doing?* Silenced it with the sure knowledge that he wasn't about to hurt her, that this was an easy, casual relationship – temporary, with no need for either of them to think beyond the moment. She was in control of her situation this time. If they wanted to kiss and share a hot embrace, why not? If they wanted to take it further ... well, there was no one to stop them – only themselves. And if they didn't – that was their choice too.

Her legs turned to jelly when Justin ran his hand over her hip and she arched to him, her fingers moving around his back so she could get closer still.

Izzie was ready to let herself drift off in a cloud of sensation when the loud, insistent *rat-a-tat-tat* of the front door knocker shocked her back to earth with a bump.

'Yoo hoo!' pierced through the flapping letterbox. 'Izzie! Can you help me?'

As Izzie eased away from Justin, she saw him close his eyes.

'I know that voice,' he said. 'Mum.'

Taking a deep breath, Izzie called, 'Just a minute!' She

straightened her dishevelled top and went to answer the call for help.

'Hi,' she said as she opened the door wide. 'Are you okay?'

'Can you come and look at my hoover, Izzie? I think I might have blown a fuse and Robert's out. I spilt something and need to get it up.'

'I've got some fuses, hang on.' Izzie gestured for Linda to follow her inside. At the same time, Justin strolled out of the kitchen.

'Hello, Mum, is it that old hoover again? I'll come and take a look for you.'

Linda beamed. 'I didn't realise you were here, son. Thanks, that'd be great as I've made a right mess. I think it's blowing out the muck instead of picking it up.'

On his way out, Justin reached down and squeezed Izzie's hand, his smile rueful. 'I've got them a new one for Christmas but now I wish I'd brought it over early.'

Izzie smiled, the yearning in her belly turning to a dull ache.

'I'll pick you up for Mick and Janey's barbeque, then, tomorrow night?' He shoved his fingers back through his hair.

'Sure. Thanks for your help.'

He dropped a fast kiss on her cheek and said cheerio.

———————

After a busy morning of catching up with Eddie and having catch-up chats with Ruby and a couple of other friends at

DAS, she began work on the first watercolour of the collection, setting up the job in the sun lounge across the back of the bungalow, where the light was perfect for painting.

Izzie also made a quick phone call to the decorator that both Justin and his parents had recommended. She thought that if she had some help she could enjoy easing back into the work for DAS, whilst still overseeing and doing some of the work herself in the bungalow.

Before Justin called for her that evening, Izzie tidied her loose curls, and flicked on some mascara and just a smudge of grey pencil around her eyes. It was a warm evening for early-October, so she settled for a white vest-style top beneath her blue and black checked shirt, dark jeans and ankle boots. She checked her reflection fleetingly as she went to answer the door to Justin.

'Hi.' He gave her a small smile and held his hand towards her. 'Are you okay to walk? It's not far.'

'Love to.' She slung her large handbag over her shoulder; it concealed all she needed for the evening, including a bottle of chilled fizz for the party table.

Any nervousness Izzie entertained at going along to Mick's barbeque was short-lived.

She was surprised that some of the same crowd that she used to belong to were there and pleased when they welcomed her as if she'd never been away.

'Izzie! Great to see you!' Janey hugged her. 'Come through to the back.'

Janey looked almost the same as she had during their lazy crazy days on the beach with a short, dark, pixie haircut, a tiny, quick moving frame and a big generous smile.

'Oh, Janey, this is lovely,' Izzie said, stepping into the welcoming garden. It was lit with strings of lantern lights along the top of the perimeter fences, background music played softly, and delicious smells rose from where Mick greeted her at the barbeque.

'Justin, hiya mate! Hi, Izzie! Great you could make it. Are you back to stay?' Mick asked as he flipped burgers and turned the skewers of peppers and mushrooms, his movements practised. 'Sorry to hear your nan passed.'

'Thanks, Mick. I'm back for a while,' Izzie said as she took a plate from Janey, who told her to help herself to nibbles. There was a table topped with salad, bread rolls, crisps, nuts, alcohol and glasses.

'Izzie, you remember Kay?' Justin guided the titian-haired, expectant young woman towards her. 'She married Tony.'

'Wow.' Izzie clasped Kay's hand. The two of them had been particularly close in the past, sharing their secrets and dreams. 'Congratulations on your upcoming baby.'

'Thanks,' Kay said as she patted her bump.

Izzie sensed some restraint in Kay, but couldn't understand why. It was only later, when everyone had eaten, drank and socialised, and Kay and Tony got ready to leave, that Izzie got the chance to speak to her alone.

Kay had already hugged Justin cheerio where he stood chattering with Tony and Mick so Izzie intercepted Kay on her way to the back gate.

'Are we okay?' she asked the friend she'd adored, but

lost touch with – mainly because that strand of her past might have led to her having to discuss Justin. It had all been about self-preservation, not deliberately intended to upset anyone.

'Just – just, don't…' She grimaced. 'Oh, it's none of my business.'

'Kay…' Izzie put her palm over the other woman's forearm. 'Have I upset you?'

'Not now… In the past.'

'How?' She frowned, desperate to know what she'd done to cause Kay's shuttered response to her – especially when everyone else had been so welcoming. 'I'm sorry I didn't keep in touch.'

'You – you and Justin. Are you an item again?'

'We're more friends than anything else now,' Izzie said. 'We've both got our own plans come the New Year.'

'Well, that's a good thing if you can do that without hurting—'

'You ready to make a move?' Tony said, interrupting as he dropped a full, fast kiss on Kay's lips and bowing like she was royalty at the exit gate. 'After you, milady! I've an early shift.'

Laughing at Tony's antics, Izzie wished them both goodbye, hoped that Kay's smile and wave meant she was close to forgiving Izzie for whatever she'd done wrong and that they might get back to being friends again soon.

As the evening drew to a close, four of them remained drinking and sharing stories as they sat around a small firepit, the orange glow warming them. 'Oh! Izzie! Do you remember those sketches you did of us all?'

'I do! Funnily enough, I found them at my nan's bungalow the other day.'

'I'd love to see them. I remember them being brilliant,' Janey said.

'You might not think that now, but I'll do some copies if you like?'

'Great. Thanks.' She lowered her voice. 'I'm making a scrapbook for Mick for Christmas. Justin's helping me out with photos from back when we hung out on the beach and since – but the sketches would be a great addition.'

'You should write out some of those truth or dares that we all had so much fun with.' Izzie laughed and caught Justin looking over at her. Once again, she saw something – sadness? regret? – in his eyes, then it was gone and a smile hitched one side of his mouth. She thought she must have imagined it ... unless ... unless he regretted not meeting her *that* day? A spear of pain shot through her and she squashed it down.

It had been all about choices – and he'd made his. And hers.

'Oh, what a great idea! Hang on.' Janey grabbed a napkin and a stray pen. Keeping her voice low, she said, 'Tell me those you can remember.' Izzie did, including the one where Mick had to run around on the beach singing 'The Hills are Alive', then she said, 'You know, in case I remember any more, we should swap mobile numbers. I'll ask Justin if he can remember any, too.'

'Fab. It's great to see you two together again.' Janey raised her coffee cup in a toast like gesture. 'You always look like you just – I don't know – belong?'

Something painful pinched inside Izzie, she took a deep breath and forced the pain away.

'It is good to reconnect,' Izzie agreed, sure that she didn't need to explain their casual relationship to anyone.

'So, tell me everything you're up to these days.' Janey asked.

'Mainly I'm working on Nan's bungalow. I'm also starting work on a remote commission for the company I've worked for since moving to London.' She finished her drink. 'It feels good to be picking up the reins of my life again.'

'So, you worked for Rufus Dean? He was your boss? And your husband?' Janey asked, then continued, 'I remember Kay told us about that. She read it in one of those glossies she loves – I think your hubby's books had just been turned into a TV series?'

'Yes.' It was strange to have her worlds overlap, especially so because she'd always purposely kept them separated.

In fact, until recently, she'd kept her world with Justin completely severed from her thoughts, her memories…

'And he died? Your husband?'

'Yes, in 2016. It'll be two years come next January.'

'Sorry to hear that.' Janey's hand covered hers. Izzie smiled in response and said, 'I'm okay.' And the thing was –

she was okay. What used to be a debilitating mixture of guilt, misery and sadness had receded, replaced by a dull ache.

'Tell me all about your wedding plans,' Izzie said to Janey, and she was only too happy to share details of all of her preparations. 'Did Justin tell you he's doing our photos as a gift to us?' She beamed from ear to ear. 'Can you imagine – blooming famous celebrity and wildlife photographer – doing *our* wedding!' She put her hand to her chest. 'Isn't it brilliant? And he sorted someone local to work with him in the day and then carry on and do the evening reception.' She smiled. 'That's so he can kick back and enjoy himself in the evening.'

'That's amazing – a great gift.'

Justin looked at his watch just then. 'I need to make a move. I've a pretty busy day tomorrow, folks. I'm shooting Eloise Porter's wedding in Manchester.'

'*The* Eloise Porter?' Mick raised his brow. 'From the girl-band?' He whistled and then chuckled. 'She took a shine to Justin here and her agent set him up doing their publicity shots when they first started and I went along to help lug his gear. She was doing the hair-flicky thing at Justin!' He laughed.

'Always a charmer.' Izzie immediately shut down a slight pang of jealousy, because Eloise Porter was marrying someone else.

'Imagine that.' Jayne clapped her hands together. 'Me and Mick'll have the same wedding photographer as celebs like Eloise Porter.'

'You will,' Justin agreed. 'But hopefully there won't be

helicopters overhead trying to get a scoop at yours. Folks! It's been fabulous, but we need to make tracks,' he said again once the excitement from his news died down.

He held out his hand to Izzie and they thanked their hosts. Izzie gave them each a hug and Justin promised to return the invite soon.

'It was a great night,' Izzie said as they walked home. She let the sea breeze blow her hair back as they neared the bungalow. 'What time do you need to leave in the morning?'

'I'll leave about ten. There's a full timetable I've to keep to for about ten hours. I don't suppose you would tell anyone, but just in case, what I'm working on tomorrow is between you, me, Mick and Janey.'

'Mum's the word, I'll not tell a soul.' She slipped her arm around his waist as he put his along her shoulder.

Chapter Twenty-Eight

Izzie

Blackpool, October, 2017

Over the following weeks, each of them had intermittent work – Justin's sometimes involved relatively local travel and Izzie's work for Eddie she mainly took care of in the mornings.

Their resolve to keep free of commitment worked well for them both. Usually, they saw one another every few days; sometimes they kissed, sometimes they just enjoyed being together. There was no talk of a future together, just their individual plans.

One mild night in late October, they walked through the illuminations together, ate chips, and Izzie remembered reading in Nan's notebook that her grandparents had done that, too.

And when they tired, they jumped on a tram to take them all the way back home, just like her grandparents had done.

All through November, Izzie felt herself growing stronger. Her connection with Eddie, Ruby and her friends at DAS continued, the plans firming up for her to return to work in early January.

By late November, she had finished the set of paintings for Eddie early and their client was happy with the photographs of her work.

As Eddie was handling all the liaising, Izzie couriered the work down to his offices so they would be ready for delivery in the New Year.

Her friendships with the beach crowd also grew and enriched her life. Even Kay had warmed up towards her again after Justin invited them all over to his one Saturday night, a week before Mick and Janey's wedding, to celebrate his birthday.

Izzie thought whatever had bothered Kay had obviously sorted itself out and let the niggle go completely.

The day of Janey and Mick's December wedding finally came; Izzie thought how it had seemed an age away when Justin first mentioned it. She thought, too, of her nan's diary, where she'd said that time sped up the less time there was. How true that was.

Izzie smiled at the warmth that bloomed inside her at the thought of Nan, at the realisation that Nan and Grandpop would always be woven through the fabric of her own life.

Justin called at the bungalow early on the morning of the 23rd December.

'I'm on my way to Janey's now, Izzie, as she wants photos of herself and family getting ready.' He patted his pocket. 'I've got their photo list. You still okay if I pick you up after I drop my gear back home before the reception? It'll be just before seven?'

'Absolutely, thanks, that'd be great.'

'You look lovely, Izzie!' Justin said when she answered the door later that evening. He took hold of her fingers and held out his arm. 'Give us a twirl?'

Delighted at Justin's response, she spun around. The electric blue dress belled then draped from her curves and silver, high heeled strappy sandals completed her look.

'Will I do, then?'

Well aware Justin was used to the stunning presence of model-like beauties at his side, Izzie hadn't bothered to compete with such loveliness. Instead, she had gone for simplicity, hair in a cascade of loose curls, clipped back at one side, and minimal make-up as she still hadn't expanded on the eyeliner and mascara that had hitched a ride in her bag when she left London in a hurry.

A quick trip out to Cleveleys had uncovered the gorgeous dress and the flirty silver sandals tucked away in a divine clothes shop.

'Are you sure I'll do? I think I could do with a lot more make-up.' In a moment of honesty, Izzie said, 'Lorna always looks so beautiful in the magazines.'

He gave a half smile and shook his head. 'She does, but I don't suppose you have ever been kissed by someone with about an inch of make-up all over their face and lips? A fake tan that leeches onto your white sheets and eyelashes that crawl down her cheek during the night?'

'No.' Izzie laughed. 'That's something I haven't done, yet.'

'I wouldn't recommend it as it gets messy, but if you do decide to try it, don't wear white.'

Izzie couldn't help laughing again, the vision of fake-tan-stained sheets just a bit too grim to do anything else.

A smile tilted his mouth. 'Your hair suits you like this.' His fingertips touched the soft copper curls where they fell against her cheek, his eyes held hers and Izzie's stomach flipped in response.

Dear God, it felt just the same as it used to, being so close to him; it felt electric, as though tingles zipped around inside her… She wanted to control the sensations, but was unable.

He smiled suddenly, as though something occurred to him. 'Do you still like to dance?'

'I do! Especially at weddings.'

'Fantastic.' He gestured towards the front of the bungalow. 'I'll go watch out the front for the cab, should be here in a minute.' With that, he left her to her final touches.

After rooting through her handbag for another new purchase, Izzie added bright blue crystal earrings, and applied a bit more mascara to her eyelashes.

That stray sensation, the spear of lust and desire that had shot through her when Justin touched her hair had sent her emotions scattering in all directions.

'How are you doing? The cab just texted to say it's a minute away.'

'Should I wear this?' She held up the blue crystal teardrop necklace that had come with the earrings.

His eyebrows raised and Izzie wondered whether that was appreciation she saw in his expression.

'Let me see?' He took the necklace from her and gestured for her to stand in front of the hall mirror. His knuckles rested against her neck and shoulders as he held the delicate necklace in place. 'I think it looks good.'

As Justin spoke, his breath broke against the skin on the back of her neck, shifting her hair just a little, and that in turn sent a sexy shiver down her spine.

'Would you fasten it for me please?'

Izzie had to take a deep breath in order to still the crazy hot quiver at his closeness.

'Aren't you taking a suitcase with you?'

Izzie laughed. 'Just a little handbag.'

'You did remember that we'll be staying in the hotel overnight, didn't you?'

'I think it slipped past me. Hang on, I'll grab my toothbrush and something to change into tomorrow.'

'Mick and Janey's idea was to have as many guests as possible at breakfast tomorrow morning.'

Everything fitted easily into her well-used rucksack. Gathering up the small silver evening bag she'd bought with the silver shoes, she took her things to the front door. 'Hang on, before we leave...' Justin held up his phone, 'Let's get a photo of us both dressed up?'

'I want one, too.' Izzie unearthed her phone and got Justin to hold it at arm's length for a selfie. He took three on the trot 'just for good measure'.

'Fantastic.' He checked the screen of his phone and then smiled broadly. 'Our carriage awaits.'

Whilst Izzie locked up the bungalow, Justin took charge of carrying their overnight bags.

She was having a job not to stare at him; he looked *so* hot in his black suit. The sharp white shirt and black and grey striped tie was the perfect foil for his fit frame. His slightly overlong wavy dark blond hair, sexy green eyes, and easy smile was also a heck of a combination.

They chatted for the rest of the journey – inconsequential stuff. It was a heady mixture of easy friendship spiced with sensual sparks.

They reached the large hotel reception on the promenade in Blackpool as other guests were arriving, the bride and groom standing side-by-side just inside the magnificent venue, greeting each newcomer in turn.

'Justin, great, you can just relax this evening instead of

being on duty!' Mick grinned from ear to ear. 'And thanks for today.'

The men shook hands warmly. 'I'll get on with processing your photos first thing tomorrow, Mick, Janey.'

Janey hugged Justin and thanked him for everything. 'It's a fabulous gift, Justin, thanks.'

Then she hugged Izzie and Izzie told her how beautiful she looked in her ecru lace gown.

Justin rested his hand at the base of Izzie's spine and they each took the proffered champagne from the waiting staff as they entered the reception room. He guided her to a large round table where they knew some of the others, and once settled, he leaned towards her and said, 'I'll nip out to the front desk and get our keys.'

'Cheers.' She raised her glass and smiled as Justin headed out of the room.

The event organiser announced that the buffet was open, and guests were free to help themselves; they also announced that the staff would be circulating with champagne.

'You coming to get some grub?' the young woman beside her asked.

'Oh, I definitely will, yes, but I'll wait for Justin.'

'No need to wait, I'm here,' he said as he materialised at her side. 'Do you want to get something now?'

'Definitely, I'm starving.'

He gestured for her to move in front of him, and as they made their way to the buffet, he leaned down and said quietly, 'I'll give you a room key when we sit back down.'

At the sizzling sensation of his breath against her shoulder, Izzie picked up a plate and shuffled around the table, which was groaning with food.

'I'm not sure I trust myself to keep my hands off you seeing you look the way you do.' His voice was a hoarse whisper when he spoke.

'You know what to say to a woman.' *Always did*, the thought occurred. As his words set that hot sensation off inside her once again, her awareness at him being close was almost unbearable.

———————————

They ate and chatted to one another and to the others seated at their table. Background music cushioned the sounds of plates and cutlery, glasses clinking and general talking and laughter.

Once everyone had finished eating, and the speeches had been applauded, the staff quickly and efficiently cleared the tables and the guests were invited to surround the dance floor whilst the new bride and groom took their first dance.

Standing beside Justin, his arm resting along her shoulder, Izzie could not help but smile up at him.

Once the couple finished their first dance, the DJ invited everyone to join the dance floor and Izzie's heart gave a little leap – no, a *huge* leap – when Justin took her hand so they could jive in amongst many others who took up the invitation.

It really was like stepping back in time. They'd spent hours dancing in Justin's parents' lounge on wet afternoons, at parties, the Tower, anywhere ... both before and after they'd become lovers.

Izzie wondered if anyone else experienced that sensation that there was one dance partner who just fitted – knew every move you were about to make and their own complemented yours; someone who smiled back when you smiled up at them and laughed when you grimaced at your own wrong-step. She felt like that with Justin, certain his hand would always be in the right place to twirl her around, his palm at the small of her back when he pulled her close and they moved from foot to foot in perfect sync. Happiness warmed her and her smile reflected that effervescent sensation.

Staying on the floor for four or five dances, they then returned to the table for a drink, and Izzie thirstily drank her glass of champagne. 'I think I need about a gallon of water,' she said and laughed. 'Does anyone else want one?'

'Yes, please, dear,' an elegant, elderly lady at the other side of the table responded. 'I'd like a pint of beer as well, please. Bitter!'

Nodding at the request and loving it because her nan had always loved a pint of bitter, Izzie turned and wound her way to the long bar. Drinks acquired, she returned to the table with a large jug of water, several empty glasses, a pint of beer and a couple other drinks requested by their companions.

'You didn't have to do that Izzie, one of the waiters

would have got those for you.' Justin helped unload the glasses when she returned.

'Didn't occur to me, to be honest. All I knew is that I needed a great big long drink, and probably not the alcoholic type.'

After drinking several glasses of water, Izzie took herself back to the dance floor and joined several ladies who looked as though they were having a good time dancing. After a while she glanced over to Justin, but he was talking to a man beside him – they looked like old friends catching up so she hadn't disturbed him.

It was kind of scary to join people she didn't know, but fuelled by far too much champagne and too little light food, Izzie sang along to the music, waving her hands in the air and being what she thought of as a participating wedding guest. She thought there was freedom in not knowing anybody *too* well, because she would not be held to task for her dodgy singing and dancing by anyone!

She only realised how hot she had become when the music slowed and as she turned to leave the dance floor along with her newfound friends.

Justin stepped towards her. 'May I have this dance?'

'Be glad to, but don't hold me too close as I'm a bit hot.'

He ignored her advice and pulled her close against him. Shivers ran all over her when he leaned towards her and whispered, 'I know.' Izzie didn't need to see his face to hear the amusement that laced his response.

Oh God! The tingles rioted through her. Again. He'd always been able to make her feel like the sexiest female on earth.

She smiled, shivered with pleasure and rested her cheek against his crisp white shirt, thankful that the loud music drowned out her soft moan of desire when his palm pressed against the middle of her back, pulling her close into his torso, the flimsy fabric of her dress no barrier to the warmth melting Izzie against his firm body. It felt right, like she fitted.

Instinctively, she smiled up at him and his own features lit with a smile that made her heartbeat literally flutter.

They danced for hours.

'Are you okay?' he eventually said.

'Great, are you?' It was getting late and the music had slowed, the DJ announcing that everyone should take the opportunity to dance to the last few songs. Justin pulled her towards him, and Izzie let her head sink to his shoulder. After all the night's supercharged fun and dancing, a slow dance fitted the bill perfectly.

Izzie clasped her fingers up around his neck, tangled in the hair that brushed his white collar; she watched his eyes darken in response to her touch, felt one of his hands shift low on her waist, pulling her into him, the other at the small of her back. She smiled, conscious that he kept his eyes on her and those darkened eyes smouldered with lust.

Too soon, the music ended and folks clapped, cheered and drifted away.

Izzie smiled up at Justin whilst he remained still, holding her in his arms. 'It's been a fabulous night, thanks. I've enjoyed being with you.'

'And thank you.' His voice was hoarse and for a fleeting moment she thought Justin was going to kiss her. A sharp stab of disappointment ran through her when that didn't happen, but then, just as she was about to take a deep breath against that feeling, his soft yet firm lips warmed hers. The charge through her body was heavenly and she responded, pulled him closer still, arched into him and he held her close.

She had no idea how long passed before the sound of the DJ's trolley trundling across the wooden dance floor brought her closer to earth. Justin's mouth raised from hers and his deep voice sent tremors through her.

'Shall we go to our room?' He gave her a small smile, a slight bow, and gestured that she should go in front of him to the lift in the lobby, where they then zoomed up to the second floor. All the while, her body craved the heated closeness of his.

A mixture of nervousness and sharp excitement fizzed around in Izzie; she had no idea what would happen with Justin once they arrived at their room and the thought sent a sharp quiver through her. She knew what she wanted to happen...

'Do you mind if I shower?' she asked him as he kicked off his shoes and loosened his tie still further.

'Not at all.'

Izzie unzipped her dress, whisked up her tiny wash bag and went into the bathroom to use the shower. She wallowed in the smell of the delicious honeysuckle shower gel provided, wondering what that smell would come out like on Justin's skin. She enjoyed that delicious thought.

There were two hotel robes hanging behind the bathroom door and she pulled the shorter one on and decided to wear it to bed since she had forgotten to pack any sleep wear. When she emerged, she asked, 'Do you fancy a cup of tea? I'll sort it whilst you shower, if you like?'

'You know me so well, that'd be great, Izzie.' He slung his tie and jacket over the chair.

Before he went into the bathroom, he smiled that smile that spoke of hot kisses, hot summer days, hotter summer nights.

Distracting herself from the thought of Justin in the shower, Izzie flicked on the telly. It went straight to a music channel so she set the remote down on the dressing table stand and let it play quietly.

It drifted through her mind that her nan always said that everything happened for a reason and Izzie wondered for a moment if her nan had brought her together once more with Justin – for a reason.

To help them both find one another again?

Or to help Izzie put her teenage first love behind her – finally – before she moved back to her chosen life in London? Or maybe to help her move on emotionally after Rufus died?

Brushing out her hair, Izzie let her thoughts wander. Did it matter anymore what had happened in the past? It was getting harder to stay upset and the anger she had felt was definitely being overwhelmed by the rise of long-buried feelings. It was becoming easier to bat down the endless questions: Could she ever trust him again? That was a tough one. But did it matter? Was it important to her anymore?

Justin had never mentioned that day in their past – the

meeting that never was – and they'd both moved on. Was there anything stopping her at this moment in time from reaching out and having this … this final fling with him?

She let the scenarios dance around in her thoughts… It was December 23rd now; he would be going away to New Zealand in just a few days. Tonight would be the beginning of the end of their fling – just friends, lovers, grabbing the moment before they would go their separate ways. Just how they intended. No commitments, no promises, no ties. No broken hearts.

Being close to Justin again, laughing, talking and dancing with him, seemed to have sensitised her entire body and dispensed with anything resembling sense or the need to know just why he hadn't turned up to meet her that day.

Part of her, an inner reckless streak, wanted to take the opportunity to be with Justin – just be with him. No future to consider, no past to throw a mental hurdle… It was tempting.

She set down a mug of tea on his bedside table and as she turned, the door to the en suite opened and steam billowed out around him. He had a bath towel fastened around his waist, wet hair darkened, lashes spiked.

His eyes held hers as he moved into the space before her, heat from Justin's just-showered skin seemed to permeate her robe. 'Izzie,' he whispered and she remained stock-still for a second when his palm moved to her waist. The breath caught in her chest.

She looked into his smoky hazel-green eyes. He wasn't asking for anything; he just spoke her name. Whatever had happened in the past, she knew she wanted him at that moment. Izzie's fingers reached around his neck to pull him closer, to pull his lips down to hers. She didn't care about anything other than melting into his kiss, his arms holding her tightly, bringing her closer, acknowledging with her mouth that she wanted him, too.

A sharp thrill shot through her when he groaned with pleasure at her acquiescence.

He raised his mouth from hers for a moment, gave her a small, questioning smile. In response, she again raised her mouth to his.

She could enjoy this for what it was.

She touched her lower lip as Justin raised his head, then touched his lower lip with the same finger. She traced his jaw and ran her fingers into his damp hair. He pulled her to him again, kissed her as though he couldn't get close enough, his mouth hot and hungry. Delicious tingles rushed over Izzie's skin as she savoured the familiar yet new Justin; sexy and so sensual it made her gasp as his palms moved to her hips and drew her against his arousal. Her pulse sped and her lower belly clenched with a physical need that had been locked up tight for years.

She was aware but did not want to admit that her locked up emotions were pushing closer and closer to the surface. But this, now – this was what she wanted. It overrode every other sensation.

They kissed, the sensual embrace making Izzie's nerve endings sizzle with pleasure. Their fingers interlaced, putting a momentary space between them, then, palms touching slowly yet insatiably, letting go and then holding one another so tightly…

She hadn't felt this kind of powerful attraction towards any other living soul, not for years.

Not since they'd been lovers.

The feel of his hot torso beneath her fingertips, his firm, warm muscles, the dip of his spine as she ran her fingers over his back, his arousal pressing hot and hard against her.

God, she wanted him so badly, her need for him fiercer than anything she'd known before. She was a little afraid of letting herself go, to let loose the tsunami of passion threatening to burst free. Yet, overwhelmingly, she wanted to reach out and take what she truly wanted.

Her body arched towards his and they held each other tightly. She breathed in, her mouth and nose against his shoulder, the decision instant.

Justin's fingers reached down and unfastened the belt of her robe. He paused and looked into her eyes for a long moment, asking a silent question; Izzie gave a slight smile and a nod, a sharp mixture of nerves and excitement causing her nerve endings to tingle relentlessly.

The hotel robe and towel dropped to the carpet, their torsos crushing together, mouths kissing more urgently, hands exploring.

Izzie thought how the sensation of skin against skin was always so tantalising.

His mouth found hers again and she laced her fingers around his neck to give Justin unfettered access to her.

'Izzie,' he whispered against her lips.

'Yes?'

304

'Don't think I can carry you up the ladder.' He gave a soft laugh against her mouth, his words a scintillating reminder of their first time making love in the loft.

'Don't think I could climb the ladder.' She smiled and he lifted her against him and sank down onto the sumptuous double bed, so she straddled him.

Izzie's hands roved over his shoulders and torso as she looked into his eyes, his own hands and fingers touching, pausing, exploring.

Heat mounted within and she sat up so he could take her nipples into his mouth, first one, then the other. He then pulled her fully against him again, his mouth and tongue finding hers.

This was what she wanted: to put out the fire that surged between them. His fingers ran lightly over her neck and shoulders, held her tightly against him, and they both revelled in the delicious sensations coursing through them. The fingers of one of his hands shifted to frame her cheek as their tongues moved hotly against one another's.

Izzie wanted him inside her so much, yet there was something so tantalising about just exploring slowly, taking their time.

'Justin…' She gasped with pleasure at his touch.

Driven by a need to drive him crazy with desire, Izzie broke their kiss and laid a trail of light kisses down his belly, then kissed his erection as it twitched with pleasure.

'Izzie.' He reached down and pulled her back up so she lay atop him, her legs splayed to the side of his hips.

Within seconds, he protected them and held her hips as

she slowly took him inside, the sensation so overwhelming it took her breath away.

She thought briefly that there must be some kind of erotic memory between them because the intervening years hadn't made them forget just what they each wanted and needed. The pleasure built and they reached an incredible climax at the same time.

'You okay?' she asked, wriggling to his side, running a finger around his shadowed chin.

'Just fine.' A crooked smile lit his eyes and his features. 'You?'

'All good.'

_____

'Morning, Izzie.' She was sleepy, warm and happy as she became fully aware of her nakedness. She lay close beside him, uncertain for a second whether this was the real world, or some perfect parallel creation of her own dreams.

Slowly, in case it was real, she fully opened her eyes to see Justin leaning up on his elbow, looking down at her.

His smile made her smile in response, swept aside any hesitation to enjoy the moment.

'Morning,' she whispered, mouth curving when he bent down to kiss her.

As his hands roved deliciously over her curves and held her against his arousal, she knew she hadn't felt this raw need for a man – *ever* – in her life. She was no innocent when it came to sex, but she *was* new to this kind of scorching need.

They lay face-to-face and Izzie saw his eyes darken with sheer pleasure as his palms explored her, fingers heightening her own pleasure. Then he held her hips as he took them both to the peak of a cataclysmic orgasm.

Aftershocks rippled through her body, gripping him, making her gasp until, slowly, their breathing returned to normal.

'Wow,' Justin whispered against her neck as he lay, spent, half across her. 'Just … wow.'

Holding her firmly in one arm, he eased Izzie to his side. 'That was something else. You okay?'

'Absolutely, more than okay. Yes, and yes – wow.'

'Thinking maybe we should shift ourselves and join the crowd for breakfast?'

'We should.' She raised her head from the pillow and kissed Justin lightly, a streak of mischievousness making her touch his shoulder and add, 'In a minute?'

And she loved it when he laughed against her mouth in agreement.

The cab dropped her home close to lunchtime and she twisted in the seat and kissed Justin full on the mouth and thanked him for a great time.

'See you later, Izzie.'

They planned to have a takeaway meal at Izzie's later and to finish reading Molly's notebook together as this was the last opportunity they would have to do so.

He had to finish editing and sorting the wedding

photographs for Mick and Janey, and do a final check on his gear to make sure it was ready to travel. On Boxing Day, Justin would decamp with all of his photography gear to the hotel at Manchester Airport so he was on the spot for his flights to New Zealand the following day.

Once she'd had a brew, Izzie spent the early afternoon having catch-up video calls with her pals in London, including her boss, Eddie.

They were all at their homes, or dashing round the shops, getting ready for Christmas Day and doing some last-minute wrapping, cooking – and, with Ruby, sleeping.

Izzie left Ruby until last as she already knew Ruby never got out of bed before noon on a Sunday.

'I can't wait to see you, Rubs.'

In response, she put her finger to her lips. 'Shh, too much gin last night… Great gig though, Paul's band was playing at Koko's in Camden.'

Laughing, they exchanged news. Izzie told her pal she'd been to a wedding of old friends and that they'd danced until late and then all met up for breakfast.

'Oh, sounds lovely.' Ruby rubbed her eyes. 'And were you dancing with any hot blokes?'

Izzie laughed. 'Of course, I'll show you photos when I'm back.' She still felt full of fizz at having had such a good time.

'Fab. I'll look forward to that. Paul says hi, and we both wish you a lovely Christmas. What are you doing tomorrow?'

Izzie explained she had been invited to join the neighbours and their son for a late afternoon Christmas dinner. 'I intend to have a long walk on the prom, then a relaxing evening with the neighbours. Then, I'll be finishing straightening up Nan's bungalow and I've a couple of estate agents lined up to value it pretty early in the New Year.'

'Are you putting it on the market then?'

'Yes.' Izzie had photographed every inch of the bungalow both before and after decorating and had packed just one bag of keepsakes.

The most important keepsake, of course, was Nan's notebook, which she would keep with her always. She would treasure it, take it out and read it through again and again, she had no doubt about that. Izzie also had the feeling that she would notice something new and different each time – a sketch on the edge of a page – a memento or words she hadn't quite caught the meaning of the first time of reading through.

'Then I'll be travelling back.' Izzie and Ruby shared a beaming smile across the ether.

'Coming home.' Ruby nodded. 'That's great!'

'I know.' Izzie felt a pang deep inside at the thought of leaving her beloved Blackpool. She still felt a powerful pull to the seaside town and the rekindled friendships she'd found here, not to mention the romance with Justin. But she squashed that down, thinking how lovely it would be to join her other friends again, her work family.

She knew Nan would be happy whatever she did.

If you're happy, I'm happy.

Izzie had asked Justin if there was anything he'd like for Christmas, preferably something useful for his trip. He'd said a lens cleaning kit would be greatly appreciated and had shown her where she could get one locally.

She'd wrapped that little box up already, but she had something else in mind – something that reminded her of those hot summer days when they'd been younger.

Something that was intended to keep him safe on his travels…

Chapter Twenty-Nine

Izzie

Blackpool, Christmas Eve, 2017

'That was so tasty.' Izzie offered Justin a wine refill and he thanked her.

They cleared up the containers from their Chinese takeaway, washed plates, stashed them away and Justin checked his watch.

'I must keep my eye on the time this evening, Izzie, as I have to get everything checked over at home before I hit the hay tonight. And I need to leave time to finish the wedding photos so I can drop them off to Mick and Janey before I make my way over to my folks tomorrow. I've still not finished.'

'Completely understand that. I've started packing up ready for going back to London.' Izzie thought how delicious it was to just spend time with Justin. She was so glad that their hot night hadn't thrown any barriers between them.

'You going by train?'

'Yup, I'm going to get myself a large wheelie case in Cleveleys.'

'Shame I won't be here; I'd have given you a lift home.'

'That's a kind thought but I'll be fine. How are you getting to Manchester for your flight?'

'Tony is giving me a lift – I'd an Uber booked, but he insisted; he and Kay are combining it with a visit to her family in Manchester.'

'Be rude not to then.' Izzie gave a little laugh. 'Have you time to have a last read of Molly's notebook?'

'I thought you'd never ask.' He turned to face her; his smile powerful enough to blast some powerful light into her soul. 'Let's do it.'

Chapter Thirty

Molly

Blackpool, Saturday June 9, 1945

There's much relief that the war is over, my Dear Diary, though much of the news in the papers is still war-related; we read that injured servicemen who were in the local hospitals were ferried closer to home either by hospital trains or by road.

Some mornings, whilst Marian is home, she keeps an ear out for Tom whilst I slip over the road to help Enid for an hour or two in the boarding house.

Once I finish, I am always eager to return to Tom; I find I miss him even though I am away from him for only a few hours.

When I went to wake him from his nap earlier, he was waiting to greet me. 'Hello, Tom. What's to do?' I leaned against the cot rails, and realised he was smiling. Then his podgy little fists pulled himself to his feet; he looked surprised and laughed up at me.

'Oh, you're a clever boy, aren't you?' He laughed his bonny, toothless grin and it made me laugh, too.

'Whatever else happens, Tom, I'm lucky to have you.' I lifted him out and carried him over to Enid's as she'd invited us both for an afternoon break – along with Marian, who was already there.

Enid made a suggestion then that when Jack came back home, the pair of us should consider taking on the Bing Lea. She said we could take over the attic rooms, which would give plenty of room for all three of us. She said she'd been thinking she'd like to take things a bit easier, get a little bungalow on the coast…

I loved it when anyone took for granted that Jack would come home; it gave me a flame of hope. I said I thought it'd be something for Jack and me to consider together, see if he fancied doing that.

'Thing is, Jack could always get another job out of season. A lot of the blokes do – like your dad did,' Enid piped up. 'And there's always maintenance to do on the rooms.'

I set Tom down on the carpet so he could crawl about and socialise; Tom grinned that joyous toothless grin when they told him how clever he was to pull himself to his feet.

We chatted for a while and then I scooped Tom up and left Enid, Marian and Agnes to chew the fat. 'I'll get out for some air whilst it's fine. Do you want anything from the shop?'

'I could do with some soap if there's any.' Enid took her ration book from the sideboard drawer and handed it over to me along with a thrupenny bit. 'And a thrupenny worth of cabbage greens if there's any about, go nice with tonight's pie.'

'Have a good blow,' three cheery voices accompanied me out of the back room to the wide hallway where I'd parked Tom's pram.

I pushed the pram towards the prom, the springs squeaking slightly as I crossed the road. I wondered how long the ration books would be used and thought how thankful I was that the fresh sea air wasn't rationed and nothing would ever stop me enjoying it.

Tom looked sleepy, his eyelids thickening as he fought against them closing.

Trams trundled along the tracks and I wondered idly if Dora was working this day. I thought she probably was, otherwise she would have joined us at Enid's. I neared the tracks, intending to walk to North Pier along the prom with the aim of getting the cabbage from the grocer's near there.

The footpaths were busy, the weather calm and I stopped to chat to Katherine, Dora's sister, as she got off the tram.

'Oh, Tom's coming on lovely, isn't he?' She leaned over the pram and offered him her finger, but he was sleepy and gave just a brief grin. Laughing, she said, 'I must hurry, I'll pop round later to Mum's for a proper catch-up. I've got the afternoon off so thought I'd do a visit; I'm hoping Mum will cook!'

I laughed, said cheerio and told her Marian was at

Enid's having a cuppa and that she should join them. 'They'll be pleased to see you.'

As I carried on and looked out to the sparkle-topped blue-grey sea, the sound of the gentle suck and flop of the waves on the sea wall was so soothing, as was the warmth of the sun delicious on my shoulders and face. I put the brake on the pram wheels and drank in the view, breathed the salt laden air deep into my lungs.

I thought about what my dad had always said: *No one's breathed that air before you do.*

'Penny for your thoughts, Molly?'

My whole body went rigid.

Was I going mad?

I couldn't believe what I was hearing.

Stunned to stillness, I clutched at the side of the pram, convinced it was a cruel trick of my mind.

This same thing had happened at night, so many times, always followed by a fast plummet into deep disappointment.

But then a shadow fell across me as he moved to my side.

'Hello, Molly.'

I spun around.

I couldn't breathe.

I stood, staring, my mouth opening.

Jack.

He looked thinner, older, with a jagged scar down his cheek, but those eyes, those deep blue eyes were the same. They glimmered with warmth.

Without conscious thought, my fingers rose and touched

his face, the sensation of seeing his slight smile making the breath hitch in my chest.

'I can't...' The words *believe it* didn't make it out. Tears rolled hot down my cheeks, cooled by the soft breeze, and his smile broadened into a full-blown Jack grin.

'I want to kiss you, but will you introduce me to my son, first?'

I gulped down an emotional sob, nodded.

'Tom, this is your daddy. He's home.' Tears rolled off my cheeks and splashed down onto Tom's beloved teddy bear.

Jack bobbed down a bit to take a good look at Tom, a single finger stroking his slightly damp forehead.

'Hello, son.' His voice was hoarse, unsteady, and he looked emotional, as if he held so much inside.

It struck me then that it wasn't the *run to you and hold each other tight because nothing else mattered* that I'd always dreamt our reunion would be.

There was a hesitant, careful feeling about it.

But I didn't care.

Jack was here and that was the only thing that mattered.

He straightened away from the pram and turned, rested his palms at my waist, leaned down and kissed me gently on the lips. I wanted to reach up and pull him closer, have him hold me tight, but instead I rested my fingers on the serge of his uniform jacket sleeve. I could feel the warmth, the strength of him through the fabric. A sob bubbled up when he made a sound in his throat, a needy sound, and his arms went around me properly. The kiss deepened and I thrust my arms around him, too, held him tight, still making sure he was real. Still terrified he would evaporate.

One of his arms held me close as the fingers of his other hand traced around my face. 'The thought of you and Tom kept me going, Molly.'

My Dear Diary, I balanced my palms on his shoulders and reached up so my fingers circled his neck and pulled him down to me so my mouth touched his. 'Jack, I love you so much. Are you back, for good?' It was the only question that mattered.

'I've to report for a medical this time next week, to see if I'm fit to work. I doubt it, though – I've a pretty damaged leg.' I noticed the stick he'd abandoned behind us.

'So, you have to go ... back to...'

I traced the line of the scar on his cheek. I just wanted him home safe. I had so many questions, so much I wanted to ask, but not then.

'I'll recover.' He laughed and pulled me close, burying his face in my neck.

About then, Tom made some little squeaky noises that he sometimes made whilst sleeping. I kept my arms around Jack when he turned his attention back to the pram. 'He's glad you're home safe.'

Jack turned to look at me and tears glistened in his eyes, his voice hoarse. 'So am I, Molly. So am I.'

Back at Marian and Bill's, Jack shook Bill's hand and he announced, 'It's grand to have you back, lad.' Marian unashamedly gave him a hug. 'I'm so happy for you both to be back together again,' she said. 'Now go, go and catch up with each other!' She wafted her hand to our room.

My Dear Diary, that was one of the happiest days and nights of my life. I had the two men that mattered most under one roof – together.

In the comfort of our room Jack got to know his baby son. Once he got over being worried that he'd break Tom if he wasn't handled like bone china, he had the laughing, squealing tot on his lap, tickling him and having Tom hold one finger from each of his hands to raise himself to standing on wobbly legs.

It was simple stuff, but I wanted nothing more from the world than Jack and Tom.

That night, after we had kissed and made love and then held one another tightly, I asked the burning questions.

'Where did you get to, Jack?'

'It's a long story, Molly. Have you got all night?' There was a slight lift to one side of his mouth.

'I have. I've got all night, Jack.'

Jack told me that their plane had been hit and he and the others had had to bail out. It was only by luck that he wasn't hit by enemy gunfire as they plummeted to the ground.

My Dear Diary, he told me that of the other five crew members, three were taken as POWs and two were shot and killed.

Jack had hidden in the woods for four days, until eventually he managed to attract the attention of a young girl working in the fields; the phrase book – which they'd all been given – helped him communicate.

She brought help and their first move was to get him out of his RAF uniform so that he wouldn't be recognised as such. They hid him with a member of the Resistance called Monique, who fed him and roughly stitched the deep cut on his cheek. It grew dark in the bedroom whilst Jack spoke, his fingers running down the scar as though he was remembering.

'Before you ask,' he told me, 'yes, it hurt. But I was free, unlike the others, so it seemed a small price.'

He told me then it had taken forever to go with his guide over the Pyrenees to Spain and eventually to Salou, where he'd learned that the war was over.

'I hitched a lift to Limoges airport and managed to get a flight home from there. I did phone the coal merchants in Manchester – they were the only ones I knew the phone number of – but when I said who I was, they said, "he's dead," and put the phone down!'

'It doesn't matter.' I felt brief annoyance that I could have known he was alive earlier but it passed quickly. As I've always said, there's no point in crying over spilt milk – it changes nothing.

'I was so afraid that you wouldn't wait for me, Molly. Joe had told me more than once that if anything happened to me, he'd be straight here and offer to take you on. He said he'd made a mistake not stepping up to the mark when you found out you were expecting...' Even in the muted lighting, I could see the torture shining in Jack's eyes.

My Dear Diary, I raised my finger to his lips and shook my head. 'It's *you* who stepped up, when you were needed. *You* I love. I told Joe that when he came here.'

'He came here?'

I nodded. It hadn't occurred to me to hide anything from Jack and I told him as much.

'When he thought you were lost.'

'I knew he would try anything to win you back.' He sighed, shook his head. 'He's always been the same.'

'I told him that he was welcome to visit Tom as his Uncle Joe, but *not* as his father. And I told him I loved you, Jack.'

My world felt right at last, Dear Diary.

Jack was home.

Chapter Thirty-One

Izzie

Blackpool, Sunday Christmas Eve, 2017

I zzie blew out and traced the words with her fingertip.
What with the lump in her throat and all the emotion on
the notebook's pages...

'I don't remember seeing a scar on Grandpop's cheek
and he didn't talk much about the war. He told the odd
funny story, but like a lot of his generation, they pushed it
aside and carried on. I do remember Dad telling me when I
was very little that Grandpop would yell out in his sleep,
frighten Nan to death in the middle of the night. Eventually
it stopped.'

'I guess wounds fade, Izzie, inside and outside. When
you think about it, most scars would fade to nothing in a
couple of decades.'

'I guess so.'

Justin shook his head, eyes shining with regret when Izzie offered him a refill. 'I'd love to stay, Izzie, but I need to get back and finish editing on the wedding photos, and get the gear checked.'

'It's been fabulous hanging out; I'm so happy we're friends again, Justin.'

Something serious flashed through his eyes, and then he gave a small smile in response. She followed him to the front door.

He leaned down towards her and she thought he was going to kiss her cheek, but his mouth found hers. Without conscious thought, her own arms wrapped around his waist and all that familiar sizzling sprang to life inside her.

When he released her, cold night air rushed between them.

'Maybe make that good friends?' She touched her lips as he gave her a sensual smile and a slight nod. 'Goodnight, Izzie. Merry Christmas.'

She wished him the same and rose on her tiptoes to kiss his cheek.

'I'll see you tomorrow evening at my folks'?'

She nodded.

Just as Molly recorded in her notebook, when you wanted to slow time, it sprinted and dashed instead. Christmas day sped by in a blur; she'd walked on the prom in the morning, then, in the late afternoon, joined Linda, Robert and Justin for Christmas lunch.

Izzie took along posh crackers, a couple of bottles of wine and small gifts, which they exchanged after they had eaten.

'These are perfect, I've been meaning to get some, Izzie, thank you.' Robert said of the trio of laurel bushes Izzie gave them. Justin thanked her for the lens cleaning kit and looked visibly moved when he opened the small box containing an engraved silver St Christopher.

He fastened it on straight away.

'It'll keep you safe on your travels,' she said.

He passed a small flat box into her hands and Izzie gasped at the rose gold Swarovski bracelet nestled in white satin. An infinity symbol was picked out in crystals on the solid bangle, a chain supporting a small love heart suspended from the band.

'Kind of a friendship bracelet,' he said as he watched her fasten it on her wrist. 'It was the colour that struck me – reminded me of your locket.'

'That's so thoughtful. I'll treasure it, thank you, Justin.' She touched the bangle that looked so delicate in place on her wrist, and thought that he was probably the closest friend she'd ever had.

They had a great game of Scrabble and there was much hilarity as Linda insisted that made-up words were fine … at Christmas.

Much later, Justin said his goodbyes and Izzie slipped away, too.

'I'll be stopping by to say a final goodbye to my folks in the morning. It'll be early, just a flying visit.'

'Give me a knock?' Izzie touched her bracelet and added, 'Thanks again, I love my bangle, Justin.'

'You're welcome. Thanks for the St Christopher, Izzie.'

Chapter Thirty-Two

Izzie

Blackpool, Tuesday Boxing Day, 2017

The following morning, Izzie was up early and made an effort to look half reasonable, aware that Justin would be round to say cheerio before flying off on location for the next three months.

She showered, styled her hair into a scruffy top-knot with little tendrils curling around her face and neck, put in dangly hoop earrings and a bit of mascara, then dressed in jeans and bright blue long-sleeved T-shirt. She rocked her head from side to side in front of the hallway mirror, trying to get her curls to lay just so.

She screwed up her nose, laughed, and shrugged to herself. 'Oh, you'll do.'

A knock on the door interrupted her efforts.

Izzie opened the door wide and gestured for Justin to move indoors; she loved the way his rangy body looked in his tan leather jacket and jeans, his white T-shirt just skimming his trim chest and abs.

'Are you all fit to go?'

'All sorted. Bags and equipment all packed and stashed in Tony's car – we took care of it when I dropped off the photos with Mick and Janey earlier – and I've done all my goodbyes with Mum and Dad. Mobile's on airplane mode, so yeah, all fit to go."

They sat at the kitchen table with their brews. Suddenly, three months sounded like an awfully long time to Izzie. 'I would probably still be scraping off wallpaper when you got back if it wasn't for you and your decorator pal.'

'You think?' He studied her.

'I do. Thanks for everything.'

'Will you miss me?' He raised a brow in question.

'No.' Then she amended. 'Maybe. A bit.'

And she thought, *A lot, too much.*

She was grateful that her actual thoughts didn't show in a bubble above her head.

He nodded, satisfied with that.

'Will you miss me?' Her question just above a whisper.

'Maybe. A bit.' He spoke her words back at her, accompanied with a broad smile, then added, 'Of course I'll miss you.' He paused. 'About the other night, it was … fun,' he said, his eyes darkening at the recollection.

'It was,' she responded, and felt warmth rise to her cheeks. Fun? That was putting it mildly.

He gave a lop-sided smile.

'So, whilst you're away, maybe you could get retro and drop me a line now and again?' Izzie asked tentatively.

'I could.' He hesitated, his brow puckered; it flickered over his features that he clearly had a problem with the suggestion, but he was then distracted, rescuing the phone from his jeans pocket, when it summoned him. 'Tony's here, Izzie.'

Pulling on her jacket, she followed him to the kerb, shared Christmas greetings with Tony and Kay, and then stood by the back-passenger door. 'You okay?' she asked Justin, turning to face him.

She put her fingers on his forearm. 'What's the problem with writing to me?'

He frowned as if it was obvious, shook his head slightly, then took a deep breath as Izzie begged, 'Please...'

As though the words were being ripped from deep inside, he said, 'I wrote *so many* times and the last time I wrote to you, Izzie, you took off and married Rufus Dean.' His features tightened. 'It was the last thing I expected.' Raw pain shone from the depths of his soul and the emotional intensity she witnessed stole Izzie's breath.

But there wasn't time...

No time to hash over the details.

What did he mean?

'Please – write?' She couldn't shake any details loose from her memory, 'Send me your address, I promise I'll write back.'

He pulled her close, fiercely, briefly. 'Izzie...' he whispered into her hair. His deep voice cracked and reverberated through her. She leaned back and glimpsed a vulnerability that she hadn't seen before when his eyes met hers, then, in the chilled morning air, his mouth covered hers and Izzie felt tears well in her eyes, her throat constricting. Her fingers spread over his jaw, skin cool, slightly roughened by the shadow there.

Tony wound down his window, 'Got to go, Justin.'

'Safe journey,' she whispered past the unexpected, massive lump in her throat. All that resolve to keep her emotions under control scattered and her smile trembled as she fought the heat of tears.

He looked directly into her eyes. 'Bye, Izzie.'

Justin shifted into the waiting car, the door closed behind him and the car drew away.

Justin's wave felt too final.

Three months felt too final.

She felt as if she had missed a whole chapter of her life and had been totally unaware it existed until now.

She felt bereft, as if there were things she needed to find out, she needed to know what she had done to cause the vulnerability in Justin's expression. Hadn't *he* been the one to turn his back and move on? To lose touch? She forced herself to face the question: Would she have said *yes* to marrying Rufus had she not been torn apart by Justin's rejection?

Justin was the only man who had ever moved seamlessly between best friend and lover in her life and the friendship he'd shown her whilst she coped with Molly's death and sorting the house spoke volumes.

The shift to something else when they'd shared that steamy night in the hotel room... To her, that felt like unfinished business, like unearthing those feelings that had been trapped away for so long. They had escaped now and she couldn't get those feelings back in the trap, as if she'd let the genie out of the bottle.

Izzie admitted inwardly that she needed to face the fact that there were some missing truths, some gaps in their past. His words, 'I wrote so many times...' The unmasked pain in his words... She knew for her own sake, and to be fair to Justin, she longed to identify these, and uncover the details. But where could she look for them?

As her nan always said, if you can do nothing about a situation, then set it aside. She would have to do just that, she thought sadly.

Justin's airport lift was long gone, the soft and the salty breeze blew against her, reminding her she shouldn't stand there staring after him all day.

It wouldn't bring him back.

Crikey, how the heck had her nan coped, waving goodbye to the man she loved when she didn't even know if she would even *see* him again, never mind when?

What?

Loved. The man she *loved*...

Returning indoors, she dashed of a text message asking, '*What? What did you mean?*' then immediately deleted it. No point. His phone was off.

Hesitating just long enough to collect her warm coat and scarf, Izzie jammed her soft woollen hat down over her head and made her way to the sea front, letting the fresh breeze sift through her thoughts.

Oh, God. Did she still love Justin? Hadn't they decided

to have a no-commitment relationship? She had the suspicion that saying it didn't actually guarantee emotions would be kept in check; saying it didn't automatically keep it casual.

She squashed the question flat, didn't feel she had the emotional bandwidth to answer it. Waving goodbye had been enough of a wrench for one day.

She considered instead whether the time she'd spent with Rufus had been a distraction. Had she been unfair to him? She shook her head and a cold gust of salt laced wind saw her pull her scarf tighter around her chin.

She thought that, at the very least, both she and Rufus had taken what they needed from the marriage and there had been real affection between them.

To Izzie, Rufus had represented her alternative path to one of pain; and to Rufus, Izzie had represented a figure who would fulfil the roles of wife, personal assistant, co-worker, companion and nurse.

A young woman ran past her wheeling a pushchair, leaving momentary tracks on the rain-wet pavement. The few people that were out had their heads down and hoods or brollies up and were being buffeted by the sea breeze as they hurried with purpose towards the dry. Izzie walked to the edge of the prom, overlooking the sea, and pulled down her scarf, baring her face to the delicious dampness of the sea-salted breeze. She forced her thoughts towards the New Year and her move back to West Hampstead. It had been the main buzz in her thoughts until that unexpectedly emotional farewell with Justin.

Chapter Thirty-Three

Izzie

West Hampstead, New Year

On the train to West Hampstead, Izzie ran through her mental checklist. She'd had a couple of valuations on the bungalow – they had both described the décor as *fresh and appealing*, and Izzie wondered what her nan would think of it. She imagined her saying, 'Oh, it's a bit plain, Izzie. It needs jazzing up a bit...' She chuckled to herself, loved that she could still have those internal conversations with Nan.

She'd told the agents she would let one of them know when she was ready to put the property on the market. It was going to be difficult to part with because of the link to Nan and Grandpop. She could take her time though, and there was still a niggle inside that part of her didn't want to sever the connection. The bungalow would give her the ability to return to Blackpool, should she wish.

But for now, she forced her thoughts onward and looked forward to joining her work family of friends in a couple of days.

She'd been thrilled that Justin had texted her a selfie of himself at the airport when he reached Auckland on the 29th December. She hadn't really known whether he would keep in touch.

Since then, they'd exchanged short, funny texts every day or so and Izzie had let him know she had left the north for London.

On reaching Farley Road, Izzie gathered up the post and then opened the back doors and windows to let some air through. The first thing she unpacked was her nan's notebook; she laid it on the desk in her office and ran her fingers gently over the linen-textured outer cover, then opened it up to reveal the inside page of mementos, her gaze resting on the small pencil sketch of a beautiful young woman, curls framing her features, a slight smile playing on her mouth...

It was stunning, Izzie thought, the notebook's inner cover and pages like a work of art. The secrets it held inside, the moments shared, purely because those secrets and those moments could not be shared with any other person. They were only safe confined within the pages of the diary, and so it had taken on the personality of a confidant.

She opened the bottom, deep drawer of the desk, and laid the notebook carefully inside, where she could take it out and pour over it when she felt the need to connect with her nan.

Izzie reflected on what a gift it had been to have such an insight into her nan's life. She would keep it safe, and keep the notebook's *secrets* safe, as her only confidant had been Justin. She had no wish to share it with anyone else.

The time at the bungalow had helped her to face – honestly face – the fact that there had been glaring cracks in her marriage to Rufus; that whilst morphing her own life to keep her promise of commitment to him, she had floundered personally, lost her identity, lost sight of her dreams, and her self-confidence had been worn down as a result. Writing down those details with pure honesty as she recollected them had helped to relieve the burden of guilt. Her own notebook – cataloguing her own emotional recovery – inspired by Nan's precious journal.

The magic of the bungalow had helped to heal the emotions of guilt and loss. The time spent at Nan and Grandpop's home had given her the chance to reset in the safest place she'd ever known. Now, she was feeling happier and actually looking forward to getting back to her life, back to her dreams.

The time she had shared with Justin had also been wonderful, a balm to her emotions.

It was a cold evening and Horace, the neighbour's cat, peered at her through the French doors as if having returned from his adventures to welcome her back. Collecting some cat treats from the kitchen, she went out to make a fuss of him until he gave her a look that said he'd had enough and wandered off. It was a lovely garden – a bit overgrown, but lovely. A green oasis in a leafy residential road. The whole tree-lined street had that feel about it.

She remembered that her neighbour, Vinnie, had volunteered to keep the garden tidy, said he preferred it to his, which was smaller. Returning indoors, out of the cold, she grabbed a notepad and wrote herself a to-do list.

Chapter Thirty-Four

Izzie

London, Monday January 7, 2018

The offices were set back from the road and a small, leafy garden softened the edges of the low building.

'Hi! How fabulous to see you!' Eddie's booming, welcoming voice filled the open plan DAS offices and pretty soon Izzie's work pals had left their desks and joined them in the reception area, noisily happy to see her.

'I didn't realise how much I missed you all.' She felt moved by the welcome. 'The offices are lovely as ever.'

Ruby grinned and gave Izzie a great big hug. 'You look great – bit of a tan going on there, Mrs?'

'Sea breezes do that.'

'Great! Have you got plans for lunch? We've got so much catching up to do!' Annette, Jamila and Portia all chirped up at Ruby's suggestion and they agreed they should have lunch in the canteen and catch up.

'Well, it'll have to wait a while.' Eddie nodded towards a visitor arriving at reception. 'Izzie has a meeting with our client.'

The others dispersed as Eddie guided Izzie and the client, author Derek Farrell, into their meeting room.

The meeting went on for several hours and Eddie and Izzie discussed what would be the quickest way to transcribe and format Derek's voice recordings and intermingled notes in order to meet an unexpectedly tight deadline for another in his series of crime books; there was also talk that his books looked likely to be optioned for a TV series, Derek told them. Because of all her work for Rufus in the same vein, Izzie was the obvious choice for the transcription task.

After the meeting, Eddie and Izzie sat down for a debrief.

'I enjoyed that, I love the brainstorming bit where everyone chips in and you get a result that suits all of us!'

'It's rewarding isn't it? And you're okay putting your admin cap back on?'

'Absolutely. You know, I never realised how much I miss everyone and the work, too.'

'Well...' Eddie tilted his head to one side slightly. 'It's good to have you back on board. We've plenty of demand for your skills. Ruby asked if you could help her with the costumes for Norma Normandez for her big night at the O2 at the end of her two-year Goth tour.'

'Really? Wow, I'm flattered. I love the variety.'

At that moment, Ruby, all long dark hair and red lips, walked past the glass walled office doing very obvious side-eyes so she could see whether their client had finished and left yet.

Eddie laughed and nodded towards Ruby, used to her outrageous behaviour. 'I think Ruby and the crew are wondering whether you're free or not yet.'

Izzie laughed with him.

She realised just how isolated she had become over recent years.

'Did you finish work on your nan's bungalow?'

'I have, yes. I haven't quite worked up the courage to put the property on the market yet though. I'm finding that thought a wrench. Are you coming to the canteen?'

'I'll join you all for a few minutes and a quick cuppa, then leave you to it.' He grinned and gestured she should move out of the room in front of him. 'Even if you decided to live back up north, Izzie, you could always work remotely. There's a few of our number now that do. They come up for monthly meetings, make the best of both worlds.'

She smiled and thanked Eddie, but didn't really take his comment on board. She was back home now, she thought.

Izzie had the most wonderful afternoon in the small café-style canteen with her workmates. There was so much laughter, so many questions. She showed them the before and after photographs of the bungalow she'd taken, photos of the sea and the beach at Blackpool. Eagle-eyed Ruby spotted a photo Justin had taken of the two of them when they were all dressed up to go to Mike and Janey's wedding reception.

'Oh! He's a bit tasty! Are you seeing him?'

Laughing, Izzie shook her head. 'No. We're friends, have been right back from our early teens. He works out of the country a lot of the time as he's a wildlife photographer and sometimes a celebrity snapper.'

Ruby screwed up her eyes. 'He looks familiar…'

'Justin Swift,' Izzie offered. 'His old mate was getting married that day,' she said as she pointed to the snap.

'Well, wow, that's a fabulous photo.' Annette held Izzie's phone and studied it, then when she handed it back, caught sight of the canteen clock. 'We need to get back to work!'

Annette, Jamila and Portia said they had to go and finish their projects.

'Before you go, ladies, shall we?' she said, holding up her phone. Izzie took a selfie of them all squashed around the table, then, to much noise and promises to have lunch again during the week, and hugs all around, the three of them got back to their desks.

And then there was just Izzie and Ruby.

'I'm done for the day.' Ruby beamed and waggled her head. 'Came in at six this morning! Well?' Ruby folded her arms, then gestured towards Izzie's phone. 'The way he's looking at you, I wouldn't be letting him go anywhere without me!'

Izzie shook her head, then did a double take at the photograph. 'Nah, Justin's used to dating glamorous types.'

'Looks to me as if he'd like an Izzie type!'

She laughed, but Ruby's observation made her think, had drawn her attention to the warmth in Justin's eyes.

It reminded her of the day at the dunes, when she'd photographed him and somehow – accidentally – caught a fantastic and telling expression. She hadn't really studied this one of the two of them further than seeing it as a memento of a great night at Janey and Mick's reception ... and what had happened afterwards. She got herself under control and shrugged, repeated, 'He works abroad a lot.'

'So? You can work anywhere! Eddie always says as much.'

Izzie found herself nodding in agreement.

She could.

She tested that thought in another version of her life, how it might feel...

A life where her need to stay at home had softened into a *maybe-I-could-travel* litany.

One where she could be with the man she loved, and still do the work she loved, still see the colleagues she adored ... and still have a home to return to, friends she could return to. But she knew now that dreams were fleeting, and often what looked perfect in a dream ... well, it only worked if the other person felt the same way.

'We have a past,' she said. 'Things changed between us.'

Grimacing, Izzie briefly explained, 'We were an item when we were younger. We're just friends now.'

Ruby did a fabulous, single eyebrow lift. 'Really?' Then she looked at her watch. 'Oh bugger, I could talk all day, Izzie, but I've got Paul home soon and we've got something planned as he's been offered a recording gig he's been after for ages.'

'Oh fantastic. No worries. I'll be back tomorrow.'

'Oh! Yes! I'll see you in the morning, then, Izzie?'

'I can't wait.'

'I just wish you were coming home with me and we could keep on catching up all night!'

'I don't think we'd get any sleep,' Izzie said. 'Actually, I *know* we wouldn't get any sleep.' They'd spent many a night on the sofa, chattering until the dawn chorus reminded them they may need sleep – back when Izzie had shared a flat with Ruby.

'And get here early enough to give me the low-down on everything!'

Izzie raised her hand in a gesture of agreement.

Laughing, they went their separate ways.

———————

Arriving at West Hampstead, the tree-lined road, leafy front garden and peaceful oasis feeling of the house was comfortingly familiar. Vinnie had kept a good eye on everything.

Over the next few weeks, Izzie sent Justin the odd message and photos – some of her with her workmates, some at her West Hampstead home, and he responded with similar. She had a lot of fun at work and thoroughly enjoyed immersing herself in the design world once again, but with a newfound honesty she admitted that there was a hole in her life, something missing, and her thoughts regularly revisited the kisses she'd shared with Justin, the hot fling in the hotel.

She touched the bracelet he'd given her at Christmas, the crystals sparkling.

'Oh, Justin.' What she felt for him was so much more than friendship.

Izzie still hadn't got around to putting the bungalow on the market. Someone had told her spring was a good time so she thought she'd delay until then, but even she was beginning to realise it was an excuse. She missed walking on the front, the sea air and just about everything that she'd enjoyed there.

Mostly she missed Justin.

She realised now that all those emotions she had ruthlessly cut off … well, they still existed. All that love she'd felt for him … it still burned strong.

Sure, they'd had a fling, but she was pretty sure he only wanted friendship now. Even the bracelet he'd described as a *kind of* friendship bracelet. She knew for sure though – she wanted far more than friendship. And so, she set in motion another huge life-change, her mind made up after so much soul searching.

She was going to sell up.

It was early February when she returned home from work to find a large, fat envelope, the edges slightly battered where it had just barely fit through the letterbox. She carried the package and dropped it on her desk.

Inside, a solicitor's letter was held in place by a band and Izzie immediately recognised the name of the firm as the one who dealt with Rufus's estate:

Dear Mrs Dean,

Our financial department has today made a transfer of funds to the following account. This represents a refund of an amount lodged with us by the late Rufus Dean to handle several personal residual matters after his demise.

Also enclosed is a letter and package that Mr Dean asked we forward to you at the same time as we present this final statement, which he requested and understood would be around two years after he died.

This letter concludes our dealings for your late husband's estate, but should you require any information or assistance in the future, please do not hesitate to contact us.

Yours…

Vaguely, Izzie wondered what the personal residual matters had been, but her attention was drawn to the plain white envelope immediately beneath the solicitor's note.

'Izzie' was printed on the front.

Curious and a bit nervous for a reason she couldn't christen, she tore it open.

My Dear Izzie,

I owe you an explanation. I asked my solicitor and dear friend, Lester, to send this on a couple of years after I pass. I hope that by holding this back until that time, you will be able to forgive me for the terrible thing I have done. Or at least try to understand.

One of the first things you did when you began to work regularly in the afternoons for me in February 2011, was to note in our online diary that you'd booked off the 11th and 12th August as holiday, visiting Blackpool on your birthday you told me when I asked. Meeting Justin, your long-distance young man, you said, the two of you intended to plan your future together.

Later that month, I convinced you it made sense for you to move into the upstairs apartment, because my previous tenant had moved out, and the friend you shared with, Ruby, was moving into her partner's house. You were actively looking for a place to rent – so it was the easy answer.

I couldn't bear to let you go to Justin; I was afraid of losing you. I knew I didn't have long, and because I knew I was becoming more unwell, I took the conscious decision to hide his letters when they began to arrive during late March, 2011, when you had been working part-time for me for a few weeks and had finally agreed to move upstairs. It was easy to pick up the post each morning whilst you were out working elsewhere. The lockable letter cage I'd had installed when I'd had a pup years ago made it even easier to continue to monitor the post.

I had looked for so long for someone I could work and live closely with, who I could trust to take on the role that you did so ably for me. Wife, secretary, assistant, carer, friend and everything in between.

You were all those things and I thank you.

I know what I've done is wrong. I thought only of myself but I have no regrets.

I thought about destroying the letters but decided against it. Yet I couldn't have them at home where you might come across them by accident.

You had spoken freely about your relationship with Justin and when the letters arrived, I read them because I needed to know whether he was a threat to my plans. I knew I needed you more than Justin did, but from what you'd said of him I didn't think I'd win you in any fair battle.

Perhaps unfairly, I thought whatever plans you were meeting up to make could be postponed to my benefit. The little phone you used to text and call one another, you thought you'd lost it, but I'd hidden that too in case Justin contacted you on it. He did. Many times. I didn't respond and eventually removed the battery. Any minor guilt I entertained was dealt with by replacing the mobile with a top of the range model I explained was 'to go with your new job.'

Someone once said it is better to ask forgiveness than permission and my increasingly addled brain could think of no other way to keep you by my side.

I hope you and Justin find one another again one day – if you're meant to.

With all my love,

Rufus.

'Dear God, Rufus.'

Izzie shook her head and rubbed her fingertips across her forehead as she tried to digest the facts. Her mouth was dry and a feeling of faintness washed through her as she gripped the edge of the desk with clammy fingers.

'Dear God...'

The writing on the bundle of envelopes was Justin's.

Chapter Thirty-Five

Izzie

West Hampstead, Early February, 2018

Taking the bull by the horns, she checked the date stamps on the envelopes, and put them in date order; all were dated through the spring and summer of 2011. The last date had been stamped on 3rd September and, unlike the others, had been posted in the UK. She opened the oldest one first, smoothed out the letter's fold and took a deep breath in an attempt to fight down the nervous bubbles that made her want to do anything *but* begin reading.

Fingers trembling and moving clumsily like lead, she picked up the first letter, but it shook too much for her to focus. She set it down on the table and began to read.

Hi Izzie,

I wanted to let you know I haven't forgotten our date on your birthday in a few months – I'm writing to see if we can alter that? There are a couple of reasons – and I apologise for messing you about in advance.

A chance to go along on an agency location photoshoot has come up and it could lead to me working on what I've always wanted.

Alongside the glamorous calendar shoot we'll be working on, there's the chance of nipping off and doing some wildlife work for my portfolio with an amazing mentor.

Thing is, to take the opportunity, I have to leave in a couple of weeks and don't have time to come home from Malta as we're working right up until we fly out to do the Sirelli calendar shoot. The job will put me out of the country until at least September, and there's a lot of travelling involved so I'll be out of touch more often than I'm reachable. I hope you'll understand I don't want to let this opportunity slip by?

How about we arrange a different date? I lost the phone you've got a number for, left it in a bar in Malta – too much Maltese pear liqueur. What a twerp! Soon as I have a replacement phone, I'll ping you the number.

If you could write back, I'll be at the address on this letter for three more weeks – then leaving for some pretty exotic locations. I have put my pal, Corey's mobile phone number at the bottom of the letter so you could send a message there – or I've also put the hotel contact number, maybe leave a message at the desk for me? I won't have an address once we leave here because we're moving around a lot.

That's the first reason. The other reason is I really need to make a go of this opportunity to secure our future as it'll mean a lot to me – and to us both financially. It'll help set us up in our own place, maybe even help us get a deposit on a house on the front overlooking the sea like we've talked about. It's taken a while to build up a reputation in the photography world and things look like they could take off even more. My thinking is that we're both young enough to alter our plans – just a bit and just by a month or so. But it depends on you? Are you okay with that? Let me know what you think when you write back?

In the meantime, always be sure I love you, Izzie.

Hope your work with DAS is still going well. Are you still enjoying all the design work? How's it working out doing admin for the crime writer guy? Write as soon as you can and tell me how you're doing. I'm sending this to your new address, so hopefully you did move!

I've to go now and get ready for the photo shoot in Valetta.

I love you,

Justin x.

Izzie shook her head. It'd all been there – all of the reasons for his no show were in this letter. He'd tried to warn her and make alternative plans.

Okay, yes, she would have been upset and angry that he'd decided to put off their meeting up for a bit, but if she'd received the letter, she would have at least *known* there was a reason. And he did know her well enough to know that she would've accepted his decision. She wouldn't have wanted him resenting her for missing his big chance.

Feeling heavy-hearted and nauseous she reached for the next letter, and had to physically force herself to focus on it. Whatever was in the next one – it couldn't be good.

Dear Izzie,

I'm concerned because you haven't been in touch. I expect you're likely pissed with me putting off our meeting date for a bit, but I'd hoped you'd understand. Hopefully you've written and your letter will turn up soon. I haven't got a new phone yet; been manic with work, but I've put the hotel number at the bottom of this letter again – and Corey's. Hoping to have time to grab one soon. I'll write again in a day or two as I'll have a copy of a photo to send you then – it's due to be featured in a British Sunday supplement.

You can have a good laugh at it – I stepped in as the male model because Corey, who was booked for the shoot, got ... well ... a bad stomach, very last minute.

Anyway, it's convinced me I'm working on the right side of the camera. Boy those models are patient –they have to hold their poses for a hell of a long time!

Write soon,

I love you,

Justin x.

Within the folds of the next letter, a photograph – a proof copy of the photograph that she'd torn from the Sunday magazine supplement and ripped into tiny pieces in anger, then regretted tearing up because she'd wanted to look at Justin's face.

The crisp, clear black and white photograph was even more striking than the colour one had been. His very slight smile as he looked down into the features of the young woman, his hair as tousled as it always was and a shadow on his cheeks and chin, the sincere light in his eyes so convincing. He was – always had been – her idea of a good-looking man. Not everyone's, maybe, but hers.

Tears rolled down her cheeks and she wished she could go back in time; read the letters he'd sent her when they'd first arrived. But would that have changed anything? She dashed the wetness from her cheeks with her fingers and stopped that thought from developing. Izzie wanted to read the rest of the letters so she could fill in the damned gap in her own past before doing any more wondering whether she would have still married Rufus…

Hi Izzie,

Okay, so you're obviously far more pissed with me than I expected. There's not a lot I can do about it from here, unfortunately. I've tried ringing your nan's house from a phone box but it's bloody useless – the money lasts no time and she says she's sorry but you're not there at the moment and she hasn't got your new number yet. She sounded worried about me, so that clearly wasn't a good thing to do. She did offer to take a message – but I said not to worry, I'd write again. In the meantime, I've written Corey's and the hotel's numbers on the bottom of this letter. Please phone? I need to clear this up with you... On another subject – what do you think of the photograph? Did I make a good model? I thought I looked better than I felt. It's a bloody tough job that.

Marissa, the female model in the photo, said all she could think about was eating a big cake afterwards. I kept wanting to laugh. Anyway, it was an experience, that's for sure. Let me know all your news?

Write soon,

I love you,

Justin x.

All this time she had been angry with Justin, blamed him for callously not turning up when he *had* written to explain, obviously thinking that it was a far more reliable way of getting in touch with her than the alternatives.

And probably because he knew she'd always loved letters...

This was the knowledge that helped to fill in that bloody gap she hadn't known existed.

But this was painful.

She touched her cheek and realised it was wet. She couldn't believe this, everything she'd thought was wrong... She had blamed Justin for everything.

Everything. But it was blatantly clear from his letters he never had any intention of hurting her.

She couldn't see for a few moments, had to mop at her eyes with her fingers.

Hi Izzie,

I'm guessing you're still seriously upset with me and I couldn't be sorrier about that. Still, I'm hoping you'll write to me before we move on from Malta. I dash and check with the reception area of the hotel every morning before work and every evening when we finish to see if you've written or left a message. I have Corey checking his mobile loads, too.

I've had the immunisations for all the places we'll be visiting – there'll be a trip up the Amazon, one to India, to the West Indies, to Morocco and loads more places. I'll take loads of photos so you can share in the good bits when we get together.

Corey, one of the models on the team, suffers from mossie bites, poor sod, his mum just sent him a package with just about every cure available packed in.

Right, better get going.

Sending you a sexy hug and a kiss – I bloody miss that.

Please write soon.

I'm happy but I miss you like crazy.

And I love you,

Justin x.

Izzie traced the words with her damp finger, blew her nose, shook her head.

'Shit, Justin.'

Her throat was tight with tears.

She wanted so much to move away from the letters and the pain they were causing her … but she'd always done that – she'd always run away.

Or in Justin's case, run away and buried her feelings deep.

She scolded herself and reached for the next letter, fingers shaking a bit with the realisation that Justin had begun to reach out towards her with more emotion in each letter.

Hi Izzie,

Right, you have me seriously worried now. I've tried phoning your nan again, but there was no reply, and Mum says she's on holiday in the Lakes just now.

Will you respond to my letters? Whatever else I thought when I asked if we could move our meet-up date, I didn't expect no response at all. I understand that you're pissed with me, but you must know I love you, Izzie.

Don't ignore me? I keep trying to work out why you wouldn't want me to be honest. I know you might not like it but we've always talked stuff over and come out the other side. It just doesn't seem like you to stay angry with me for so long. You certainly haven't before. And I can't for the life of me work out what's going on in your mind; that's pretty unusual.

We're here just one more week now and then off travelling and we'll all be out of touch. I'm anxious to hear from you.

At last, I have a new phone, number at the top of this letter, ping me a message so I have your number – I must have remembered your number wrong, coz no response to the dozens of calls and messages sent from Corey's phone, or my new one.

Love you so much,

Justin x.

Izzie's sight was blurred again. She gasped, a sob erupting as she touched the words of Justin's penultimate letter, wanting more than ever to hide away from what she was uncovering. She paused long enough to blow her nose and go and splash her face with cold water before picking up the last of the letters, the postmark two weeks later than the previous one.

Izzie,

To say I'm gutted is an understatement. I just wish you hadn't left it to Kay to tell me about you marrying your boss.

So that's it. There's nothing more to say. I would wish you well, but at the moment I'm too fucking angry and upset to write any more.

I never thought it was possible to hurt this much.

Justin.

'Oh, God,' Izzie whispered as wrapped her arms around herself and gasped for breath.

Sobs rose noisily and she ached for all the pain she'd caused Justin – unwittingly caused, but caused all the same.

Anger ripped through her. 'Rufus, you bastard!' She shook her head. 'That was so … so … *wrong!*'

Even with the proof in front of her, she struggled to believe what he had done. What right-minded person would interfere in someone's life like that?

Inconsolable, she laid her head on her arms and sobbed great noisy, angry snotty sobs. There was nothing she could do to mend this; she knew that she couldn't turn back time and undo the harm. She couldn't confront Rufus and let rip, pummel him with her fists.

'It was wrong! So wrong!'

Her phone burbled away on the kitchen table and unthinkingly she answered. It was Justin calling via a video call on WhatsApp.

'Hey.' His cheerful greeting gave her a moment to blow her nose yet again and wipe her fingers over her cheeks.

'Justin, hi.' She cleared her throat, it ached with misery. 'How are you?'

'Better than you, by the looks of it.' He gave her one of his to die for lopsided smiles. His hair was blowing across his forehead then away with the wind, and the sky in the background was intensely blue.

That made her laugh, snottily, but she laughed. 'I know.' She took a deep breath, 'How's work going?'

'Fantastic; the scenery is spectacular. I'm in the north at the 90 Mile Beach. Look.' He panned the gorgeous endless golden beach, the lace edged blue waves. 'It's about seventy degrees and beautiful. I'm on my way back to the camper van now and I wanted to see you, find out how you are.'

'Justin...' The tears began to pour freely down her cheeks again. 'Something happened. I need to tell you...'

'What's happened? Izzie, are you – are you pregnant?'

She shook her head, the words *I wish* floating uninvited through her mind. Her nose and her eyes ran. Much in the same way as he'd shown her the gorgeous scenery by panning around with his phone camera, Izzie sniffed and did the same thing with the letters that she'd read, then set them back down on the table, the last one on top.

'I don't get it.' The warmth drained from his manner. 'Why are you showing me those?'

'I'm so sorry, Justin. I'm sorry. I never *got* them.' She wiped her fingers down both cheeks, attempted to stop the hot flow of tears without success. 'I got some letters from before these that Ruby passed on after I moved to the upstairs apartment here in West Hampstead, as she handed them to me at work.' Her voice was hoarse with emotion. 'But these I've only just received. They were sent on by Rufus's solicitor, along with a letter from him saying he'd hidden them from me along with my phone.'

He was silent for what was probably only a second or two, but it felt so much longer to Izzie.

'I'm so sorry.' She couldn't look at the screen any longer, the slight time delay accentuating his slow response.

'Have you read them now?'

'Yes,' she gasped. 'I never would have ignored you; I didn't know you'd written!' She grimaced then. 'I waited for you all day on my birthday, thinking you would come. When you didn't, I assumed you didn't want me.'

'Shit!' He looked rattled, raised his chin as if to stop his own pain from spilling out. 'It never occurred to me you wouldn't get the letters. I sent them with loads of time for that reason. I didn't want you travelling up to Blackpool thinking I'd be there.'

There was a long pause at Justin's end and then he shook his head. 'So, you thought I didn't turn up and that was it?' He blew out a disbelieving sound. 'You thought I would finish what we had without a word? Izzie?'

In response, she nodded.

'I thought – thought it was all your fault. I blamed you and thought I was blameless. *I wasn't.*' Her words were barely audible. She grabbed a tissue to wipe her face and blow her nose. 'I wasn't blameless. I let myself be manipulated by Rufus.'

'What Rufus did changed our lives, Izzie. He kept those letters because he wanted you for himself, not just to work for him, but to be his wife,' Justin said.

'That's why he did it.' She shook her head, still struggling to process the whole debacle. 'That's what he said in his letter.'

He looked pale, angry and confused. 'I thought you'd been dazzled into falling in love with your famous boss and sacked me off.'

'No, Justin. I was in so much pain because I thought you had moved on, got involved with one or another of your glamorous models. There seemed to be photographs of you with them everywhere I looked.' She dashed tears from her eyes. 'I'd told Rufus about you, of course, and thinking back, he listened, but didn't comment much. He obviously took a lot more notice than he seemed to. And you're right, Justin, I was dazzled, but it was the timing.'

Justin raked his fingers back through his hair. 'I need to go in a minute, Izzie, the others are back.' He glanced away, out through the windscreen of his camper van. 'We need to go through today's shots.'

'I just – I need you to know I would never have hurt you

that way, Justin. If I'd known, I would never have ignored you.'

He nodded and that warmth Izzie had always loved shone briefly in his green eyes, then flickered away. 'It didn't feel right at the time.' He blew out. 'And I guess I was too distracted by beckoning success to do more about it.'

She wiped the hot wet tears from her cheeks and whispered, 'I'm just so sorry.' As she spoke, she was shocked to see from Justin's expression that he was struggling to control his own emotions: his shadowed jaw was tense and she couldn't be sure but she thought there might be a tear shining in his eyes, too.

His voice was huskier than usual when he spoke. 'I know.' The sound of his co-workers entering the camper van signalled the end of their exchange. 'Izzie. Keep in touch?'

'I will. I've some photos to send you – I'll do it soon.'

He smiled, but it didn't reach his eyes. 'I'll look forward to that. Bye for now, Izzie, love.'

The connection cut, Izzie hugged herself again, wishing that she could feel Justin's arms around her, like when they'd burrowed into the sand dunes at Starr Gate for the day all those years ago, their picnic lunch in her rucksack along with her sketch pad and towel. They'd revelled in holding one another tightly whilst they laughed and kissed. They'd thought there was all the time in the world, thought that they'd always be together.

Instead, their promise to one another had been broken, their bond destroyed by someone she'd trusted completely.

She sat there for long moments looking at her blank phone screen, and was startled back to life by the buzz of a message arriving.

Sadly, we can't do anything about what's already done, Izzie. Don't forget to send your photos to me? Speak soon, keep in touch, love Justin. X

Smiling, she ran her fingers over his words. She'd heard her nan say something very similar when things went wrong. *Don't cry over spilt milk...*

Blowing out and standing up, she went and washed her face with cold water, brushed her teeth and then sent him several of the latest photos she'd taken with her work pals during one of their lively lunch breaks.

And for good measure, she wandered out into the garden and took a selfie of herself with her thumb up. She sent it off to Justin, realising too late that she had absolutely no make-up on and the selfie showed her eyes still swollen from her crying jag. She sent a hasty message to follow the photo up.

Without any adornment! Love from Izzie.

She put a row of kisses and a smiley wink face emoji.

Justin had sent a picture of himself and his work colleagues – they were all windblown and smiling, leaning against the outside of the camper van, waving towards the phone's camera. The message was:

Everyone says hi xxx

NB All of us also without any adornment.

She laughed, felt better.

She thought that she'd search out her notebook and carry on writing down how she felt about what had happened – much in the same way that Nan had. Somehow, just thinking about doing that made her feel better. She now understood fully why Nan kept the record of her emotions and events in her homemade notebook.

One of the first additions she wrote in her notebook were the words Justin said when she'd asked him if he'd write to her, which only now made sense: *'I wrote so many times.'*

Something else made sense too. Kay had been slow to warm to Izzie at first when they'd met up again, despite their firm friendship in the past; if she'd been the one to tell Justin about Izzie and Rufus and had seen his reaction … that would explain it.

As Molly had done, Izzie wrote an entry in her own notebook in the form of a letter to Justin; she would show it to him if things worked out the way she was now certain she wanted them to.

Dear Justin,

It didn't seem right to tell you this in a text message, and I would love to be able to tell you this face-to-face but as that isn't possible, writing it in a letter seems like the second-best thing to do.

Besides the letters I never received, Rufus also admitted to taking my mobile phone, said he monitored the messages you sent then eventually removed the battery. He bought me a new one, saying it was a new phone for my new job.

I should have asked more questions at the time; I should have tried harder to get in touch with you. Your last letter was filled with such raw pain; it mirrored how I felt after waiting all day, having no idea you'd written to change our plans.

I know it sounds like I'm being dramatic, but I felt like a jilted bride in my new dress, complete with a picnic and a bottle of bubbly.

By the end of the day, I just felt like a fool. I can honestly say I couldn't deal with the agony.

Instead, I shut down all my feelings for you and ran away; I accepted the road out of the pain that Rufus offered.

You asked me if I loved Rufus. I did. But it was a different kind of love to what we had. I have only realised that in hindsight.

I have realised too that I love you. I always have and I'm sure I always will.

Izzie x.

Chapter Thirty-Six

Izzie

West Hampstead, March 9, 2018

'Yes, I'm happy with that completion date,' she had assured her local solicitor on the sale of her West Hampstead home, '6th of April is perfect.'

Izzie was certain this was what she wanted. The emotional whirlpool caused by Rufus hiding Justin's letters was beginning to settle, but it had the effect of springing her into action. The first step had been to sell the house. Luckily, she had an eager buyer. Her neighbour, Vinnie, a retired, very successful actor, loved the area and had always preferred Izzie's house because the garden was bigger. For years, he had asked Rufus and Izzie to give him first refusal if they sold and he was delighted to accept when Izzie approached him, happy to have all the furnishings too – as Izzie had no need for any.

Now she knew what she wanted. Who she wanted. Without any doubt. She was going to reach out and attempt to make it happen – any way she could.

At the same time, she intended to finally finish putting her own world to rights.

Blackpool, Friday April 6, 2018

She wanted to have that day – the day that had been robbed from herself and Justin through Rufus's deception. She'd been doing her best to set it up without him knowing. Izzie got a little thrill because she had deliberately led him to believe she was still in London, their exchange of messages indicated that she'd travel to Blackpool at the end of the following week for their first meet up since his return from working on location in New Zealand.

Justin's mum, Linda had helped and was sworn to secrecy; she had established for Izzie that Justin would be working away from home for the entire week until around midday…

Unloading all she needed from the cab, she entered the code into the concealed key safe, let herself into his house, propped the door open with her picnic hamper, bulging wheelie suitcase, rucksack, rug - and then returned the key to its safe.

Wasting no time, she unloaded her hamper of food,

glasses and plates onto the table, then grabbing the picnic rug, unfolded it, raised it up and let it billow and open, settling on the wooden floor. Then, with her focus on getting everything else ready, she emptied the bag of ice into the cooler, enjoyed the sound of it rattling as she pushed in the bottle of bubbly.

'He'll think I'm crazy…' She half-laughed, nervousness mingling with excitement, carried on setting out the spread; the delicious finger sandwiches, tiny scones, grapes, dips and breadsticks; everything and more she had taken to the beach last time. In addition, because this time was indoors, she arranged several sets of fairy lights artfully around the table, draped homemade bunting bearing pictures of the sea and sand between Justin's photographic artwork.

She stood up a home-made card on the table in the middle of all their favourite snacks.

It said, Happy 23rd Birthday, Izzie. Yes, it was six years and seven months late, it was inside rather than outside – still too cold outside for a beach picnic – but the way she saw it, that was no reason to wait any longer.

As a finishing touch, she set the soundtrack of gentle waves breaking on the shore, the hypnotic sound of the shifting water was layered with the call of gulls, the subtle shift of pebbles scuttering against the sea wall.

She glanced at the clock, she had just a half hour left to get ready; grabbing her change of clothes Izzie hurried up to the bathroom.

The yellow sundress she'd made years ago had never been worn again, but was screwed up and shoved in the deepest eave in her attic bedroom. Izzie was thrilled when after a wash and good press and with a bit of wriggling to accommodate her curves, it looked pretty good. She shivered, it really wasn't warm enough for this, but, what the heck…

The top button pulled a bit tight, kept popping open when she breathed. 'Oh well,' she grabbed her makeup and put a couple of coats of mascara on, then teased her hair into a top knot, let curling tendrils frame her face, hoop earrings glinting in place.

Her breath literally caught in her throat when she heard the front door open. 'Eek,' she whispered to herself, 'you're early…'

Hurriedly, she hooked on her flip flops and moved to the top of the stairs.

Luckily, when she glanced down the stairs, the front door was propped open with an equipment case and no sign of Justin…He must be unloading his gear. She dashed downstairs and was suddenly gripped by intense panic; almost gratefully, she sank to the rug, closed her eyes, made herself take some deep breaths. Her pulses pounded so loudly in her ears that she didn't hear the front door close.

'Izzie? What the – what?'

Slowly, she opened her eyes to see Justin's half puzzled, half amused expression as he pushed his fingers back through his hair and looked around the room, the room she had transformed into a magical pop-up beach and picnic area.

'Hi.' The word squeezed out past her nerves. Oh, God, why was she putting herself through this? It had seemed like such a good idea.

'This looks – amazing.' His gaze stayed for a long moment on the birthday card on the table and its message. 'But it's not till August.'

'I want that day back. I don't want to wait.' Her pulse banged so loudly, she thought she'd explode, her palms were sweating and her mouth was suddenly, completely dry.

He sank down onto the rug beside her and took hold of her hands.

'You think I'm crazy don't you, Justin?'

'Yes. And I love it. Happy birthday.'

Izzie wound her arms around his neck and squeezed him tight, crushing her face into his neck. 'It's so good to see you'. Her fingers spread over his firm, strong shoulders, the fabric of his jacket shifting beneath her touch.

'How long are you up north for?' His warm palms felt so good against the cool skin of her upper arms.

'For good.' She watched his reaction, terrified because she had promised herself to be completely truthful, not waste any more time, whatever the outcome. 'I've sold the West Hampstead house, I'm back here now. I want to be here, in Blackpool. By the sea. With you. I've realised it's where I belong.'

'Seriously?'

She nodded. 'I realised too that I was always going to feel aggrieved – unless I took my day back. Our day back, Justin. When we were going to make all our plans.'

He studied her for a moment as though considering her words, and whilst he did, her mouth went completely dry again, a cold sweat broke on her whole body.

'If you don't feel the same, just – just be honest?'

Although if he didn't feel the same, she thought she might well pass out completely right here on the picnic rug.

He took a deep breath, rubbed his jaw between finger and thumb. 'I wrote you a letter while I was away, because you asked me to, but that's when I knew I needed to give it to you in person.'

'You did? Will you – will you read it to me?'

'Shall we open the bubbly, then I'll nip up and get it from my desk.'

Just minutes later, Justin had retrieved the letter from his study and they sat facing one another on the thick picnic rug, propped up against a bank of cushions, glasses refilled to the brim.

'You really going to make me do this?' His expression was filled with fun, like he really didn't mind, but was still mildly embarrassed.

She nodded, leaned in and traced her fingertip down his cheek. 'Yes.'

He blew out slowly as though steadying his nerve, took a swallow of bubbly and then set his glass down.

My dearest, funny, beautiful Izzie,

I am writing this because you asked me to write and I need to express something and admit to something; I've never done this before, so it may not be beautiful.

I love that you shared Molly's notebook with me, something so private and personal about the grandparents you loved and admired so deeply.

I feel free just being with you. I felt that way when we were lovers in the past, too.

Now, here's the truth: I do want you – any way you'll have me.

You make me happy.

We enjoy one another's company so much and I want it to carry on. I want you as more than a friend if you'll have me. I want you more than I've ever wanted any woman.

Would you consider travelling with me sometimes? I am thinking I would like to spend time at home with you, too. That's a weird feeling because I have never felt that before. Maybe we could do both? We can keep our own homes – or share – I do not care.

This is the closest I've come to commitment since the time we should have got together and I know it's what I want. But only if you do too.

I need to admit that soon after I wrote asking if we could change our plans, I had regrets. Huge regrets. When I heard you'd married Rufus, I was devastated. I was way too emotionally depleted to look for any answers and so I worked and didn't come up for air for a very long time.

I love you, Izzie. Forever and always, I love you as my friend, my lover, and hopefully, one day, my wife, if we both think it's a good idea.

All my love,

Justin x.

'Oh', a soft squeak left her, she reached out and wrapped both arms around him and kissed him through her hot tears. She thought she would burst with happiness when Justin held her just as tightly.

'Thank you.' A letter could mean so much, hold so much promise. But that he had chosen to keep it and give it to her in person meant everything to her. It was almost as crazy as her determination to claw back this special day.

'There's something else.' Justin grimaced, 'I'll admit this had to be rescued, I lobbed it out of my bedroom window in a rage more than once, kicked it under the car wheels, but it kept turning up. I think maybe this is a good time to finally give it to you.'

She frowned, couldn't think exactly what he could be retrieving from his jacket pocket; 'In the end, I stashed it away with my passport.' He picked up her hand so her palm was open and dropped the delicate gold ring, complete with a small, rough, honey coloured gemstone in its filigree mount onto her palm. 'It's Maltese calcite.'

'You – you bought this for me… In Malta?'

He gave a single nod.

Izzie thought she might never swallow again past the lump in her throat. 'Oh, Justin, I don't know what to say.'

One of his eyebrows raised a touch. 'Yes?'

She laughed and sobbed all at once, let Justin pull her into his arms.

She had it all – her special day had turned out very special this time.

At that moment, she fancied she felt Nan's presence, her guiding hand lighting the path to happiness for them both. The right path this time, the one that was always meant to be.

Izzie was home.

YOUR NUMBER ONE STOP

ONE MORE CHAPTER

FOR PAGETURNING BOOKS

One More Chapter is an
award-winning global
division of HarperCollins.

Sign up to our newsletter to get our
latest eBook deals and stay up to date
with our weekly Book Club!
<u>Subscribe here.</u>

Meet the team at
<u>www.onemorechapter.com</u>

Follow us!

 @OneMoreChapter_

 @OneMoreChapter

 @onemorechapterhc

Do you write unputdownable fiction?
We love to hear from new voices.
Find out how to submit your novel at
<u>www.onemorechapter.com/submissions</u>